God's Bridge

A NOVEL OF BELIEVING

Jack Perkins

God's Bridge: A Novel of Believing

Moosewood Editions
3916 Casey Key Rd
Nokomis, FL, 34275
jackperk@mac.com

Publisher's Note: This is a work of history-based fiction. Some names, characters, places, and incidents are a product of the author's imagination. Locales and public names are sometimes used for atmospheric purposes.

Book Layout ©2017 BookDesignTemplates.com
God's Bridge: A Novel of Believing/Jack Perkins -- 1st ed.
ISBN -13-978-0692825822

*For the tenders, toll takers
and travelers of Dingmans Bridge*

We build too many walls and not enough bridges

—*Isaac Newton*

AUTHOR'S FOREWORD

Don't be misled seeing my name on the cover as author. The book is *by* me, yes, but it is not *about* me. It is about my brother.

His name? Depends whom you ask. To a devoted television public over years he was simply "Perk." I'll let him explain the Perk quirk for himself. But first, let me set up some history.

Years back, as breaks broke, my older brother and I both became TV correspondents, he ahead of me in both years and reputation (his getting blown up that time significantly boosted his rep; not that I envied.) Something he and I agreed upon early was that the only story neither of us would be qualified to report honestly, with balance, would be the story of himself. A reporter needs to be objective. He can't be about himself. So, we pledged, were it ever needed, to serve as the other's Ghost, writing his story for him. Hence, this book and my author's credit. Also, though I already announced the book is about him, I should tell you it is about other people as well and – oh, yes! – always it is about a bridge.

A bridge? A bridge built by our family well over a century ago. Peerless it is and sturdy, surviving today where three prior bridges long ago collapsed. A bridge of history lovingly

1

held, of today embracing yesterday, a sweetly lyrical bridge and to some people, holy. A local pastor called it God's Bridge.

It was our grandfather and his two brothers who birthed this bridge across a major river between states. Their heroic roles encourage us, their descendants, to write this account. I confess up front that it is a story where some of the things told might not have happened exactly that way and a few of the people described frankly never were, meaning that pulling together the tale required both painstaking research and loving imagination.

Which is to forewarn: there is fiction here, there is fact. A reader inclined to fret over which is which, I remind that all truth does not reside online. Google won't locate the Google my brother knew, the one who saved his life.

For now, I propose to let fact and fiction dance together to tell the full story, or better put, *stories*. Tales interweave; warp needs weft. If I start by introducing one small town and some of its people, there is still to come another small town and down the road (or is it up?) yet another. Not immediately, of course. Continuity is not a straight line. Time leaps ahead, then turns back on itself, ultimately seeming irrelevant. The bridge testifies that in the end, philosophically, there is no *Was;* there is no *Will Be;* there is only *Is.*

Among the people we come across in these three towns (and crucial visits to a couple of explosive cities and two "wars"), some are believers, some doubters, some deniers. Nor are the villains always deniers. Some most fervent in their believing are most wicked. I shall enlist on neither side in these pages. As a guest in readers' minds, I shall not try to proselytize. I will though report faithfully my brother's own faith and how it traveled and matured over time.

Of the three towns considered, I might alert that one barely exists anymore. That town has no *Will Be* left. It was mostly erased a while back, stolen away, the town and the hearts of its people, by something that never should have happened but did. That human-made, government-perpetrated disaster not only altered ineradicably the area around the bridge but in the end delivered the greatest gift God could ever have given a man, the gift of Himself, of His Holy Spirit and ultimately one of His comeliest, personally assigned angels.

Now, if fact and fiction are to play together, pray let the music begin, that my brother may dance.

CHAPTER ONE

YOU SHOULD BE PROUD OF YOUR GRANDFATHER
--Our grandmother holding a fading photograph

Call me Perk, just Perk. No need getting hung up on given names. Names given are often not kindly received.

As a boy, I adopted a mutt off the street. (What kid hasn't, or wanted to?) He was a frolicking, playful pup. Wishing to accord the homeless urchin dignity, I proclaimed that henceforth he would be known as *Sir J. Butchingham Dog.* As soon as I told him, he went into a funk. The more I repeated it to him, the more despondent he got. Only when I decided the hifalutin' name wasn't suited and assured him that, okay, he would henceforth be known as simply "Butch" did he become once more the exuberant fellow I had saved from the streets. Names matter.

Mine?

I assume my parents wished to accord me the dignity of family heritage, selecting for my first name that of one of my father's uncles. Even years later, when I finally met my namesake, bib-overalled out in his fields near Medina, and was taken with his soft-spoken Ohio farmer ways, I still wished I hadn't been stuck with his name – *Morton!*

"*Nyaa, nyaa, nyaa,*" mocking kids pestered, "Morton isn't a person, it's a kind of salt. *When it rains, it pours.* C'mon, Morton, it's raining, let's see you pour." Cracks like that were why I swore never to let them learn my middle names. Those had been taken from my mother's side of the family to make things even, I guess. Her maiden name had been Bryte and she had two aunts she loved, women with the curious names Birdie Belle Bryte and Liberty Belle Bryte. Mom chose the latter, thoughtfully dropping a terminal *e* to make it seem masculine and I officially became **Morton Liberty Bell Perkins.**

As I said, call me Perk.

My younger brother got lucky. He was named simply Jack. Not even John. Jack. The folks had spent their creativity.

Our hometown had a name problem of its own. Strangers rarely said it right. It was simple: Wooster. Wooster, Ohio. But how many times did we have to tell outsiders, "No, the double O's aren't like *Rooster.* They're like *look* or *book.* Call it *Wooster.*"

"The good thing about the folks who mispronounce us," said Mr. Pollock, my high school speech coach, "is that they won't be moving here. We don't need any more people. Ten thousand's just right, and at least we know how to spell our town unlike those unreconstructed Brits back in Massachusetts. *Worcester*, indeed. That isn't a town; that's a sauce." He always found the fun way to twist things.

The heart of our town, as it ought to be in a small town, was Public Square. There loomed the gray stone buildings of county government. There too, the bank where we kids would take what money we'd been able to make pulling dandelions or buckweed from neighbors' lawns or sorting tomatoes at the greenhouse up the street. Dutifully, we would buy war stamps, make deposits and have our passbooks hand-stamped.

Also on Public Square was Dick Morrison's barbershop where we made biweekly visits I always looked forward to. This was where townsmen clustered Saturday mornings, reading magazines not welcome in their homes, reading and talking, mostly talking. "So Truman's comin' to town, didja see that?"

"Oh yeah, 'round midnight tomorrow. Whistle-stopping. Anyone going?"

"For Harry? Not a chance. Now if it were still FDR — Rest his soul — I'd be there in a heartbeat."

"What about the man on the wedding cake?"

"Dewey? Not me, thank you."

These were the town criers of news, fancied adjudicators of disputes. Dick Morrison was a negro. We didn't notice. I surely never heard anyone speak of it, let alone call him a "nigger." We had our prejudices, I guess, but only in the abstract. Dick Morrison wasn't an abstraction. He was a friend.

The greatest pride of our town was The College of Wooster, a renowned Presbyterian school just a block from our home. I loved the college for its colorful Kiltie band, skirling about in yellow and black MacLeod tartans, the high white socks and sporrans, the bags and chanters. What was it about the drone of the pipes, the steady, melancholy drone over which danced the lilt of the chanters' familiar tunes:

Highland Cathedral, Scotland the Brave, Amazing Grace. Cries of banshees, brandished bugles of saints, grounded, always grounded by the Rock of many ages. A man or woman -- and certainly an impressionable youth - could not but be thrilled on hearing the pipes.

There was another reason for pride in the college; two reasons actually: the brothers Compton. If many Woosterians could never calculate the dimension of their contributions, they were proud of both. They knew that the Comptons had been associated with our college, and gone on from there, Karl to work on development of the A-bomb and head M.I.T., Arthur to win the Nobel Prize for Physics. Wooster's gifts to the nation.

There was another, for a while. Each year the town erected a Christmas tree on Public Square to honor a man named August Imgard. From Bavaria, he had come to America back in the 1800s, settled and begun working in a tailor shop in Wooster. His first winter, he found himself yearningly homesick so he went out into the woods, cut down a fir tree, brought it home, set it up and decorated it with colorful hand-crafted ornaments.in the German tradition. It was quite a sight, stirring such interest with neighbors that come the next year many chose to do the same. For a century, then, Wooster was known for being the town that gave America the Christmas tree.

"Vell, dot's a nice story," said Willi Schreiber. "But, dot's all."

He was the father of one of my best neighborhood buddies in those school days, B. Schreiber. That's how he was called, just "B." His father was Dr. William Schreiber, head of the College of Wooster's German department and he fit the role, gruff and sternly Teutonic. Though, contradictorily, he was also the man who introduced me to the records of the brilliant parodist, Tom Lehrer. For that, I was grateful. For another revelation, though, I and the town would never thank him. His devotion to truth, he felt, outweighed his commitment to his hometown. That, though I certainly didn't appreciate it at the time, was a valuable lesson for a nascent reporter to learn. Dr. Schreiber spent long hours researching and ultimately proved that, no, Wooster had not produced the first Christmas tree. Other cities beat August Imgard. We weren't first; we weren't unique.

But we did have another distinction. We and our adjoining county were the largest concentration in America of the Amish. Saturdays, our main street was lined with buggies, Amish folk come to town for weekly shopping. There they were, women in black dresses and bonnets, no makeup, of course; men also in black, bearded if married, clean shaven if not. No zippers, even buttons on their garments, rather snaps or hooks-and-eyes, for some reason.

"Curious," my mom would say. "They are most curious people." She was wrong, I was the most curious. I didn't understand Amish ways. Why no cars? Telephones? Radios? Colors in their clothes? What about barn raisings? Shunning? A grownup, confronted by the unknown, fears or mocks. A kid, unless swayed by adult biases, simply wonders. I knew whom to ask.

Dr. Schreiber knew the Amish, had made extensive scholarly studies and written about them. About their pacifist ways, their devout beliefs, their underlying principle that if the rest of the world around them, the "English" they called us whatever our national origins, did not believe in their ways, then they, as much as possible, would remove themselves from us and our ways. I was increasingly intrigued and so he arranged to take "B" and me one week out in the country to attend one of their worship services. Not in a church for they had none but in a home. Worship, they believed, did not need its own edifice; it should be with them every day in their own homes, their barns. This week it was to be at Eli Hersberger's place outside the little town of Sugar Creek. Church leaders were chosen, Dr. Schreiber told us, not through appointment by some ecclesiastical hierarchy, not through election by parishioners, but simply by lot. That, they believed, let God make the selection. Cynically, I wondered: Would our nation do any worse staging elections by lot? No need for "whistle stops."

I thought about that and a lot more that day because I had a lot of time. The service lasted four hours. But then, the food. From the barn it was up to the Hershberger's house for a fulsome Amish Sunday dinner — roasts of pig and beef, pot pies of chicken and vegetables, mashed potatoes and broad egg noodles bathed in a cream-rich gravy. And on and on through three kinds of flaky-crust pies — lemon, apple and coconut cream. All made on the wood stoves of several neighboring homes and with no electric appliances. Any "English" who thought the Amish a simple people never took Sunday dinner with them.

For our family, usually, Sundays after the hollow holiness of church meant my dad, brother and I (not Mom) would head along Liberty street as though we were going to the movie house to get some Sugar Daddies and settle in to see the weekly cowboy double feature starring Gene, Roy, or Tom. But before we got that far we had to enter into what my brother called "The place I hate most of all."

We would climb the stairs at the tired Wooster Hotel, up three flights to a small room, musty and bleak, and there, visit Grandmother Perkins. She was the reason we never went to a certain church because she went to that church and my mother could not brook being with her. That never seemed churchly to me.

Nor did my brother and I enjoy those stilted visits, Grandmother P. was a proper figure dressed in lace and blue, almost always blue, seated in a turned cherry wood chair, dad taking the desk seat, hardly large enough for him, while we kids either perched on the windowsill or if it was winter and the window cold, plopped on the floor. It was close and awkward, like visiting an inmate in her sorry cell, a stranger I never really came to know.

After all this time, the one thing I wish I had learned from her was more about her deceased husband. All I knew was that he was a primly handsome gentleman in an ancient photo in a silver frame on her desktop. Straight of stature, bright white hair and mustache, honest and forthright look. A man I would like to have known but never did. Who was he? What had he

11

done, the distinguished-looking Grandfather from the photograph?

"Very handsome man," I said to her one day.

"And a very good man," grandmother quickly added. "You should be proud of him and how he helped so many people."

"I'm sure I would be." (If I knew him, I thought.)

"And proud as well of your father," she added. "My son."

"Oh, of course. We are," we said.

And that's all. All the conversation among us that stuck with me. I knew only that at one point grandfather James Stoaks Perkins and she were from another small town, this in New York State and named Horseheads. That was funny. My dad once gave me a small leather wallet stamped with the likeness of two horse heads and under them the words, "Horseheads Bridge Company."

"You keep this, son, to remember your grandfather," which I couldn't do since I hadn't known him. Just that he had something to do — and I didn't know what — with bridges. Especially, with one particular bridge in another strange sounding place, a place my folks went to every year and told us that we kids should start to go too, although, confusingly, they also said that the place they went to didn't really exist anymore yet they still went. It was in Pennsylvania and it was called Dingmans Ferry.

CHAPTER TWO

"I WANT TO GO AWAY, FIND A PLACE AND MAKE THAT PLACE A SOMEWHERE. THIS IS GOING TO BE A GREAT COUNTRY ONE DAY. I WANT TO BE PART OF THAT."
--Young Andreas Dingenman to a friend

There would never have been a town of Dingmans Ferry, Pennsylvania if there hadn't been a Dingman.

There would *still* be a thriving town of Dingmans Ferry, Pennsylvania if there hadn't been the grasping tentacles of government.

Before the screed, though, the man. The man who appeared long before a bridge of any sort existed along this reach of the Delaware River, though there was long a felt need for a way of crossing between Pennsylvania and New Jersey here, even before those two were states.

Andreas Dingenman was one of the first arrivals from Europe. When his parents brought him to this country, it wasn't yet a country. There were dreams, hopes and determination: there were colonies and commonwealths and vast tracts unnamed and unexplored, adventures awaiting. But there was no United States.

13

Arriving from the Netherlands, the family settled in the mostly Dutch village of Kinderhoek, in New York's Hudson Valley. He was a visionary, the young lad who would Americanize his name to Andrew Dingman. Always had dreams which he shared not so much with family but with a buddy his age, Robertus Wilhelmus Godefritus Van Gennip.

"Rob," he told him one day in their teens, "you know I'll have to leave here before long."

"Leave here? Why, Andreas?"

"I have to do something with my life."

"Why not do it here? We can do something together. Something to make a real difference."

"Rob, this is nowhere. It'll always be a nowhere. I want to go away, find a place and make that place a *Somewhere*. This is going to be a great country one day, one day soon. I want to be part of that."

He had good instincts. When, in his early twenties, he set off for the far side of the great Delaware River, he was basically crossing the young land's frontier, the lands on both sides of the Delaware, near the conjoining of what would be New York, New Jersey and Pennsylvania were thriving. Grist mills and sawmills were humming alongside the river itself and those waters that came to be known as Dingmans Creek. (He had simplified the name and given up the possessive form, losing the apostrophe he always forgot to put in anyway.) Dingman himself had built a wooden flat boat tethered to a line running across the river, creating the Dingmans ferry, a name that would long outlast the ferry itself. The ferry operated on no set schedule. A customer from the New Jersey side would clang a big bell over there to summon the ferryman on the Pennsylvania shore who would then take to the flat boat, propelling it by hand-over-hand pulling on the cable suspended above the route. It was not quick or easy or in bad weather pleasant but it served.

Andrew Dingman was doing what he had promised his youthful friend he would do: He was making his new home a *Somewhere*. Indeed, for himself and his generations to come he created not just a *Somewhere* but a dynasty. Next down the line would be son Daniel, to become better known in those parts as The Judge, a state representative then district judge, a man of character, a character of a man, conducting his judicial business in bare feet on the lawns of the great stone house he built in 1804 right on the softly sloping shore of the Delaware. He would live there with his family and eventually other kin, including one outsider he could never have imagined.

As he sat out on his eastern porch, gazing at the river and the occasional crossing of the flatboat, he began dreaming of what, perhaps, should happen next. Something he himself would never get around to but his kin would as they carried on.

What they did, with their Dingman dreams and determination, was to go to the appropriate government officials in both states, Pennsylvania and New Jersey, and apply for and ultimately succeed in acquiring a charter to erect and operate a bridge over the river. That year was 1834, and as playful fate would have it, the seventh president of the United States was Martin Van Buren, a man who like Andrew Dingman a century earlier had left his hometown of

Kinderhoek, N.Y. to find his *Somewhere*; in Van Buren's case, the White House.

For the younger Dingmans it did not seem a great challenge to build a bridge. There were many already spanning the Delaware river upstream and downstream from their site. Most were wooden and some covered. The Dingmans would also do wood but save time and money and not add the cover. Construction went well, took a couple of years and in 1836 the first Dingmans bridge was in business. The first. *Just the first!*

After only five years, came a frightful storm. Would the bridge hold? A couple of the brothers spent the night by the rough little toll-takers shed.

"Why do these things always happen at night?" asked one.

"Evil inhabits the dark," replied the other. "Testing us, Andrew."

"Testing our beautiful bridge, you mean."

"May the Devil take the hindmost. But not our bridge."

"Amen. Speaking of which, a prayer might be in order. You think?"

"Shine or rain. Always is." And right there by the end of their bridge, rain pelting, skies boiling, river raging, the brothers knelt, disregarding the muddy roadway and, holding hands and looking upward to the Source, prayed. Then sang. Just the two them, their voices challenging the roar of the storm as gustily they sang out:

> *When peace, like a river, attendeth my way,*
> *When sorrows like sea billows roll;*
> *Whatever my lot, Thou hast taught me to say,*

16

It is well, it is well with my soul.
It is well with my soul,
It is well, it is well with my soul.

The bridge survived that night although with morning the Dingmans began hearing of one bridge after another downstream that had not made it. When all reports were in, at least five other bridges -- those at Reiglesville, Center Bridge, New Hope, Taylorsville, and Yardleyville -- had been torn from their bases, broken, and floated away in that Great Flood of 1841. The wives of the mud-kneeling brothers of Dingmans Bridge uttered not a niggle when washing their husbands' trousers that week.

That was 1841 and blessed years lay ahead. Ever-increasing river traffic meant increasingly prosperous times for the bridgemakers. They were not gouging their neighbors. For one thing, under the terms of their original states-granted charter, what they might charge per crossing was directed, specifically and unequivocally in language redolent of the 1800s:

. . . for every coach, landau, chariot, phaeton or other pleasure carriage, with four wheels drawn by four horses, the sum of fifty cents.

If drawn by just two horses, the charge would be only *thirty-one and a forth (cq) cents.* While

. . . for every chaise, riding chair, sulky, cart or other two wheeled carriages or sleigh, sled, . . . with one horse, eighteen-and-a forth cents.

For a single horse and rider, twelve and a half cents; for every foot passenger, two cents: every head of horned cattle, three cents; every sheep or swine, one cent.

There were, however, specific exceptions. The bridge must permit free passage for anyone bound to or from school, church or a funeral. (That would much later be tested when during America's Prohibition days, an inordinate number of funeral processions took free crossings with notably over-burdened hearses.)

These were good times for the bridge, for the Dingmans.

But then, 1847!

In a sense, it was the cruelest of fates that could befall the Dingmans that storm season because their bridge did just fine through the onslaught of another demoniacal storm and all would have been well if only the Milford Bridge several miles upstream had behaved as conscientiously. Instead, it washed completely off its moorings and rumbled recklessly southward, its timbers and deck boards becoming projectiles driven by flood waters directly down toward its Dingmans cousin. Relentlessly, it came, the noise of its thundering approach competing with nature's own thunder. When it was clear to the Dingman men taking refuge in Judge Daniel's storm cellar beneath the Stone House that what they were hearing was no longer just the cacophony of nature's thundering but something closer and more menacing, they raised the slanted doors and crawled up out of the cellar to witness inescapably the slow-motion destruction of their own beloved bridge, the Milford pummeling it into the same fatal fate it itself had just suffered. They saw their dear bridge being first struck and then struck again until soon their own timbers and deck boards were crashing downstream with the rest. There was no stopping it, saving their bridge. It was being splintered, washed away, inexorably annihilated in an awesome maelstrom of roar and destruction.

Numbly, they watched. Finally, one spoke.

"It's too late, brothers, to pray for the bridge. But not too late to pray. And again they stood there, hand-in-hand, hardly believing what they had just witnessed.

God, dear God of what we understand and what we do not, help us accept the unacceptable. Help us find promise in the wreckage of our plans, our work, our dreams. Gratitude in accepting that not our plans and dreams but thine are what we need honor. Even when we don't understand. Even, dear God, like now.

The very next week, they dug out the old flatboat and Dingmans Ferry was back in business.

For three years. By that time the enterprising family had built and erected, yes, a *new* bridge. This one was covered, quaintly attractive but that quaintness also added labor in winter. Someone had to go out and fetch wagonfuls of snow to haul back to cover the bridge floor so that sleighs could make passage. They didn't have to do that for long, of course. After four years this bridge too was felled, this time without any assist from the Milford Bridge upstream. It collapsed on its own in especially ferocious winds.

Back to the ferry. And another couple of years till the family, with more hope than memory, unveiled their *third* bridge.

Guess what. After just six years, it needed neither assault by neighboring bridge, ferocity of wind, or any other alien instrument; it was just so poorly made that one day, seemingly unmotivated, it collapsed on its own.

That was enough. Finally, the Dingmans, heirs of a determined, never-give-up clan of proud Dutchmen, gave up. They had worked, they had prayed, they had failed. For another decade they would run the ferry boat — people over on the Jersey side clanging the big bell there to summon the ferryman, one of the local physicians needing passage when a ferryman was not to be found, looping his special basket carrier to the overhead cable and hand-over-handing his way across to his emergency call. Ten final years of that and the Dingmans were done. They sold the property to a relative, John W. Kilsby, who would operate things until the dawning of a new century at which point the curtain on the next act would lift on a completely new cast of players. From yet another small town.

CHAPTER THREE

"WE NEED TO STRIKE WHILE THE IRON IS WROUGHT."
-- *Will Perkins, punster of the family.*

The villagers of Horseheads, New York had known a grisly moment of history, which, curiously, they chose to memorialize in their town's name. They were that kind of people.

September 1, 1779. The French and Indian War had mostly run its course in the southern tier of New York State though there were still disputes among white settlers, Frenchmen, and Indians of the Iroquois confederation of tribes, still need, that is, for occasional military interventions. One mission brought 5,000 men and scores of Army pack horses to transport great burdens of heavy equipment 450 miles through densely wooded lands starting from Easton, Pennsylvania, up the Susquehanna River past Elmira and onward to the Finger Lakes region, then west to Genesee. It was a grinding trek for the men and the horses hauling the heavy gear. So much so that, as the return trip began, it was clear that many of the beasts would never make it. Out of mercy, commanders ordered the horses be put out of their misery. Dozens of horses were killed and left along the route. Sometime later, Iroquois warriors collected sun-bleached skulls and laid them out in a line of horse heads to warn white men that death would be theirs should they come that way again.

The nearby village folk could have reacted negatively, cursed the impertinence, rekindled the hatred, but, displaying a wiser sense of balance, chose rather to use the grim scene to enhance their own positivity. They named their village Horseheads.

Horseheads was never a big place whether as village or town. Just before centuries rolled from nineteenth to twentieth, census takers couldn't uncover more than 4,944 citizens in all of Horseheads. Three of those were named Perkins — the brothers E.A. (Arthur), James (J.S.), and Will.

The middle of the three, James, was my grandfather. He had been born in Ohio, in a small town near Wooster. But he and his brothers backtracked to New York State to go into business, an endeavor that would be productive for them and for history. With keen minds for mechanics and design and science, they founded what they named the Horseheads Bridge Company and soon were known throughout their field and kept busy. More than once, records would show a jurisdiction desiring a bridge constructed would have to wait because the brothers were busy building another somewhere else. At times, as entrepreneurs, they created their own projects.

"Gentlemen, here's an idea," said James one day to his brothers in the small room they used as their office.

"Just what we need," said E.A. cynically. "Another job when we can hardly keep up with all we have."

"Ah, but this one," countered James, "is not us undertaking somebody else's project. This will be *us* creating *our own*. We're the finders, the buyers, the builders, the sellers, and ultimately the owners, making money all along."

"Tell," said the taciturn brother, Will.

"Let's go over to Maisie's," said James, "have a bowl of soup, and I'll fill you in. It's a good one."

Maisie was a pleasingly plump woman (such was the expression in those days) who enjoyed cooking and, apparently, enjoyed as much eating her cooking. She got the men seated, told them the specials, took their orders, walked away and the brothers fell to talking. Mostly, James.

"Two projects, gentlemen. One being the perfect resolution to the other. Here's what I have in mind. You know that abandoned railroad bridge up near Muncie on the Susquehanna? I hear that, from disregard and disrepair some of the structure is threatening to fall into the river. A good storm come up, maybe the whole thing. Abutments and supports not maintained. It's good iron, though. Trusses and spans mostly sound. Good materials, from the boys at Phoenix. Good stuff and certainly not just good for scrap if we move quickly."

"It could be good for *us* somehow?" E.A. was skeptical.

"If we can find it another home."

"For five spans of wrought iron trusses, a new home?" Will this time.

"I think I've found one," James beamed excitedly.

"Chowder," cried Maisie, balancing her tray. "Who had the chowder?"

E.A. claimed the chowder; Will, the meat loaf special; James thanked Maisie for the chicken noodle. She moved on and the men settled back to their planning.

"We have to move fast," urged James. "Lock up salvage rights on the Susquehanna as soon as possible."

"Need to strike while the iron is wrought," joked Will, the punster of the family.

"If you say so, Will." James rolled his eyes.

"And then what?" Both brothers this time.

"We go down another river," said James. "And we should be doing both of these things simultaneously. Set aside other work temporarily. We have to hurry. We need to head down the Delaware to our old friends who control things down there.

"We've never met them," said E.A.

"We will. And make them best friends by extending an offer I think they'll be very grateful to hear. They've already lost their bridge three times over the years, each time having to go back to the old flat boat they've kept in storage and restart their confounded ferry boat operation again. Folks down there are getting pretty tired of it all, I'm told. So we come to the rescue."

"How do their measurements and ours jibe?" asked E.A.

"We'll have to check, but what I hear, we could rebuild their crossing with only three of the five spans we'd be getting up north."

The brothers fell to silence, considering, as they consumed their soups and meat loaf.

"Coffee?," asked Maisie, dipping by. "Desert? Have a fresh huckleberry pie just made today."

"Just coffee for me," said Will.

"Coffee," echoed E.A.

"Well, Maisie, you know I'm not much for coffee," said James, "but I sure could go for a piece of wonderful pie. Assuming . . ."

"Assuming I have ice cream, and of course I do."

"Then you have a customer."

"Be right back," she almost sang.

James turned back to his brothers. "I say one of us should head off to the north, one to the south. Immediately after Christmas next week. If we're going to make this happen we have to move fast on both ends."

Will was always the cautious one. "If E.A goes up the Susquehanna to check that bridge and you, James, ride south to plot the purchase, I'll stay here to coordinate. Don't let us buy something we won't have a place for. Or buy a place and have no bridge to span it. Telegraph me as you negotiate."

"Sounds good," each agreed.

"*Looks* good," blurted Will as Maisie brought pie ala mode to James. "I'm gonna have to do that too, Maisie."

"So will I," joined E.A. "I do believe we're celebrating."

"Leaving?" asked the small woman who at the moment did not feel small at all. "How can you think of leaving right now, James?"

"I'll be here with you and young Howard for Christmas. I won't leave till the day after or so."

"I'm not thinking about about Christmas. Or about Howard," she said, peeved at his stubbornness, his disregard for their family, their *growing* family. "I'm thinking about Little Ruth. Or Fred. Whoever the dear one turns out to be," and she softly patted her abdomen, plump and ripe with the babe due next month.

"Dear, there is not a chance, I promise you, that I will miss the birth of our baby. I'm as eager as anything to meet her."

"Her? You are so stubborn, James. I know you hope for a girl, men always do, but will you be so pained if your daughter turns out to be your son?"

"Of course not, dear. I will love whoever God chooses to place in our care."

"*Our* care, James. *Both* of us. From the *start.* That's why I don't want you to go off on this trip."

"Helen! Doctor says the last week of January. I'll be leaving last week of *December.* Fully a month before. I'll be back in plenty of time. Promise. This deal could be very important to us. You and me. And, eventually, to Howard and . . . whoever." He hoped his loving smile would carry his case.

Helen wasn't happy but knew his mind was set and she felt that her role, satisfied or not, was to be a good wife and honor his decision. That way was marital concord.

"I'll be eager to hear how your plans go," she said, yielding.

"And I shall be *very* eager to follow every report I can get through E.A. on how you and the bump are doing. I love you, dear."

"And I, you." She showed him.

26

Next morning, the brothers met to coordinate. They would start their two-pronged assault a few days after Christmas. Will laid out the plan:

"Next week. E.A. goes upstate to the Susquehanna to check out that abandoned bridge, five spans of wrought iron. Worth trying to salvage? How to do that? What crews needed? How, then, to transport the chosen sections? How many men? Barges? How and where to get them? What routes through the rivers and canals? What permission needed? From what authorities? E.A. would work on these questions from up north, me from here. And you, James., ride down to Dingmans Ferry, scout out those folks. See what our buy would take. *If* E.A. says it's a go from his end. Busy time coming, gentlemen."

"Busy time *following* the busiest time, the one called Christmas shopping," said E.A. "Need my sizes, brothers?

It would take two years. Two years to run their twisted timeline of research and purchase, research and purchase, and it was not always easy or smooth and there'd be some nerves twisted as well.

Starting with E.A. in the upstate New York town of Muncie. It wasn't hard to locate the old railroad bridge, abandoned by the railroad but still mostly intact though here and there parts of the structure had collapsed, fallen, now lying forlornly in the murky waters of the Susquehanna. Still prominent on both sides of the standing iron trusses were words he had never seen before yet knew well: *Phoenix Iron Works.*

Phoenix Iron Works, of Phoenixville, Pennsylvania, had produced most of the cannon for the U.S. Army during the Civil War. It would create rails for the expanding Pennsylvania railroad. Nor was it a local or even just national phenomenon. It's puddled iron had gone into the creation of the Eiffel Tower in Paris just a decade earlier.

Heading into town, E.A. quickly got guidance through the local newspaper office to the owners of the bridge property and further learned that they had just been served papers by government authorities requiring the owners to pay to have the debris cluttering the valuable waters removed within the next six months or be severely punished and fined.

Eager they would be to listen to this stranger from Horseheads offering, possibly, a way out. E.A. had come prepared to offer whatever it would take to buy the bridge. Now, though, he began to think it might not take much at all. If anything.

"I've had a long trip, my buggy and me, a busy time. It's great to meet you and I feel confident we can help each other. But what I need most right now — and I hope you'll understand — is dinner and a bed. You're invited to join me . . . in the former."

All laughed, all accepted and they retired to the local hotel's dining room for a filling if not flavorful dinner courtesy of the Horseheads Bridge Company.

E.A. was certainly ready for a good night's sleep. But he couldn't sleep. There was far too much to think about. Numbers and strategies tumbled through his night-mind, diligently denying sleep. Come morning, he knew what he wanted to do to make the deal and how he should try to do it, but he wasn't sure he could even stay awake.

Coffee flowed. So did enough maple syrup to bathe a double stack of hotcakes. After some fruit, E.A. felt ready to confront a day that could prove quite important to him and his brothers. He hooked up with the locals back at the office where they met the day before. Now they exchanged the niceties of the day and E. A. got right to it.

"Gentlemen, I have an offer for you. I spent a lot of time after our lovely dinner last night considering your situation and sympathizing with your plight. You face some harsh possibilities but perhaps we can offer help to obviate those for payments and penalties."

To their questioning looks, he began laying out the plan. The gist was simple yet daring. He told them that with their approval and appropriate legal review by attorneys, the Horseheads Bridge Company would have papers drawn up to assume all rights to the bridge including sunken elements of same in return for the pledge to make payment-in-full for all necessary salvage to totally remove the sunken materials as well as the standing portions of the bridge structure. Further to exonerate the current owners of said property from any current or impending punishments or penalties due to said bridge remains. "You win by clearing yourselves of all problems and threats. We win, once we are able to effect the clean removal, by transporting the structures to a site we have located where the pieces can be reassembled to serve a new and needy river community. We each win. Great deal, I believe, for both sides. What say you?"

He could see relief in their faces but see also the smart businessman's learned reluctance to signal it. Finally, the one who seemed mostly the leader, a portly chap with pince-nez said, "Mr. Perkins, we are delighted to have your carefully reasoned proposal. And, yes, before responding we shall wish to consult counsel as you suggested. He's out of town for a couple days, back later in the week. Do you have things to attend to meanwhile?"

"I certainly do. For one thing, could you provide me with the prints, specs for all of the bridge? Once I get those I want to drive back out there for some more reconnoitering. Though first, where's the telegraph office?"

Collecting the papers from the bridge men, he headed down the street to send a briefing wire to Will writing in the strained language of telegraph-ese where charges were per word and punctuation had to be spelled out.

WELLGOING HERE STOP DECISION FORTHCOMING
WEEKWISE STOP HOW DINGMANS ENDIT

Taking his rig, he rode once more out to the bridge to draw pen-and-ink renderings of all he could encompass. Going up onto the bridge, where the tracks remained, he spent two hours recording measurements and doing more drawings. Eyeballing, it seemed to him from what he knew of the Dingmans site, its needs might well be accommodated by just three of the five trusses of this bridge. Perhaps they could sell the remainder for scrap perhaps even sharing those monies with the Muncie men. Sweeten the deal if needed.

In coming days, he would begin searches for sources of barges, cranes, workers willing and equipped for underwater salvage, and any locals who could help him lay out the route of waterways between here and the Delaware. Shouldn't be difficult, so many cutoffs and canals already constructed throughout the area. Much planning to be done. But for E.A., much encouragement and enthusiasm. This, he was growingly confident, could work.

If things were *wellgoing* on the other end, too.

CHAPTER FOUR

"THE DINGMANS KEPT BUILDING THEM, THEY KEPT LOSING
THEM. THE RIVER DIDN'T WANT THEM. YOU'VE GOT TO
RESPECT THE RIVER."
—*Pastor John to visitor James Perkins*

To the first time visitor, the little town of Dingmans
Ferry was a serenade, lying liltingly beside the great
river to which it was both caregiver and ward. The
village bade brother James welcome home although he had
never been there before.

Nor, he came to realize, was it just a waterfront venue. It
was not lifted in mountains like the Jersey side but ascended
gracefully from its lowly shore, climbing hills until it reached a
proper mount for its centerpiece, the stalwart Methodist
church already most of a century old. James went there his
very first day after arriving by buggy from Horseheads. He sat
alone in a pew for a long while in quiet to pray -- for his
venture, yes, but also for his wife and son and child to come.
Then off he went to seek out the clergyman.

Pastor John, as he introduced himself, was a fastidious
fellow, happy to welcome James and offer whatever assistance
he could give to the stranger. "Actually, though," he caught

himself, " to me, to the church, to God, there are no strangers in His house. We all are His people."

"To be sure, but we strangers can be grateful for guidance. First, I would say, to a worthy hostelry."

"Follow, friend. In season you must realize this is quite a thriving tourist destination. Now, peacefully quiet.""

He steered James along the street past many baronial if rustic establishments. Two story, three. Spacious and empty. Closed for the winter.

"In summer, hundreds of rooms available for basking visitors. Town's jammed. Old ferry down there (pointing down the hill toward the Dingmans) keeps busy. Just hope we can keep it going down there. Don't know what we'd do . . ." his voice trailing off as he led James up the steps of a large house saying, "This is Dingman House, open all year. Nice place. You'll like it." He led James to the wicker rockers on the broad front porch where with sun on them were still warm enough, winter or no. "Have a seat."

"Thank you, pastor . . . "

"John. Small town."

"John. Might I prevail upon you for one more favor?"

"Of course. Speak it."

"I've heard concerns about the ferry down there."

"Money, taxes. I'm not saying what's not known in town. Current ownership — for many, many years it was one family, the Dingmans, good family, holy people but they sold out not too long ago and present owners are better ferry men than businessmen. Have themselves squeezed. With the bank, with

34

the taxmen. Tough times for them. Word's about they might even lose it."

"The ferry operation?"

"The whole thing. Rights, land, all. That'd be terrible."

"Used to be a bridge there, right?"

"Bridge after bridge after bridge. The Dingmans kept building them, they kept losing them. The river didn't want them. You've got to respect the river."

"John, I need to tell you more about myself. Do you have some time?"

"Let's get you registered and take a pause in their tearoom."

Which they did, James presenting his business card from Horseheads Bridge Company, and briefly outlining the proposal to purchase a structure up north and transport it, disassembled, to the Dingman's site where they would reconstruct it and, having purchased the proper authorities and permits, they would undertake to operate it with as many local employees as possible. He and his brothers, he assured John, were good bridge men and good businessmen. What at this point he would ask of John would be continued guidance and counsel and help connecting with the right people. "I assume you know most of the folks hereabouts."

"We're the only church. Methodist or not, if they're believers they come to our church. So, yes, if they're believers, I know them. And if they're not, I'm trying to get them to be, so I know those too. How about I help you set up a meeting of the movers and shakers?"

"You know the Shakers too?" Wry smile. "I'd be honored to meet with all. Whenever you say."

"Next Sunday afternoon. Not tomorrow. Week after. I'll need time to enlist people. So Sunday the ninth. Let you know what time."

"Doing business on the Sabbath, pastor?"

"Think of it this way, Mr. Perkins, if you can really do what you have in mind to do, it'll be a Godsend. Those are permitted on Sundays." His eyes crinkle-smiled.

James walked with the preacher back to the church to fetch his rig and head to the telegraph office. *Closed for the Holiday*, read the sign on the door. But of course. So wrapped up was James in his project, and his travel, he had let it slip his mind. It was January first! It was 1898! A new year and new plans and — oh, my gracious — sometime late this month, a new child! What graces does God bestow upon the faithful and true?

On down the hill he rode, down by the Dingmans' Stone House to the site of the ferry. Dingmans Ferry, no longer Dingman's. We are fast approaching a whole new century, he thought. This dear, nestling town needs a bridge. We have to make it happen.

Next day, Sunday, he faithfully attended the only church in town, praying especially for his wife eager to hear of her, from her and to let her know that he would be home, he planned, well before the last week of the month. Long before their child would arrive. That, he would not miss.

On Monday he sent a telegram home via Will.

DINGMANS DOABLE STOP WORKING PROAGREEMENT TWO WEEKS STOP RELAY LOVE HELENWARDS ENDIT

Tuesday he took his horse and rig across the river on the ferry, the 120-foot-long, 60 foot wide flatboat. As he crossed, he sketched and made notes, paying special heed to the remnants of support piers from bridges past, what remained of abutments at either end; rolling up onto the Jersey side, he paused to look back at the hills of Dingmans Ferry. What a gloriously bucolic vista, what a vacationers' paradise. What an opportunity.

He followed a steeply ascending shale road as hills climbed abruptly from the river toward the village of Layton. It was orchard country, trees bared now by winter but throbbing still with their appley promise of next season's buds, blossoms, and autumnal fruit to be crunched, squeezed, canned and pied. James loved apple lands

Layton was a simple crossroads properly accoutered with a general store, an ice cream stand, closed for the season, a few houses, and all around, farms. He stopped for coffee at the store and got chatting with a gaggle of welcoming fellows who acknowledged to him that, to be sure, having to clang the bell to summon the ferryman and then wait for the crossing first this way then that in order to get to Dingmans Ferry was a sorry inconvenience and, yes, they'd love to see a bridge back operating there. Make lives a lot easier. And lure more tourists over to the Jersey side, too. Did he have an idea there might, one day, be a bridge again? "Could be, could be," he tantalized them. And was on his way, taking a doughnut with him for the road, a road that they had told him would take him, "should you want to go there and had time and patience for the travel, down to New York City itself. Or making a right turn you could circle around through the lovely Peters Valley to another postage stamp village called Bevans."

He chose that way. Classic black walnut trees formed a canopy arching over him as he drove, a pleasant way to journey. The road climbed then dipped again, all the while without sign of traffic or houses for a long while. Bevans was no more of a town than Layton but a place to make a hard right, as he had been guided to do and climb a much steeper hill rising past a few rock houses surrounded with farmlands, dark red berries still clustered on spent sumac, until finally the road began descending again. At one convenient stopping spot, he pulled up simply to look, look around at the steel gray waters of the river flowing slowly below, innocent waters, incapable, so they would have the dreamer believe, of the cruelly destructive nature at times ascribed to them. It hurt them, the waters whispered, to think that any would think them capable of evil. *Gaze upon us, you up there. Gaze and see for yourself, we are waters of peace. No fears need you have in bridging us. As we welcome the traffic that floats upon us, we welcome too that which spans us. A magnificent bridge does not demean the waters it crosses but enhances them. Bridge-builder, bridge-builder, when you do it, and we know you will: Make it magnificent!*

Back at the hotel, the river still with him, he enjoyed a dinner featuring one of its former denizens, a Walleye, respectfully sautéed, nested among mashed potatoes and green beans. These sent him contentedly up to his room and to his journal to set down the words he actually heard from the Layton gaggle and those he fancied hearing from the river.

Bridge-builder, bridge-builder, when you do it, make it magnificent. Those words went with him to sleep.

Next day, Wednesday, he drove the ten miles or so up alongside the river to the county seat of Milford, Pennsylvania. It took several hours and visits to many offices scattered around town to get the information he had intuited. Information that should make his assignment much easier.

Now, Thursday, he was back down at the river to hunt up Mr. John W. Kilsby. Years earlier, that gentleman had married the daughter of Andrew Dingman III and taken over operating the ferry. He had been off yesterday but James knew now he needed to talk to him and what to say.

"Mr. Kilsby, I have a business proposition that I think can be beneficial to us both." They talked for an hour, back and forth, perched on the gunwales of the ferry boat, James never directly revealing the results of his survey of county offices and records day before. Saying nothing about tax debts or the possibility of impending tax sale. They spoke of assets — mainly the boat, abutments east and west, the Stone House and the land it sat on, a handsome property of discernible value, the business, good will and -- significantly-- the governmental authorizations and licenses from the states on both sides. These were the greatest assets, as James understood. He briefed Mr. Kilsby on what Horseheads Bridge Company had in mind and assured him they had both the know-how and wherewithal to make this work, to render this much needed service to the communities around and their hoteliers and merchants. A deal could be good for everybody.

He also promised Mr. Kilsby employment once the new bridge was in place.

He was persuasive. He and the urgent need Mr. Kilsby felt to disentangle from problems that till today had felt to him insoluble. He was relieved and most happy to have this New Years gift extended. They agreed they would see lawyers and bankers tomorrow and get the transfer started. They would . .

CLANG, CLANG. From the far shore, business summoned. "See you tomorrow, Mr. Perkins. Rest well, I know I will." And as his guest disembarked, the ferryman set off toward the New Jersey side for, symbolically at least, one of the last times.

Friday was a billow of busyness. This office and that, these lawyers, those lenders. Counsellors and amanuenses. In its essence, it was two men trying to make complex matters simple that never should have been complex. Each sought the same result, whatever the paper people said. They were comforted by their shared determination to get things done such that their tentative acquaintance was annealed as a friendship by the time the day was done.

"Tea," asked the soon-to-be old owner.

"Let us," replied the soon-to-be new one.

In the tearoom at James's hotel, they sat at a corner table, finally relaxing, the billow dissipating. Things weren't done, of course not. But the progress and amity seen today deserved celebration. There would still be papers and interrogations but neither had doubt: It was indeed going to happen. The Horseheads Bridge Company was going to be buying the ferry operation with the full intent of constructing a new bridge across the river at that site.

From across the room strode a purposeful Pastor John, beaming as usual. "Gentlemen, you both seem lighted by good fortune pending. Do I read you right?'

"You do, indeed, pastor," said Mr. Kilsby, smiling the answer such that his words were unneeded.

"Well, Mr. Perkins, I have everything lined up a town gathering Sunday afternoon if you still think that useful."

"Thank you. I do indeed. In a way, more useful now that we have something significant to report. What time?"

"Say three, at the church."

"Perfect. And thank you."

A run to the telegraph office to report the good news, send wishes home once again and then supper, journal, and early abed. Not to sleep much, not to sleep, but to welcome a waking dream that was soothing and sweet.

Saturday morning. Oatmealed, coffeed and fruited, shod in work boots, James headed toward the river. The day shivered clear. He had no intended destination. The most salubrious walks do not. He padded pleasantly along unconsciously humming a favorite hymn, "Just a Closer Walk with Thee." Was he a godly believer? His dad and mom had raised him to be; he would raise his kids to be. But he? Was he a believer?

He was a mechanical engineer. He dealt in coefficients, structural integrity, angles and radii. His pocket was never without his "slip-stick" as he called his slide rule. With it he was like a Chinaman with an abacus, fingers flying, able to solve anything, so it seemed to the dazzled onlooker. So, yes,

James Perkins was a believer -- in himself and in his talents. But, too, he never referred to his talents, aloud or silently, without inserting the phrase "God-given." His God-given talents. He never failed to acknowledge.

Just a closer walk with Thee,
Grant it, Jesus, is my plea,
Daily walking close to Thee,
Let it be, dear Lord, let it be.

Especially since Howard was born, he had inwardly accepted and outwardly acknowledged his faith. How, having been so intimately involved in the miracle of birth, could he not? To be sure, many experienced without accepting. That happened, but not with James and Helen. Occasional churchgoers before the birth, they became regulars as soon as parenthood permitted. They would never again, they vowed, deny their faith nor fail to proclaim it.

He came now upon a farm here at the edge of the river. A sign announced *Riverside Cattle Farm* and, indeed several dozen head could be seen ranging the land from the shore up to what appeared to be an earthen dike either constructed or natural. What a wonderful place for cattle as it would be for people. He wondered if the farmer ever just came down here on a sun bright day like this, sat himself down on a hillock of grass and imagined.

Let us gather by the river,
The beautiful, the beautiful river,
Let us gather by the river
That flows by the throne of God.

What a challenge to work these acres in this relatively remote setting without a bridge to get the farm's products over to the marketing possibilities that lay across the river. In so many ways, the new bridge — the *old* bridge made *new* in this new location by him and his brothers -- can bless these good people, if . . . if they find the strength. And he knows they can. He picks himself up and sets out once more.

I am weak, but Thou art strong,
Jesus, keep me from all wrong,
I'll be satisfied as long
As I walk, let me walk close to Thee.

Through this world of toil and snares,
If I falter, Lord, who cares?
Who with me my burden shares?
None but Thee, dear Lord, none but Thee.

Not true, that verse. Not for him. 'Who cares?' Not only did his God care, so did the loving mate God had given him to share all. She would love this countryside, he hoped. She was greatly on his mind as he pondered the future, his and hers -- *theirs.* Especially was she with his thoughts because of what this night portended. He read it on the hotel calendar. Full moon. The full moon always called forth a ritual between the two of them. He must be outside tonight.

For hours he walked that morning till it was no longer morning. At one point he came upon a small store whose proprietor agreed to make him a sandwich to take along and directed his wandering to a glorious little waterfall tumbling down a chute of rock, the spray as it cascaded being transformed by light beams into magical, vertical rainbows.

Into a placid, leaf littered pool the waters gathered, exhausted from their ride, taking ease. As did James, seated poolside with peanut butter and jelly. And expectations. And challenges. And hope, mostly trust in God and hope. He lay back, head cradled by a cushion of leaves and closed his eyes.

How long lay he there? What is the distance from waking to sleep? How far to fragments of beckoning dream? What speed is needed to escape the now and pass into timeless time? Can a slide rule calculate that? Only by stopping to think and the purpose of lying there was to not to think but to be open to thought received, come from rays of sun. Gold. Silver . . .

Soon we'll reach the silver river,
Soon our pilgrimage will cease;
Soon our happy hearts will quiver
With the melody of peace.
So let us gather at the river,
The beautiful, the beautiful river . . .

It was dark by the time he had returned to town, dined and set off again for his special rendezvous. The sun had long since set but the moon was full and must have been at perigee, so large did it loom in the east. As he got closer to the river it seemed to unroll a luminous carpet across the water before him, inviting, inviting.

Long distance telephone service had been successfully tested a few years earlier permitting phone calls throughout a network put together by AT&T from Chicago to New York but it did not reach into small towns like Horseheads or Dingmans Ferry. That lack would not deter James, however, because he and Helen had found years before that the only communications medium their souls needed was the beacon of a full moon. James, gazing at it here, knew that where she was, she too was gazing at that same wrinkly-bright face, thinking, first, her own thoughts and then hers miraculously merged with his, however distant he may be as his were merged into hers, a blessed psychic union of the two of them, no AT&T required.

So he assumed it would be this night, two souls communing by the glowing, shared moonlight. But, gaze as he might, reach out best he could, however much he enjoyed the scene, he did not feel connection. Somehow, he did not sense a presence reciprocating.

How foolish! The man of logic and science muddled by failure to "sense a presence." Illogical. Still, as he walked back to his hotel up the hill, he could not help feeling uneasy. Was something wrong?

CHAPTER FIVE

WHATEVER SIGN IS ON IT, IN YOUR HEART YOU WILL KNOW IT
IS GOD'S BRIDGE.
                    — Pastor John, prophesying

H e didn't sleep well that night and come Sunday morning was eager to go to church for special prayer. He sought out Pastor John, was assured that all was ready for the town gathering that afternoon, so took a seat in a front pew and bowed his head. Prayer was the one form of communicating that had never failed him and he had plenty to talk to God about this morning. Praise, gratitude, intercession on behalf of Helen, that she was alright and God be closer than ever to her in these last days of his absence. He would be leaving for the trip home in another week. *Keep her and the unborn in Your loving arms until my return,* he prayed.

The pastor, selecting scripture for the morning's service, had purposefully turned to the Book of Joshua, passages as Moses' people were about to cross over into the Promised Land and were instructed to have the bearers of the holy Ark of the Covenant step first into the waters of the River Jordan and as they did, the waters would suddenly stop flowing, the river dry up, permitting safe passage. Then, after the people had crossed, the river once more gushed into life. The point he wanted to make was that such heavenly assistance was required in those days. "But in these days, we are expected by God to learn to solve our own problems for and by ourselves, although with His guidance."

"Brothers and Sisters, a man has come to our town. I don't know him full well but I assure you he is a man of God and of purpose and devotion. He does not carry with him the Ark of the Covenant, nor can he make the waters of our river stop even should he wish, but he does, I truly believe, have the grace of God with him and can give us a sturdy and sound way once again to cross that river in a way more keeping with our time than Joshua's." There was tittering in the congregation, at the reference back to Joshua, he guessed, but he saw no shaking of heads or any signs of disbelief.

Though embarrassed by the biblical hyperbole, James was encouraged by the seeming acceptance as the pastor went on to invite any and all to the meeting that afternoon, as he put it, "It's time to get our new bridge a-building."

James hoped, if all went well, to be able to spend yet another week beginning to line up the personnel to run this end of the operation: builders, steel men, laborers, money men, legal counsel, the like.

If all went well. And it did at that afternoon's meeting. For a few minutes. Then an unexpected reality crashed its surprising way into the proceedings.

The pastor had started the meeting in Parish Hall and it was filled, every seat, good sign. James took over to report the deal he was making to purchase the bridge right-of-way and proper licenses and authorizations, the Old Stone house and remaining bridge abutments and piers. He told of the old railroad bridge over the Susquehanna by Muncie and how his company would be disassembling and barging its pieces to here on the Delaware. "A new Dingmans bridge arriving in kit form," he joked. But this bridge of sturdy iron to last not just a few fleeting years but, he pledged, "a century or more." He saw eye rolls of skepticism, ignored them, intending then to begin his pitch for men to join the effort not by giving money but by making it, working on the project. He was in the midst of that when the door creaked open and a most uncomfortable little man, twisting his hat in his hands, apologized his way into the room asking if there might be anyone there named Perkins.

With James' reply, the man apologized again and explained. "Sorry to interrupt you gentlemen -- er, and ladies -- but not finding anyone around, I was told most everyone would be here. So here I came. Again, forgive the intrusion. I was told the message was most urgent, deliver at all costs. Your local telegraph office is closed Sunday's so the message was routed to our office in Milford with instructions to get it here as quickly -- absolutely as quickly as humanly . . . "

James interrupted. "Please, sir, if you have a message for me let me have it." Especially after his concern not having been able to communicate with his dear Helen under the moon last night, he was filled with dread as, finally, the messenger handed it over and clumsily, nervously, James ripped it open and read. From Will.

BABY BORN EVENING EIGHTH STOP ALL WELL MOTHER CHILD STOP HELEN SAYS LOVE STOP FRED SAYS COME HOME POP ENDIT

"Pop" dissolved. Clutching the telegram, he plopped onto his seat and unabashedly quivered and cried.

Pastor John rushed to his side. "What's the problem, friend?"

"Read," he handed him the message. "Our baby, our *Fred* was born last night." Likely while he had been out moon-gazing, wondering why he felt no return impulses. She at the time was in labor about to birth their son weeks early. He missed it. He swore he wouldn't but he did.

Finding the deliverer of his good news, he pressed upon him a handsome gratuity and asked if he would be able to courier an urgent reply. "Just say 'tell my wife I love her and tell baby Fred I'm leaving here tomorrow for home as he instructed.' Got that?"

"Yes, sir. And congratulations, sir." He left in apparent hurry which pleased James who turned back to the crowd he'd been addressing and explained the interruption though did not apologize. Let them share the universal Father's celebration.

"Dear God," the pastor intoned and the room fell silent, "We pray for the baby just born."

"Fred."

"Baby Fred. We pray for him and for his mother and especially for our new friend, his father. It was to be here to help us, our town, that he was not there to meet Fred's arrival. Bring him home speedily and safely to his family and then, when he returns to us, let us help his mission in every way we can. We pray in the mighty name of Jesus Christ, Amen."

"Thank you, pastor. May I ask of you all that you forgive my abrupt departure in the morning. And that you let Pastor know which of you are willing to work with us on this project. You'll be most fairly compensated, I guarantee you.

The room was slowly clearing, many coming by to shake James' hand, offer support, let him know they would sign up with Pastor John in the morning.

Pastor John, as all had finally left, turned to James and said, "I'm proud to know you. Proud that I've been given to a wee bit of prophecy for you."

"You're a prophet, too? A seer?"

"Let's say a dried up prophet. A sere seer."

Brother Will will like this fellow punster, thought James. "And your arid prophecy?"

Softly, sonorously, he laid his words before James as a sacred offering. Simple words they were, but in their simplicity was their power. James absorbed them in memory and as soon as he returned to his hotel room, before he started packing for his joyous drive home tomorrow morning, his returning to dear Helen, his meeting young Fred, congratulating Howard for having become a brother, a big brother — before any of that he took out his Journal, collected his pen and put down the words he would never wish to forget.

"Here is what I see in your future, son," Pastor John had prophesied, "Yes, you shall build your bridge and it will be magnificent as your voices insisted and people will think of it as *your* bridge but in your heart you will always know that in so many ways it is much more than yours and your brothers'. You will not give the bridge your name because you will know it is not yours. You build it for God. Whatever sign is upon it in your heart you will know it is Holy. It is and will always be a *God's Bridge.*

And one final prophecy: Time will come that your son, the one just born, will take charge of that *Holy Bridge*, and one day *his* son, while living at the bridge, will meet *God's* son. That will be truly *Magnificent!*"

CHAPTER SIX

"THIS IS GOING TO BE FUN, IF IT DOESN'T DRIVE US ALL CRAZY."
— *Brother Will Perkins at the new bridge site*

Never," thought James, "never since Jesus returned to heaven has there been a more joyous homecoming." A boisterous confusion of celebration it was, that Horseheads evening, Helen excitedly meeting him at the door, the two embracing, tender, heartfelt but brief, before she proudly rushed him over to the cradle where he stared adoringly at his baby son, Fred, stroked his sleeping, almost hairless pate, only then to be interrupted by an insistent tugging on his trouser leg, son Howard demanding at least a share of what used to his father's full attention before this intruder butted into his family. James bent down and scooped him up. "How is the little man of my life?" At which point, Helen was back and the three were in one awkward embrace which, given their love, was not awkward at all.

James was home.

"Come," said Helen, "have some tea."

"I'll get my things and take care of the horse. Then I have so much to tell you, good news. And I want hear from you why Fred chose to get into the act so early." He headed outside, she to the kitchen to get water going.

As they were enjoying tea and talk an interrupting knock on the door heralded two excited visitors, brothers Will and E. A. "Just sugar, no cream for me," blurted Will not waiting to be asked. This was family; that was fine. "Straight," said Will. And as Helen gathered cups and began serving the chatter began. It quickly grew cacophonous but it was not idle chatter; not small talk but big; not the logorrhea of flapping minds but the intensity of purposeful men catching up, briefing each other without having once to say STOP or ENDIT.

For most of an hour they sat at the kitchen table sharing their packets of good news, figuring next steps, roughing a calendar. "Just so he gets to spend enough time at home to get to know Fred Morton Perkins," insisted Helen.

"That's great, dear." Hearing the name, his new son's full name for the first time, surprised him. "We hadn't even discussed middle names."

"No, that we were going to work on when you got home, as promised, 'well before the baby is born.'"

"She got you there, Brother." Will's kind contribution.

"Thanks for noticing. But, dear," turning to his wife, "I love the choice. Uncle Mort will be thrilled." Morton was one of the clan back in Ohio, farming around Medina. Nor was baby Fred to be the only Perkins to bear Morton in his name. So would one of Fred's own son's three-and-a-half decades later. Which is to say, as I've explained, I.

Next day, in their small office, the principals of the Horseheads Bridge Company set to work. Yesterday, over tea, they had speculated and dreamed. They knew generally what they meant, what they intended. Now, they had to get specific,

54

make it happen. That meant marshaling numbers and schedules, estimating needed personnel in two locations, figuring budgets, arranging swing loans, assigning priorities in both time and geography. They spent the day working on it, so immersed that they called Maisie to ask if she would kindly send over some sandwiches and soda pops. And did she still, by chance, have any of her huckleberry pie? She didn't. They allowed as how they could somehow survive on apple. Ala mode, please.

Who would figure the best route and means of transportation for the "bridge in kit form" as they came to call the pieces they would salvage from up on the Susquehanna. What to do with bridge sections unneeded? Who to oversee that phase? Presumably E. A. who had done the workup. Similarly, James should be key man initially at Dingmans Ferry although it seemed wise for E.A. to take over there to operate it once constructed. Also, since the brothers' first task was to head north to get that end going James would have time at home for a while with his growing family. That's how it would happen.

Winter — with snow, ice, storms, cold — wasn't the best time to begin on the Susquehanna. But a perfect time for E. A. to start lining up equipment, men, barges and permits. By spring, then, he was ready to start.

It would take most of that summer of 1898 to dredge, dismantle, raise, select, arrange in collections those span components to destroy or sell as salvage and those to be loaded and barged to be reassembled miles and states away. . .

. . . where James would have his team ready to receive. Not that he had been slacking off in the meantime, he and brother Will. With an insistent backlog of jobs, they joined another firm to assist building a bridge down by Port Jervis, New York. A bridge and a separate structure as a live-in toll house.

Now, with 1899 gleaming over the New Jersey horizon, they were all gathered on the expectant shores of the Delaware to begin playing "puzzle-piecing," as they called it.

"This is going to be fun," enthused Will. "If it doesn't drive us all crazy." Actually, James with his "slip stick" and Will, the draftsman, prepared blueprints of their detailed plans while understanding that the best plans oft overlook some factor, that is, don't fit as planned. But let's say the brothers were as ready as they could be as the barges under "Captain" E.A. began floating down from up north burdened with gargantuan pieces of iron puzzle.

To this day there is a photograph in the annals of the bridge company showing what appear to be daredevils perched high atop the new Dingmans Bridge a-building. They aren't daredevils, of course — no Spandex, spangles or catch nets — and while perched precariously, the men seem to be making every effort to look insouciant in their brimmed hats (no baseball caps in those days and with no OSHA, no hard hats). A few wear baggy dungarees but, if eyes don't mislead, some of the men are wearing the recent rage for laborers: denim. Levi Strauss' original 501 jeans had been introduced just a few years before. Most wear long sleeve white shirts, seemingly a dressy cadre there on the iron. But no, look again.

It is not iron they surmount and cling to. The horizontals, verticals and angled members are timber, a wooden exoskeleton within which the iron trusses and spans are being bolted together. The cocoon, referred to as false work, in which is to be birthed "Magnificence."

Frozen in the single photograph, it seems an endless process, this creation. It must have seemed so, too, to the folk of the area awaiting anxiously the freedom of passage for people and products. It must have seemed so, as well, to the brothers, their investment, their risk, their dream so slowly taking form.

Just over a year it would take. Sour cynics watching from afar with memories close, wondered how many years it would be before *this* Dingmans Bridge would itself be blown down, washed away, crashed into and destroyed as every predecessor had been. How long?

The brothers didn't worry. They had three things going for them. They had raised the rock support piers even higher above normal river level. They were building with iron, not wood. And, with Pastor John leading, they had blessed to God their labors on the day work began and, again, in the early months of 1900 as laborers scrambled to the top of the three trusses to mark the "topping off" ceremony. All prayed while raising over the eastern truss the flag of New Jersey, over the western truss that of Pennsylvania and over the center truss the proud forty-five Stars and thirteen Stripes of the United States, two of those states now more firmly united than ever. As agreed by the brothers, E.A. would operate the reborn bridge, acting himself as toll taker and manager for its early years. Which would not be without challenge.

To be sure, in 1903, another fearsome storm would rampage down the Delaware and the waters would roil and the winds would rip and people would fret and when it was over, indeed, the crossing would be have to be closed for two months. But not because of the bridge. It survived unmarred. It was the roads leading to the bridge that failed. From the brothers, learning details, there was a flush of great personal pride. They had indeed built a bridge for a lifetime. That glowing pride was the first reaction, understandable but unwarranted, they unanimously agreed. For in their hearts they understood: It may have been their minds that made the bridge happen but the thoughts placed into those minds were not their own but had been given them, deposited by the sustaining life-force they knew as the Holy Spirit.

Their pride quickly morphed into prayers of gratitude.

The next menacing storms -- and they would be historic; hurricanes no less -- would not slam into the bridge until more than forty years later. Then, a new generation would be tested.

CHAPTER SEVEN

"... GREATEST NATURAL CATASTROPHE IN THE HISTORY OF THE
UNITED STATES."
    —*National Weather Service on Hurricane Diane, 1955*

In August 1955, Jillian Amacher was sixteen and about to
start her last year of high school. She was fair and bright, a
towhead who neither wore nor needed makeup even
when summer sun accentuated the freckles on her cheeks and
her button nose. Natural and content to be surrounded by
nature, she loved where she had lived all her life, here on the
shore of the Delaware River, on what her grandfather had
long ago named the Riverside Cattle Farm. What she
preferred to call their "ranch." She was born to the peace of the
place. Still, excitedly if a bit reluctantly, she would be leaving
before long, heading off to college. She hoped to attend Ris-
Dee, the Rhode Island School of Design in Providence, her
dream ever since she first started putting the pictures in her
mind onto paper, then canvas, then molding them from clay,
sculpting with plasticine. She tried woodcarving and pottery,
weaving and macramé. She learned a little in each discipline
and wanted to learn so much more. She had considered Pratt
or Parsons in New York City but they were in New York City.
Her folks had taken her there once. Once was enough.

Carnegie Mellon in Pittsburgh would be fine and in-state but RISD was her dream. She had already applied and now, anxiously, waited.

Her dad didn't much like the idea of "losing my daughter to some snooty New England place." Meaning her going away *anywhere.* Of course he knew that that couldn't be. Shouldn't. His wife, Bernadette, was right in telling him he needed to ease off. He wasn't about to lose his tomboy daughter. He was allowing his beloved fledging to learn to fly on her own. Wherever she flew, she would always return to the nest, to her dad. He and she would still have their precious times in the woods or on the water, she being the son he used to wish she had been. Under his tutelage over years, she learned to shoot; she could fish (though was never easy cleaning her catch). She and he loved camping in the Poconos down the way. Hiking the forest, inhaling the perfumes of the summer woods. Sometimes her mom would be with them. Jillian liked that. But without Mom, Pop taught her camp cooking. He was very good. She got pretty good. And enjoyed doing it knowing that when you're camping, everything you cook is *Haute cuisine.*

This particular August afternoon, Jillian was on the porch, looking out at the rolling river, rushing much faster than usual. She sat in a favorite wicker rocker, the chair needing no human propulsion, a freshening wind doing the rocking for her. Darkening skies and the radio agreed: heavy weather was coming. Very heavy.

"Another hurricane maybe." It was her dad taking the chair beside her. "We got a frightful soaking from the one last week. That miserable Connie. Now this one is supposed to be called

Diane. Why do they always have to name them? Take a lovely girl's name and ruin it. Glad they haven't tried to call one of their storms *Jillian*. I'd blow my stack."

"We're gonna have more than your stack blowing around here tonight, it appears."

"I don't worry as much about the wind. We're pretty well battened. Johnny Popper is safe in the shed."

"You love your old tractor, Dad."

"Not the most powerful John Deere ever made but the most reliable. We may need it after the storm passes to help clean up. Meanwhile, cattle can take shelter. They can handle it. I worry about the rain. If we have too much more rain, the ground's already saturated. Can't take much more before it just starts washing away and down the river. Riverside Cattle Farm would have no more farm."

"We'll be fine, Dad."

"Howdya know?"

"I've been assured."

"Got the word straight from Upstairs?"

"You taught me: Go to the Source."

"Trust Him always."

"*I* trust *Her* always."

"Ah, my burgeoning feminist. Would you compromise? Trust Him/Her always?"

"Always "

Skies were ominous. The wooly clouds now were mostly from black sheep. Fast ones at that. "Let's do what we can to be sure, Jilly. Come on." And he led her on a tour of the property, just the two of them, securing storm shutters, weighting down loose objects, hauling porch furniture inside, securing doors, the sort of things a father would normally do with a son. She was up to it and happy for the chance to work with him, to be trusted to do it. Many of her girl friends around the area would not think of being asked to do manual labor. Her pal, Susie, would never do it. She always said, "If it was meant for women to do, they wouldn't call it *man*ual."

They had dinner and in spite of the threatening storm, each headed off to bed, hoping perhaps to be able to sleep if for only a while.

An hour was all Jillian got before being roused by her Dad, jumping from bed, still clothed, and following him back out to the porch. A full moon, alternately obscured then revealed by scudding clouds transformed the scene into an old time stop action movie. Jerkily flashing before them was a horrible scene. Down by the river, two or three dozen head of cattle were out on the ridge, that rise of high ground running parallel to the river bank. Between the ridge and the main pastureland was a gully some twenty feet wide. In normal times, that hollow, though four feet deep, was no impediment for cattle traversing it. But this time was not normal. The gully was a lake, so saturated the soil by last week's Hurricane Connie that it could not absorb the pelting rains Debbie was mercilessly dumping. What could be done?

"Need help, Chas?" Neighbor Hank Lawson had to shout loud to be heard over the raging winds.

"Please," hollered Jillian's dad. "Gotta get those critters off the ridge, down through the gully somehow and up where they'll be safe. How?"

"We always loved playing cowboys, Chas. Giddyup." And he and Chas set out running through the slashing storm toward the wayward animals, Jillian, unknown to them, racing right behind.

"Gotta spook 'em," yelled Chas. "Get behind 'em. Force 'em this way, drive 'em right through that new river as they see it."

"I'll go over to the ridge," shouted Jillian, surprising them and taking over as her dad always enjoyed watching her do. "You guys close off both sides."

"How're ya gonna move 'em?" her dad shouted.

She said only, "Watch." And slogged through the slough up to the ridge by the river and once past the animals she reached down into her parka pocket and pulled out the revolver her dad — much to the dismay of her mom — had given her for her sixteenth birthday a couple months back. Aiming it into the sky, she fired three shots. *Blam! Blam! Blam!*

Startled, the cattle bolted with fright, rushing to get away as fast as possible, thundering, splashing through the gully, water or not. Through that ravine and up onto the level pasture land where, the "cowboys and cowgirl" felt they at last they would be safe.

"Hey, kid. That was great. As for you, Gene Autry." said Chas to Hank, "Come in. Have coffee."

"Thanks, Roy Rogers, but I better get home. You gotta be mighty proud of your Dale Evans there. She's sumpin."

Early next morning, storm mostly abated, Jillian and her dad went out surveying Diane's destruction. Didn't take long to see evidence. Johnny Popper's refuge shed was collapsed, the tractor wearing its fallen roof. Chas rushed over to examine it.

"Not good," was his crestfallen diagnosis. "Gonna take some serious work."

Out in the river, dashing along, they saw what seemed to be — what *were!* — pieces of houses being ripped downriver. Incredulous, they watched. Another piece, looked like a corner of a small barn. And then — No, *a car!* "'49 Studebaker," Chas told his daughter as though it mattered. Around their farm itself all else seemed well. Some shingles off, a shutter ripped down. All the herds seemed safe, intact. Back inside they checked the radio, hearing stories fearfully fraught. Numbers of people missing, maybe washed away; buildings leveled; roads awash; and up and down the Delaware, *many bridges completely destroyed!*

"It will be a very long time before this area can regain anything approaching normalcy." So the *theys* on radio were prophesying that awful August morning in 1955.

On one hand, they were right. When governments, which have always been better at tabulating disasters than preventing or ameliorating them, had done their assessments they would proclaim the enormity of two historic hurricanes, one right after the other, less than a week apart, Connie then Diane. What one damaged, the other destroyed. What one soaked, the other engulfed. Depending on how much of their swaths were counted, those unladylike ladies were responsible for dozens, scores, even multiple hundreds of human deaths.

The National Weather Bureau would later insist: "The hurricane season of 1955 was the most disastrous in history."

Adding this specific superlative: "Hurricane Diane was the greatest natural catastrophe in the history of the United States."

But, as several proud kin of three brothers from Horseheads named Perkins would happily learn: The Dingmans Bridge had survived! Fundamentally intact. None of Diane's floating projectiles of debris had struck it. Support pillars had recently and wisely been raised just enough that her surging waters climbed just to the level of the bridge's wooden floor planks before safely subsiding. Abutments maintained. Shorelines held. *The Dingmans Bridge withstood!*

For the most part, the town and people of Dingmans Ferry fared relatively well. The several churches of the town gathered in earnest prayers of gratitude that Sunday morning, echoes of the many private prayers whispered or spoken across the land in preceding days.

What the thankful people had yet to learn was that however horrific nature's fury might be, other forces in coming days would prove even more evilly ruinous.

CHAPTER EIGHT

IF YA GET IN A TOUGH PLACE, DITCH YOUR I.D. TELL 'EM, HE'S
BARNEY GOOGLE, MY NAME IS DOOGLE
— *Friend, rehearsing our escape from the KKK*

H ow did it happen? Without planning, almost
without my knowing, that's how it happened and I
had a career.

Bless something or a series of somethings, I thought, not
yet entertaining the idea of a *Someone*. The Someone, were I
pressed to name one, I would have said was obviously myself,
a guy with both talent and persistence who knew how and
when to take advantage of opportunities. That's how it
happened that the high school speech tournament winner was
awarded a job on the local Wooster radio station, WWST, to
deejay a show called *Hi-Jinks Harmonies;* from there moved to
the big city, Cleveland's WGAR to do news; then start a news
department at a Cleveland TV station from which there would
be occasion to feed stories across the country on NBC's newly
inaugurated *Huntley-Brinkley Report,* those stories well-crafted
and well-received by network executives such that suddenly —
so it seemed in the scheme of things — while still in my
twenties I had climbed the career ladder to that rung labeled
"*NBC News Correspondent.*" (As the fates or whatever would

have it, my brother was not many steps behind me on the career ladder.)

My immediate boss at first was the best of the breed, the peerless anchorman, David Brinkley, among broadcasters, the master of concision. *Say it simple; say it once. If you leave something clever out, don't fret. No one knows that you* didn't *say.*

A son of the South, Brinkley was distressed by the way some Southerners were treating other Southerners of different colors. It was a shame at the least, a national travesty at worst, and he believed his network ought to be "reporting the hell out of it." He explained, "What's happening is certainly an evil; hell is being visited daily upon a people who have done nothing wrong but to wear skin of a color some bastards down there don't like."

When Brinkley said "down there," he meant where he came from. Wilmington, North Carolina had been home. And to be sure, southern courtliness still tinged him but southern bigotry, bias, and hatred were anathema. "It's hell. So how do we help exorcise the hell? By shining our lights, by reporting the hell out of it." He said it simple, said it plain. And saw to it that his newest colleague would be assigned to the story.

Over coming months, pursuit of that Story of the Century would send me careering from Jackson, Mississippi (where NBC's local TV affiliate station refused to carry my reports on their station) to New Orleans, to St. Augustine (where bullies in official positions dragooned me out of town), to Atlanta, to Birmingham, to Selma, and back to D.C. for what would prove to be an historic culmination called The March On Washington. Hundreds of thousands of people poured into

68

the nation's capital strewing themselves across National Mall from the Capitol to the Lincoln Memorial where, with the Great Emancipator looking down on it all, Joan Baez sang, Bob Dylan sang, Mahalia Jackson sang. Many people sang and many people spoke but in the end, one — just one — would truly be remembered. He was a man despised by some, feared by others, threatened often, jailed frequently and ultimately murdered, but by many people of varied stations and colors at that time admired, even idolized.

And never forgotten.

The memories of his soaring oratory that day might get twisted. Jumbled. Things happen. What once is indelible in the mind, can evaporate like fog words breathed on a window.

Or like when something you could never have expected to happen — happens. And you, incredulous victim, can't for the longest time understand.

What was it? I don't know. There's so much I don't know. I listen. I listen and I hear but what? And what does it mean?

Peace they cried, but peace was not.
Once the charade-parade had passed
It seemed so clear it could not last
For there were anger, boiling hate
And hate and hate and hate and hate.

I'm muddled, I'm muzzy. And all that comes is verse? Elliptical verse? What good is that?

What happened? I lie here, unseeing, unhearing and don't know what it was but something, something horrible happened. Something hateful I seem to sense though with

what sense or senses I cannot tell. What was it? Is it?
Something put me here. Where is here? I am here but where?
Why?

Hate happened. Hate and hate and hate. That's what. How?
Hate happened somewhere. Where? Somewhere else. How?
Exploded. Hate exploded. Hate exploded and I heard it. I was
there. I must have been there. Where? I heard it. I felt it. I feel
it yet. I lie here and still hear it and feel it happen there. Not
here. It wasn't here. I'm sure it wasn't here. But where is here?
I am here. I am awake. Was I asleep? Here? There? Where?
And why? And how long? If I've been asleep why and how
long?

I hear it. Again I hear hate exploding. Or still. What do I
feel? What do I see in this gauzy place I do not know?
Questions whirl but answers don't whirl with them. Even if
they did I couldn't catch them. You can't grab hold of answers
that whirl. Whirl like a room that is spinning, insanely
spinning in bursting, numbing noise. The noise, the noise of
silence.

Silence and pain. Torturous pain stabs in parts of me I
never knew could hurt. Aren't only muscles supposed to hurt?
I think my bones hurt. Every movement hurts. And mostly my
mind. My mind is pained. It is pained I believe by what it
knows but will not tell me. Not yet. It knows where I am and
why and what it means and maybe what's to come of it, of me.
It bears a frightful burden, my fright-filled mind.

What? Where? Why? Who? When? The classic reporter's
questions. Am I a reporter? If I'm a reporter how did that

happen? What am I supposed to be reporting? This reporter on this day — or night — cannot answer. That hurts too.

I fix on these things for a moment or hour or day until they dissolve. No. That's not right. They don't dissolve. I do. I dissolve back into the nowhere I came from. Into the whiteness, gauzy whiteness everywhere, everything . . . white.

A week later, or a month — there is a clock on the white mists of wall but no calendar. I cannot know the day or date and of the time only the number eight. Morning? Night? As I puzzle this latest conundrum there softly materializes from the cloud that masquerades as wall, a form, an apparition approaching, a vaporous vision. As it nears there is a ghastly scream of terror and then another, piercing. Followed by a soft assuaging voice, that vaporous woman trying to soothe the paranoid screecher before her.

"How are we feeling today, Mr. Doogle?"

What? "No, no!" I insist, my voice more normal (if I remember what my voice used to be), no longer screeching, "I'm not, I'm not . . ."

"Now, now, Mr. Doogle, I just came in to see how you're doing."

"You're wrong." Why can't I get through? "I'm not . ."

"Not going to get any more injections until the doctor comes by in a little while. Don't worry."

"Please, ma'am, nurse, whatever, I'm trying to tell you. I'm not what you called me. Not Doogle."

"Now, now, we'll get it all straightened out. You just rest. The doctor will be here soon."

"But I'm not . . ."

Yet as she walks away, disappearing once more into the vagueness of white, I wonder. Am I? Maybe, from what happened to me, whatever happened, I truly don't know who I am anymore. Maybe I *am* Mr. Doogle. The name does sound familiar. Somehow familiar. Doogle. Maybe I am.

No. I'm — think, think hard. It's in there, my name, who I am, really am, why I'm here with all these wires and tubes sticking in me. It's all in there, up there. Think.

Or sleep. Maybe I can find what's in there, up there, in sleep.

Too many. I don't drink beer. Hate the taste. Dirty socks squeezed through a wringer. Remember wringers? Mom used to use one to squeeze the beans out of the lima pods from the garden. Pods go one way, beans fall into a basket. Lima beans, socks, beer. Too many beers and Bunky and I get to plotting. Bunky! He and I have worked so many stories together I never use his full name. He's happy I don't. *Farnsworth Buncombe?* That was a county in North Carolina. Buncombe County. Its congressman made a speech once. A colleague called the speech "So much Buncombe." Word got shortened to "Bunk." So much bunk! Can't blame Bunky for not wanting to be Buncombe.

So there we were, Bunky and I, playfully plotting. "If they ever come after us, ever come after us, here's what we do. Give 'em phony names. Ought to have code names." Made perfect sense in the beer-fog of the moment.

"Why the hell we need that?"

"The *Northern* press. That's what we are," he said. "The enemy."

"You're paranoid, man."

"If we don't tell the stories, how the Bull Connors of the world, his police dogs and firehoses, and the Klansmen down here are treating folks, black folks, nobody'll know, nobody'll care. It'll keep happening. They want it to keep happening so they don't want us down here telling on them. Have another."

I remembered one day there was a comic strip character called Bunky. He said, yeah, and another one named Barney Google. *Barney Google.* That was something. How? That still, it seemed, was something. What? Why?

Sleep. Find the answer in sleep.

Or in pain. Everywhere pain.

Bunky. Bull. Barney. Barney Google. There it was! Code name. That's what we agreed on that beer-sodden night at Dennery's in Jackson, Mississippi. Great place. That's where we connived. "Get in a tough spot, ditch your I.D. They ask your name, tell 'em, *He's Barney Google, my name is Doogle.*"

Doogle!

I ring for the nurse. Same one as before. "I've got it. You're right. I *am* Mr. Doogle.'

'Good. Things are coming back. "I'll be right back, Mr. Doogle."

There was an unreadable smile on her face as she walked briskly out and down the hall, to return not more than a minute or two later, accompanied by a woman in business suit with short-bobbed graying hair, handsome and business-like. "This is our hospital director, Mr. Doogle."

"That'll be all, Nurse Edwards. Thank you." And the nurse closed the door behind her, leaving the two of us alone.

Her name tag read *Eugenia Palmer, Director, St. Anthony's Hospital.* Business-like, she launched in. "Let me tell you what I know, Mr. Doogle. First, that you're *not* Mr. Doogle. I know your name, who you are and why you're here. Your friend, at first he called himself Barney but I know his name too, brought you here seven days ago. Been checking back with me — only me — twice a day. Gave me the whole story which I have not yet shared with anyone else. Though people have certainly tried. I'll get to that in a moment. You need to know all this. Your doctor believes you're ready for it though he himself doesn't know what I'm about to tell you. What do you recall? Shall I call you Mort?

"Mort, that's it. Thanks. But, no, I'd rather Perk.

"Well, Perk, you were at a church. Remember that?"

"Me in church? Not really."

"Sunday morning. 16th Street Baptist. Just before services. Down in the basement with the kids. Remember at all?"

I did. A bit. Murkily.

"Take your time. No rush."

There's never a rush in the Civil Rights Movement. Run on their own time, those brave — some say foolhardy — civil-rightsers. 16th Street Baptist. Birmingham, Alabama. I could see it, three-story brick, handsome place. Been there many times. When King, Abernathy and Shuttlesworth got together to plan things. They trained their Children's Crusades there.

Children! I saw it. Through the murk, I saw them, dozens of Negro youngsters, ten, eleven, twelve, mostly girls, and I was right there with them when . . .

74

. . . I felt it. I felt it again and I heard it. I grabbed a couple of kids, fell on them, clutching them. The explosion, the explosion of hate. But what was it?

"Let me take over," Ms. Palmer says. "That explosion, that bombing about ten-thirty that morning killed four of those dear little girls, little black girls down in that basement. Blew the whole wall off. You were in that basement when it happened. Your friend told me that. He had gone out to get shots of people coming in but you were down there in that basement, trapped.

"You know, Perk," she continued, more personally reflective now, "when Bull Connor was finally voted out of office a few months ago, I had hope for our town. For way too long his police had terrorized Negroes of all ages around here, all stations. You know the stories. The firehoses, dogs turned loose on 'them uppity damn niggers,' he called 'em. You probably reported some of those stories yourself."

"More than I might have wished."

"But now even with Bull gone, his Klan henchmen are still around, still cruel and vicious and mostly still in control. Untouchable. You can bet some of them were behind this. Speaking of which, you had visitors today. Just a few hours ago."

"Bunky? Barney?"

"No. No one you know or want to know, believe me."

Her way of speaking was casual but the import insistent. She was not here just to talk. There was urgency to her tone.

"Three men. Asking for you by name. Your real name. Don't know how they got it but our receptionists, not knowing your real name, it not being anywhere in our records, had them see me. I know one of them, man named Bobby Frank Cherry. Definitely Klan. Maybe they knew that you, that damned northern troublemaker, had saved two of the girls' lives, and want to teach you a lesson in southern manners. You may be at risk from more than your medical problems. Those will take time, rest, therapy and lots of good doctoring perhaps for months but not here. Here is no longer safe for you. Not as long as the Klan's so close on your trail. Nor can you count on protection from our local gendarmerie. It doesn't work that way down here. You know that."

"I do. So what's the answer? Ideas?"

"Not just ideas. Plans."

But at that point came a discreet knock on the room door and a tentative voice. "Ms. Palmer, something urgent,"

"Come in. Nurse Edwards," she said impatiently, "I didn't want to be disturbed. What is it?"

"Sorry, but I thought you needed to know there was a man just here looking for,. for . . . He said another name, not Doogle, but I thought you should know. Might be some connection. I know it's not my business but . . ."

"Who was he? What did he say? What did he want?"

"His name, he said, was Chambliss, Robert Chambliss. He said he'd heard that a man who had been hurt last Sunday in the explosion at the church, that the man was a dear friend of his and he wanted to see him."

"And you told him? What?"

"We had no one by that name. He said was I sure. I looked again through the patient log and said, yes, I was sure. So he left. I came right here. Just didn't feel right about it. Or him."

"You did right. Better get back to your station. Oh, and have Dr. Bullock paged to this room, stat." As the nurse withdrew, the director said to me, with urgency sharpening her voice, "We have to go."

"Go? But I . . ."

"You'll be alright. Dr. Bullock will be with us. We've planned the whole thing. Your friend says your bosses approve. They're paying for it. We had hoped we wouldn't have to do it, not so soon. But we're ready."

"For what?"

"To save your life."

A doctor entered. Name tag: Zachary Bullock. He spoke hurriedly with the director, gave me a perfunctory greeting, and produced a needle. "Best get you ready for a little trip," he said with no explanation. "I assume you know what I mean." But before I could reply . . .well . . . er . . . I couldn't. Words came tumbling forth but their laces were untied. They made no sense. Instead I began hearing myself singing. Feebly, off-key, singing: *We shall over-* . . . *overcome, shall come* . . . *Deep in my heart* . . . *over* . . . Baez . . . Dylan. Quarter million people. Quarter million, someone said. "Not here to tear down walls but to build bridges," boomed a stentorian voice. And I heard. I believed. Bridges. We all need . . . have a dream. All need. That was three weeks ago, only three weeks ago and I was there hearing about the great man's dream and dreaming it with him. Now? Now forget dreams. I'm running for my life.

God's Bridge

Trying to find a bridge that leads out of hell. Bridge from hell to where? Where are these people I don't know taking me? Where's Bunky? Barney Google? My name, sir, is not Doogle.. .. not Doog . . .not . . .

CHAPTER 9

ON BEHALF OF THE UNITED STATES AIR FORCE WE ARE PROUD
TO WELCOME TODAY A MAN WE CONSIDER A HERO.
--Commanding Officer, Stewart Air Base

Where? With whom? Do I know any of these people around me as I find myself foggily coming to with the drone of engines and the familiar jostle of an airplane in flight.

"Doogle!"

I see him. I shout. "*Barney Google!*"

Those around exchange smiles of satisfaction at my recognizing my old buddy, while Bunky himself falls into character instantly.

"Ah, yes, I do believe it's none other than Mr. Doogle himself. I've gotta tell you fella, it's mighty damn good to see you here. Awake. Hell, better than that, *alive!*"

"I'd say praise God, if I believed in one."

"We've still gotta work on that, friend. I'd think after all you've gone through and facing all you aren't yet *through* going through you'd be a candidate for a revelation."

"Hell, man, how can I be praying about a deity when I have no idea where I am, who these people are, where we're headed or why. I don't even remember much about why I'm here. Wherever 'here' is and wherever we're going."

"So the Giver of Information wants someone to give him some. Howdya like those turned tables, Perkins?

Perkins! First time I've heard my name, my real name spoken for . . . how long has it been?

It's a small plane. Charter type. Bunky gets up from his seat across and works the aisle like a Stew, pointing to people as he goes, introducing:

"Most important, your attending physician and secondary plotter in this escape — and believe me, Perk, you needed an escape —the eminent Doctor Zachary Bullock. A man history will one day either praise or condemn for saving your sorry butt. And most of your other parts."

"Just most?"

"All you're gonna need. And this," continuing his tour of introductions, "is the lovely if not always wholly compliant — as, sadly, I have discovered — Nurse Sally Beckwith."

"Give him an 'A' for effort, though," says the young nurse, smiling.

"I can see why he'd try," I laugh, quite agreeing with my friend's judgment.

"And, Perk, guess by whom the good nurse was hired. Who's footing the whole bill for hospital, doctors, nurses, charter flight and has made all the plans for your next stop. Guess?"

"Bull Connor?"

"Oh, man, you're close. Bill McMurphy."

"Mac? The network?"

"But of course. The Peacock. Which brings me to our next introduction." A young man, out of place in a suit and tie, steps forward from his seat, "Mr. Arthur Gradszinski. Don't try to spell it, you have enough problems. Arthur is the Unit Manager New York sent to arrange things and most importantly, pay for them. Perk, I tell you, the network folks seem to like you a lot, value you highly, though I can't figure why."

"I love you, too, man." And turning toward the new fellow, "Pay him no heed, Arthur. And if I'm not wrong that'd be G-R-A-D-S-Z-I-N-S-K-I."

"Correct. I'm proud to know you, sir."

"We'll get along fine, Arthur. And let me say one thing more to all of you good people here. Thank you. For more than I know. More than I'll ever be able to repay. I guess, from what little I do know. Thank you, simply, for my life. And with that, I am done talking." But far from done crying. *My life.* Even if I don't yet know details, the *how's* and *what's,* I am powerfully persuaded that these people around me right now saved my life. Or to put it another way, gave me a new one.

I melt.

The doctor steps forward. "Sir, I don't want to give you any more shots unless you feel need. What's your pain level, one to ten?"

"I'm okay. Say three or four. I'm just pretty overwhelmed by everything, everyone. Wouldn't want a shot against loving gratitude even if there were such a thing."

"Oh, there is. I wish there were some inoculation I could give against hate. That's what's needed in our lives these days."

"You're a Southerner, Doc?"

"Who doesn't feel a need to raise himself up by grinding others down. Some would call such as me fools or hypocrites."

"I call you rare."

"Not as rare as you may think, or as your newspapers and TV report. I tell you we reasonable ones are the majority of Southerners, albeit a far too silent majority. Intimidated, fearful, given of good intentions but timid expression."

"What's the answer, Doc? Is there an answer, one answer?"

"Let me ask you this." He leans forward to impress his sincerity and devotion to what he is about to say. "Where were you when you were injured? What were you doing there? When the explosion came, why, instead of seeking shelter for yourself, was your first instinct to shelter those two little girls near you? Why did you risk your own life that way to save theirs? You didn't know them. Why?"

I close my eyes. Sheltered in darkness, through a kaleidoscope of tumbling thoughts, I try to find the words, the answer or answers for him and mostly of course for myself. Engines drone, plane-mates chatter in hushed voices, sounds that themselves ask questions though none of them, I sense, as important as the ones Dr. Bullock just asked. Why? Why did I do what I'm told I did? And why, most of all, am I so tightly bound these days in a cocoon of *Why's?* Will this butterfly ever be free to fly?

" . . . at 18,000 feet. Speed 350 against slight headwinds. ETA Stewart, about forty minutes from now."

The pilot's report brings me back. Back to even more questions. But, somehow, I still feel the ones Dr. Bullock posed are more important. Opening my eyes, I see him still there, waiting.

"Doc," I say softly, talking to him only, not others around. "I can't reply. I mean, I can reply but not answer. I don't know why I did what I did. Never been the hero-type. In a way, I guess, I'd have to say I didn't do it. Something else, maybe *someone* else did it."

"Which means you ought to get thinking more about what your friend was suggesting a few minutes ago."

"What's that?"

"That with what you're going through, you ought to be a candidate for a revelation."

"God talk from my doctor?"

"Who better than a person who sees God's miracles around him every day. The miracles of the inconceivably complex machine that is man. The miracle of its functioning, its ability, in most cases, to repair itself as needed with only slight assistance from a human physician who, of course, will take all the credit as he debits the patient."

"You're different, Doc."

"Because, though I believe in myself, my learning and abilities, I believe mostly in the Great Physician."

"God?"

"God."

If I am not comfortable with his talk, his God talk, I am glad for him.

"Starting our descent . . . " the pilot again. "Should be landing Stewart in just under twenty minutes. "

"Okay, folks," I put it out to the crowd. "I'd be really grateful if someone would fill me in. What the hell is going on? What and where is Stewart? Why are we going there? Or anywhere?"

Bunky goes first. "Perk, you were in danger as long as you were in Birmingham. The Klan had word that a northern spy — you! — had butted in and saved two little *nigger kids* and they determined to teach you and any other northerner interlopers who might have ideas about butting in to their good ole southern ways a lesson they'd never forget. And any other intruders would be scared off by. At least they'd maim you, maybe kill you to warn others away. The fact you're one of the hated northern press made it all the better. Somehow, they learned your name — I think one of the local papers reported it: I didn't see — but we had very carefully registered you into the hospital with the code name you and I agreed on long ago and to only the head of the hospital did I tell the full story. Everything seemed covered but when Klansmen who were covering all hospitals came nosing around we began -- she and I and New York and the good doctor here -- began making escape plans. Doc naturally wanted to hold off as long as possible to get you stabilized. But then when the last visitor came, a guy Ms. Palmer knew by rumored reputation as a Klan executioner, that was too much. We had to act. That's when Arthur very quickly got wheels turning."

The young man in the suit gets up from his seat, takes over the account.

"Not wanting to wait even till morning, I ordered the plane to be ready to take off by oh-three hundred. That's three in the morning, Mr. Perkins."

"Yes, Arthur. Thank you," I say it without sarcasm. It's no time to belittle a rescuer.

"Where we're going is a hospital in Port Jervis, New York. St Francis Hospital. It gets you well away from the South and the resilient, vindictive Klan while also keeping you away from big cities which I know you do not favor. Yet you'll be only ninety minutes from the Apple and network brass. And yet will have superb big-city quality care. Your new friend, Dr. Bullock, has a brother named Jack who is the head of cardiology at St. Francis and, all in all, influential and respected throughout the hospital. Indeed throughout the medical profession. We checked him out, of course. He will oversee your entire program of rehabilitation in coming weeks. He'll be personally responsible."

"Great. Thanks. And Stewart?"

"Home of an Air Force base, Stewart Field. It's the closest field for us. We had to make special arrangements through the Pentagon to permit this civilian plane to land there and our ambulance to be waiting to pick you up. Took a lot of effort and no little exercise of political influence."

"You're the man, Arthur. "

"Maybe, sir, but you're the reason."

The rest of the briefing includes a cursory discussion of injuries and prospects. Till now, treatment has been aimed at stabilizing me. Now, at the new hospital they'll be able to take it from there, diagnose more precisely the extent of injuries, select best modalities of treatment. It'll take a while, I'm told, and the network is fully supportive regardless the time and expense it may require.

"You're a hero, as they see it -- as the public sees it too," says Arthur. "New York is very proud."

Hero. The word bothers me. I shake my head not only to deny heroism (it isn't heroism, I figure, if you don't know you're doing it) but also hoping to feign humility which has never been my métier.

"Good to hear. Thanks, Arthur. Are you ever Art?"

"To no one but you, sir. Please."

The plane lands soft as an angel and pilot's back on the p.a..
"The ambulance has already been pulled into position and the support car. They're ready for you, folks."

Ready, we find, with more of a welcome than we intruders on their military base expected. The sun is just rising, a small brass band playing, flags waving, a squad of uniformed airmen standing at attention as my gurney is rolled down a ramp, at which point an officer steps forward, gold braid gleaming, to read a document.

"On behalf of the United States Air Force and the men and women of Stewart, we are proud to welcome today a person we consider a hero." That word! "Not a serviceman doing his military duty but a civilian going far beyond duty to save lives of some of the most vulnerable of our citizens: children. We stand here today to honor you, sir, and pray you a quick and total recovery. Signed by me as commanding officer, Stewart Air Base." He leans down, hands me the document, comes erect and salutes. It is a salute that physically I am unable to return so I respond in the only way I seem to know lately. With a gusher of tears. Clenching my eyes, I turn aside, hoping he and his men will understand that my weeping expresses a profound gratitude for an honor I know I don't deserve.

It takes just under an hour to reach the hospital in Port Jervis where another embarrassment awaits. I shouldn't feel this way, I know, but crying in public challenges the ego. This time, no martial band, no military formation, no commander's proclamation. More moving even than those. A *Welcome Perk* banner rough-scrawled over the hospital entrance, and maybe a dozen nurses and doctors standing outside softly applauding as I am wheeled by. The faucets open again.

One of the waiting doctors steps forward and I ready my attention but he slides right past me to the man at my side. The two doctors Bullock, Zack and Jack, embrace heartily, greet warmly and only then turn my way for introductions. "Mr. Perkins," says *my* Dr. Bullock, "meet your new Dr. Bullock. I place you in the hands of the second finest physician I know, Doctor Jack Bullock."

"Doc, nice to meet you. You can call me . . ."

"*Mister* Perkins," Bunky interrupts.

"Ignore that guy, Doc. He used to be a friend of mine."

"Yeah," Bunky says, "until he became a big time celebrated hero and dumped his old buddies."

"I do think," New Doc observes, "you guys argue too much to be enemies."

"I got me a pretty smart doc, Bunky, don'tcha think?"

"Smart enough to put you in your place."

"And at this moment, son," insists New Doc, "your place is inside in bed. We have a lot of work to do, you and I. We'll start this afternoon. See, I'm a nice guy. Give you a whole half day to sleep. Of course that's mainly so I can catch up with little brother. Here we go."

Two orderlies push my gurney through the doors, down a corridor, down another and into a room, a private room I'm glad to see which, I guess, will be my home for a while. A while.

CHAPTER TEN

I SHALL SOON LOSE MY LAND, MY LEGACY AND MY LIVING.
DAMN IT TO HELL!
-- *Chas Amacher to government officials*

The United States Army Corps of Engineers was founded by Thomas Jefferson in 1802. Initially based at West Point, New York, for decades it was the only engineering school in the nation.

Over years, the Corps was active in the Civil War, building fortifications, pontoon and railroad bridges and roads. Several Corps-trained commanders led men into battle: Grant, Halleck and Meade for the Union, Lee, Johnston and Beauregard for the Confederacy.

During both the First and Second World Wars the Corps was counted on and heroic. Helping end the war with Japan were Corps contributions to the Manhattan Project. Add to their proud list of achievements: The Pentagon, (built in just 16 months!), the Gatun Locks for the Panama Canal. the Kennedy Space Center, Washington Monument, Bonneville Dam, restoration of the Everglades, and across the country, being the largest provider of recreational space in the nation. The Corps also maintains inland waterways from the Ohio and Mississippi Rivers to lakes, canals, and locks and bridges and dams.

Dams. Great affection for dams. And now the Corps had plans for another. They had had the plans for many years, tucked away on a shelf all this time. Someone in the Corps — whether needing a new project to bring attention to his career or needing a way to expend funds and thus keep his department from the risk of its annual budget being shrunk — Heaven forbid! — had begun dreaming. Dreaming of what would be known as the Tocks Island Dam. Had a nice ring. Unless you knew where Tocks Island was and what a dam there would mean to hundreds, thousands of voiceless people.

Oh, to be sure, the project as dreamed could provide some always needed drinking water for thirsty Philadelphia and New York City. That could help sell the scheme. Too, it would create a beautiful, broad lake, forty miles long, a mile wide, and 130 feet deep, great for sportsmen, fishermen, boaters, water-skiers.

Some would love it.

Some would hate it.

Countless would suffer.

Tocks Island, you see, lay smack astride the Delaware River between the Delaware Water Gap downstream and Dingmans Ferry upstream. The town and its bridge under this dream, this plan, would end up fully submerged beneath the new lake. Not partly, not somewhat, fully!

The people, hundreds of people, would be driven away, whether or not they wanted to go. Dingmans Ferry, the popular, quaint, quiet refuge for metropolitans seeking a natural escape would no longer exist. How could that be permitted to happen? It mustn't. Don't worry, so far it was only a bureaucrat's dream. Plans on a shelf, drawing dust. Easily forgotten. Easily.

Until those pernicious ladies, Connie and Diane, came calling. Now someone in Washington — perhaps a congressman hoping to get his name on a dam or, even better, on that beautiful new lake — urged the guy at the Corps who had told him about the plans years before to dig them out; this might be their time. They could be sold as future storm protection for the whole area, flood abatement. The Corps could have another feather in its cap. Better move fast. But, of course, nothing in Washington moves fast. Even things that mean some bureau or agency or department or Corps gets to spend money.

Indeed, the coming months and years would example how cruel — many thought dictatorial — the American government could be. It had powerful tools available. Confiscation, eminent domain, outright seizure. As a local paper wrote, federal enforcers swarmed over the land "some say like storm troopers, others say like locusts" devouring all before them.

Jillian Amacher was home when they knocked on the door at the Riverside Cattle Farm. For several years she had been back from her college time, those four exciting and fulfilling years at Rhode Island School of Design. She was a talented freelance artist, working several accounts including American Greetings for whom she illustrated greeting cards while so pleasantly living back where she belonged, here on the farm with dad and mom.

Answering the knock, she saw a pasty, self-important Caspar Milquetoast of a man, flashing government credentials, gilded, embossed and meant to impress if not downright intimidate. The credentials were far more imposing than the man.

Jillian was not surprised by his arrival. For months they all had heard of confiscations beginning. They knew their farm might be next. It was not a surprise. Nor did they have any valid idea what to do about it. Even to forestall it. Talk around town was that when these guys were finished there wouldn't be any town. No one could fight it however hard they might try. (Which was not true; we'll get to that.)

Valid as people's objections seemed to them, they did not seem so to pasty Milquetoasts. Milquetoasts, thwarted, could simply step into phone booths and come out Supermen armed with writs and injunctions and powers of expropriation and dispossession against which no mere citizen could prevail. Simple Americans have no writ of right.

"You are the owner here?" Caspar asked her.

"No. God owns it. He owns the land, cattle, sky above, river flowing out there. Some men think they ought to own those things but frankly . . ."

"Please, Ma'am, I need to speak to the owner of, er," consulting his papers, "the Riverside Cattle Farm."

"Good idea. I think we all should to talk to Him every day. Thank Him for all of the beauties and the privilege we enjoy being permitted to live here and . . ."

"I am trying to be polite."

"He likes us that way, I think."

92

"Ma'am, it's up to you. You can play games, if you wish . . ."

"Okay. Your favorite, I figure, would be *Monopoly*, right. Leaving the rest of us *Sorry?*"

"That's it. I will be back. And when I come tomorrow, I will have with me a federal marshal who has arrest authority. We *will* get answers.

"Thanks for stopping by, Mr. Federal Man. I didn't get your name but your credentials were really impressive. Do come back. You're welcome here anytime . . . that no one's home."

He stomped out the door with a decidedly un-Milquetoast stomp.

"And so it begins," she thought. "The end."

Next day, as promised, two men knocked on the farmhouse door. This time, Chas was home and Jillian was relegated to observing.

"Gentlemen," Chas said ushering them in. "Let me clear the air with, no not an apology but an acknowledgement of your meeting yesterday with my daughter who, I understand, was flippant if not disrespectful. Let me assure you, I shall not be flippant but as respectful as your mission here deserves."

"I assure you, sir . . . " Milquetoast began until Chas cut him off.

"Gentlemen, please, as long as our family has lived on these acres, in this house, three generations of us now, four counting my daughter, we have had two rules: One, do not interrupt the head of the house. Two, be civil. I would appreciate your accepting those two simple rules while with us. All right?"

Each muttered a reply.

"Not too many years ago, gentlemen, I was fighting for my country. Today I am sorry to find, *it* is fighting *me*. I fought to keep alien hordes from taking over our country, seizing our properties as their dictators wished, making us totally subservient to their commands. And now? Now, same scenario but the hordes are not aliens, they are *us*."

"Now that's not fair, Mr. Amacher . . ."

"Sir!" Chad erupted. "*Rule One!*" And, calmly, he continued. "What you are talking about, gentlemen, with these outrageous plans you represent is to destroy homes and farms, lives and history, for what? To take a live and life-affirming river and dam it. *Damn it!* You would replace it with a still and stagnant artificial lake. Why? To create recreational opportunities for Americans, you aver. Americans who have recreational opportunities here already: Hunting, fishing, camping, climbing, splashing in waterfalls, basking in the quiet of fir-scented woods. They have all these. We have all these. Already. So what is to be gained? New Yorkers and Philadelphians might get some drinking water? Yes, while losing the quaint old vacation hotels at which they have found yearly surcease from the frantic lives in those poisonous cities.

"Gentlemen, I thank you for hearing me out so courteously, I realize you are not the makers of these tragic plans, only some of the implementers. But I don't have much chance to be heard by the makers. Especially now that it seems a *fait accompli.* So, thanks to you implementers, I shall soon lose my land, my legacy and my living. *Damn it to Hell!'*

Which ejaculation propelled him from his seat, sent him striding angrily over to the window where slowly he would keep his fury but at least regain his composure while gazing out at the cattle, the lands, the river all of which would soon, he knew, be lost.

No one spoke. Not a word until, at last, Chas, without turning, said softly, contritely, "I myself just violated Rule Number Two. For that, gentlemen, I apologize." He turned back to his guests. "Now, your turn. For what have you come here today, to apologize?"

Warily, Milquetoast reached into his briefcase and extracted a bulging folder that simply screamed *Legal!* He stood erect, empowered it seemed by that folder and the unarguable authority he was about to wield.

In coming days so many more homeowners, business keepers, and sorry, helpless souls like Chas and his family, would be confronted by the same Incontestable Authority.

Incontestable yet furiously contested. Groups gathered, organized, marched, protested and felt altogether justified doing it. They also felt the futility. *"Damn the Dam,"* their signs and placards screamed, but screamed into ears not deaf perhaps but surely not caring.

Why should we care what the people think, Government seemed always to be saying. You are the public, we are public servants, yes, but never forget: We know better than you what's good for you. Just leave us alone. Let us steal your homes, your businesses, your schools, your churches, your livelihoods, your lives. Don't you understand? We know better than you. That's how we serve you. Don't forget.

Only years later, would someone in government with more candor than shame finally tot up the total destruction done on behalf of the Tocks Island Dam scheme, and not until the new century would an enterprising graduate student at New Jersey's Seton Hall University, Kathleen Duca-Sandberg, find and publish those truths in a thesis. She reported that by the time all the seizures, forced sales and federal confiscations were done, ten thousand properties had been taken, many from people like the Amachers whose families had been on those lands for generations, some since Colonial days. Three thousand homes were razed, 25 summer camps destroyed, 125 farms, more than a hundred businesses, seven churches and three schools were destroyed or abandoned. On both sides of the great river, towns became ghost towns. In Pennsylvania, Dingmans Ferry and Bushkill were basically gone. On the Jersey side, Wallpack shrank from 384 citizens to 67.

Oh, and The Bridge? The proud Dingmans Bridge and the Old Stone House adjoining it? What became of them through all this and all to follow? History happened but not in the same toxic way it happened elsewhere.

CHAPTER ELEVEN

WE GUESS WHAT WE WANT TO SAY IS PRETTY SIMPLE. THANK
YOU FOR OUR LIVES.
        -- *Beatrice and Camille, church bombing survivors*

T hink you're ready, Perk?"
        "Doc, if I had waited until I was ready for the
        various passages of my life, I never would have
passed. What do you have in mind?"

Doc took a seat in a chair across from the bed to which I
sought refuge between the excursions each day for both
physical and occupational therapies.

"Actually," he said, "it's what several people have in mind."

"Like who?"

"Well, your bosses of course. One of them, the man named
Mac, is waiting to come see you as soon as I say you're up to it.
I listen carefully to him since he's the one still paying the bills."

"Hope you're charging him good."

"Actually, giving him our standard "Hero's" rate. Proud to
have you here. Getting lots of publicity for it."

"You know what he wants?"

"Think it's about the timing of a new assignment he has in
mind for his hero. Take advantage of your renown."

"Damn! And who else?"

"Well, my brother has wanted me to pass along some news to you. The hospital director down there . . ."

"Wait, I remember. Give me a moment. Got it. Palmer," I said, proud of reclaiming that memory, "Eugenia Palmer, right."

"Actually, I don't know. Not sure I ever heard her name. If I did, then your memory is now better than mine. I like that."

"And so do I. What did she have to say? Miss me?"

"Zack said she wanted to make sure you got the news that Birmingham police have arrested a man for setting the bomb at that church that Sunday morning. He's going on trial for murder."

"Good. They didn't fool around."

"And here's what she most wanted you to know. His name is Robert Chambliss. Mean anything to you?"

I puzzled. Sounded familiar, that name. Robert Chambliss. Where had I heard it?

"She said he was one of the men who came to her hospital looking for you and they wouldn't tell him you were there."

"And if they had, if they had, I might not be *here!* Thank God for her wise decision to keep me anonymous from even her own hospital staff."

"What did you just say, Perk?"

"...from her own hospital staff."

"Before that. You said 'Thank God.' Glad to see you coming around. Always a good sign when a patient begins to recapture reality. Thanking God for His mercies is acknowledging reality."

"C'mon, Doc. We had an agreement. But that's good news, his arrest and all. Chambliss. Hope she'll keep us informed. And you said you had other news?"

"This, about your dad. You know, ever since I met him one of your first days with us, back when you were scarcely aware he was here, I'm afraid, I've been a fan. He's a distinguished and intelligent man, soft-spoken, very bright. I like and respect him. So he's one of the fellows run the bridge down there, the Dingmans Bridge? Sure hope the government doesn't take that away too."

"Why would they?"

"To clear the way for a gargantuan dam they 've been threatening to force on all of us. Haven't you heard your dad talk about the Tocks Island Dam?"

"Never paid much attention to stuff about the bridge. Just know he was the president of the little company and still vice-president and secretary, I think. He and my mom go down there every fall for stockholders' meetings and such."

"And those meetings are next week. He hopes to be here then to see you again. Hopes you might be able to go to the bridge next week, see it, attend the meetings, get to know the people. Hopes you'll get more interested in it, especially since it's right here in what, for the moment, is your back yard."

"How far?"

"From the hospital here in Port Jervis, a half hour's drive. From our home in Milford where you dined with Patricia and me last week, fifteen minutes tops."

"Man, that was great."

"What?"

"That meal Patricia put out. You are one lucky man, Doc."

"And believe me, Doc knows it. And, he knows something else. Perk, hear me out." Now, I sensed, he was getting to the purpose of his being here. "I am a cardiologist. I have no right telling you how to handle your bones, your joints or organs or any of the other parts other doctors are working on for you. I also have no right telling you how to live your life. But, hey," he broke an impish smile. "that's what I do."

"So do it."

And he gentled into his avuncular say-so. "I told you what I think of your dad. What troubles me is that you don't seem to feel the same way. Never seem to feel much at all about him. This bridge down here is important to him. A great source of pride for him. It was his own father, your grandfather, who with his brothers built it. Many had tried before and failed. Your dad's dad succeeded. Great reason for your dad to be proud. And now he's helping run the company and that's reason for you to be proud. Yet all I get from you on the subject -- and I think all *he* gets is -- disinterest, dismissal. I think that hurts him. I know it does. But I also think he's not the sort to tell you it hurts him. I, on the other hand, *am.* As a cardiologist I deal with hearts and my diagnosis in this case is that his heart breaks a little when you dismiss what is important to him, what he's proud of."

"You ended that reproach with a preposition, Doc. Can't I ever teach . . ."

"Stop! He might allow you to launch such a diversion, but I won't. I will not allow you to avoid the point with distracting drivel. Answer me."

It was a flinty obduracy I had not seen from him. Nor did his penetrating eyes let me evade it. I knew he was right. Long I had known it. Maybe it was just how we were in our family. We were practiced avoiders, skilled slipabouts. My dad had never discussed with me his pride in his dad's history-worthy accomplishments, nor had he ever acknowledged to me any pride he might have about my own successes these recent years. We didn't talk of such things. Good or bad. Unpleasant things as well as prides and joys, we kept them all to ourselves in our home, in our lives.

"Doc, I accept your diagnosis. I'm afraid it's accurate. So, I'm grateful you're a cardiologist because I guess I need a consult on my heart, too. What should we call it? Not open heart surgery, not that, but some kind of heart-*opening* procedure is needed for sure."

"You are the only one can perform that procedure, Perk. It's your heart. Although you might bring in the Great Physician to assist."

"We had an understanding, Doc. No God talk."

"I'm only recommending what I know my patient needs."

"Your patient who is growing impatient."

'OK. Here's my prescription. Welcome your father when he's here. Go with him and your mom to the bridge and be proud of it. I don't know how you couldn't. And tell him you are proud. Let it boggle you, the thought it could have been done and so lastingly by his family, *your* family all those years ago. And, of course, let him know that you are proud of him as well. Go to the meetings, meet the people, take interest in them and in the business. That'll be your most sincere gift to your dad. And, you know what? Gift to your own healthy heart as well. Doctor's orders."

Before the bridge, though, came Mac. Bill McMurphy, head of network news in New York showed up in my room with a firm and warm greeting almost shouted as he entered.

"Perkins! It is so damned good to see you when you know you're being seen. Not like the last time, several weeks ago. I'm sure you can't even know I was here but I wanted to get here as quickly as possible to tell you how proud we were and are of you. I speak for us all at 30 Rock — you are our hero."

That damned word. My instinct, again, was to disown it. But perhaps as part of my *heart-opening* procedure I needed accept it even if hearing it displeased me; if it pleased the person speaking it, I should be grateful and . . . Silent!

"Anyhow, I'll let Art Gradszinski give you the details but I wish personally to tell you that the network's gratitude is going to be demonstrated financially, a substantial raise for you." He cited an amount. Generous indeed.

"Thank you, Bill. Thank you."

"And I have one thing more.." Art, standing at the back of the room, stepped forward with a gift box, not professionally wrapped, I was happy to see. No corporate gift from Tiffany or Bloomies. Instead, a package that appeared home-wrapped by a real someone, a personal something.

"From a few of your fondest fans, as you'll find." And he passed it to me.

The envelope outside was handwritten, addressed in a hand not familiar to me. It said simply, "To the Brave. From the Grateful." There was a short note inside:

"Dear Mister Perkins. We guess what we want to say to you is pretty simple. Just sincere thank you. Thank you for nothing less than our lives. We are told if it had not been for you, we would probably have been killed that morning in the basement of the church. Now, we're told you are in the hospital and not in great shape. So we thought you might be able to use this there on your hospital bed. We made it, just the two of us, and we went to the church and asked God if he would please bless it and while he was at it would he bless you too. We pray you will get well soon, Mr. Perkins."

"P.S. We would love to meet you again one day when you're all better." It was signed "Beatrice and Camille."

Beatrice and Camille. I hadn't known.

In the box, which I opened slowly to delay the tears I knew would come, was a blanket, knit, clearly handmade, all in peaceful pastels of blue, lavender and yellow, beautiful, soft. Very soft. I clutched it to my face against the weeping I should not have shied from, but in the presence of my boss who had just accorded me the professional tribute of a significant raise, it seemed puerile to bawl.

"If you don't mind, Perkins. . ." he said as Art stepped forward with a camera at the ready. "Picture to send to the girls of you and their gift. Here, let me step in with you if I may." And he did and Art did and then, of course, Art did again. I had tried to dry my eyes but may not have succeeded in time. What the heck, it was just for the girls. He said.

"I'd like to write a short thank you note for you to pass along to them." Ever-ready Art produced pen and paper, I scratched out a few wavering lines, hoped the girls could read them, and handed the paper back to Art. "Thank you."

Art retreated but from the boss' look, he still had something to say. "One last thing, and you may think when I tell you this so deep in our talk that I buried my lead. It's this. This is what I've been waiting for the doctors to okay my coming so I can tell you in person."

He gave me the lead. As soon as I was able -- it would depend entirely on my complete recovery, the network planned to launch a new documentary magazine program to be called *Perk's Journal.* A regular show in prime time. He had already begun assembling a staff subject to my approval. The concept was that I would travel the world reporting what stories I chose. We would bring together an hour's worth of my best each month. I was the boss, I and an executive producer to be chosen soon with, again, my consultation and approval. It would be my show. Playing, of course, (though it remained unsaid) off the attention the network was still getting from the Birmingham affair.

"The iron is hot, Perk." he told me earnestly. "Let's strike."

I had only one question. One word. "Bunky?"

"Yours full time."

I reached out from under the softness of the blanket and shook his hand.

How could I not have been thrilled? My own show. Prime time. My control. Stories I chose.

It whirled in my head most day and night. Who as exec producer? Paul? I once told him that he was one of only guys I'd worked with that I would follow anywhere. Maybe him? And what stories? Should I revisit the two girls in Birmingham? Be a great story but might it target them, endanger them? Risky for them and risky maybe for me? Ought to get to Vietnam which looked to me like a war in the making for America. Do stories there. See what other Asians thought. Talk to Jim Robinson, our correspondent out that way. He'd know. Always stories in the Middle East. Didn't we used to call Israel and Palestine the Near East? Now, the Mideast? What happened to the Near? Maybe whoever knows the answer to that should be the new Exec.

So much to think about. And so urgent the need to get out of here. Therapy nurse came an hour or so later and found me for the first time eager to go and get working.

CHAPTER TWELVE

SON, YOU'RE A REPORTER. YOU MUST KNOW THAT WHAT YOU
SAY IS NOT NECESSARILY WHAT PEOPLE HEAR
— *Dad to son*

D ad and mom arrived Thursday, although mom didn't come in to the hospital at first. She waited in the car. Dad told me she wasn't sure she could stand to see me all broken and hurting. "I didn't do a detailed job describing what I saw when I visited you here that first week. Still . . . been tough, hasn't it son?"

"You know what it's been, Dad? It's been humbling. Very humbling! Maybe I needed that. Everything had always gone so smoothly in my life. Everything I wanted, everything I tried, worked out for me. Big TV guy, so full of himself and suddenly he's here, in a town he'd never heard of, among people he'd never known, struggling to learn again how to walk. Thirty years late for that. That's why I say humbling. Fortunately, there was no significant injury to this mug of mine. Some internal stuff. Two surgeries already rebuilding things down there. Really amazing, we have all those miles of colon twisted around down there just waiting to be of some use. Like backup parts. So they take some of that, measure off what they need and use it to build a new bladder or whatever and you're back in business. Fortunately, in my case, with no need for a colostomy bag or lifelong restrictions. Except be more careful in the future. Bombs, I'm advised, aren't the gut's best friends."

"Well, you look good to me, son."

"And I want to say, Dad, how great, how really great, it is to see you. To have you here. I don't say this much. Never have. But I love you, Dad." To obviate a reply I kept going. "I reckon we needn't go through the medical details with mom, huh?"

"Wise. I'll get her."

As he left, I scrambled as best my scrambled gut muscles and still weak legs permitted. I doffed the hospital garb and grabbed civvies, khakis and T. And just in time. The door swung open, hesitantly, anxiously, and there she was, in purple with the string of pearls she was so proud of, her hair blued just enough that it didn't look blued. Heart-shaped face with the "widow's peak," she called it. Never knew what that meant. But she looked good. "Hi mom."

"Oh, you're sitting up." She stepped toward me though did not reach out. Ours was never a physically expressive family. "I was so afraid. Your father told me what you looked like before, all tied up with tubes running in and out everywhere. That must have been awful."

"Yeah," I joshed, "I'm glad I wasn't here to see that."

"What?"

"Nothing, mom. Good to see you. And do you know what? The doctors have cleared me — if it's okay with you — to join you for a couple days at the bridge and the meetings. They figure I've got to start getting out of this comfortable nest a bit and I figure that it's about time I know more about that part of your lives . . ."

"*Your* life as well," Dad jumped in. "You're going to be a stockholder, too. Starting at this meeting. You should be getting involved. I'm glad you'll join us."

"Yes," said mom, coming at it from her own point of view, "I want everybody to meet you. Show you off a bit. They all know about you, of course. They'll be thrilled to meet you."

"Well, mom, feel free to parade me around like a prize poodle with a pink ribbon in my hair . . . "

Dad, forestalling a quibble: "Don't you think the ribbon should be blue, son?"

"Guess you're right, Dad, and I don't want to be a poodle. Maybe a mutt like Butch. Remember him so long ago? No, he was never allowed in the house. I wouldn't like that. Anyhow I'll be there for the bridge and proud to be."

"Have you seen this, son?" Mom held forth a newspaper, I couldn't tell which one at first, but I could clearly see the photograph she had folded it to. There I was in the photo Art had made here a couple days ago, the picture they told me was "just for the girls." Girls of the PR department, I guessed they meant. So there was I, cuddled in the hand-knit blanket dear Beatrice and Camille had made. Caption: **Girls Saved in Bombing Knit Blanket for Hospitalized Hero.**

Quickly perused, the story included the text of the girls' note including — Dammit! — their names. Just first names but still . . .

It also named this hospital. Maybe I didn't need to worry about that -- we were up north now -- but I wished it hadn't. After what I'd been through, I knew not to underestimate the enemy. Many had learned that lesson about the KKK and its evil disciples. I needed to tell Doc to have security alerted.

"Well," I said to mom, "they spelled my name right. And not such a bad picture, ya think?"

"Why, it's terrible. You look all shrunken up like a ghost or something."

"Zombie, perhaps," I suggested.

"Don't make light. This makes my son look pathetic and I am not one bit happy."

Checking the masthead, I promised her that, "I'll tell the New York Times how unhappy you are next time I see Punch Sulzberger."

"You know him? He run this paper?"

"He does and I don't."

"Well, I'm mad."

"Duly noted. So," turning to dad, "when do we go to things?"

He filled me on the schedule for the weekend. When they would pick me up, what to expect. The exuberance of his recital made me very glad I was going to do this though it wouldn't be easy, mentally or physically.

"I'll walk you to the door." To show mom I could. I saw her blanch as I reached over to get my walker. "Only temporary," I assured her though I was not sure it assured her.

"Lead the way, folks."

Mom wanted to stop at the public restroom, to get her composure, I figured, after seeing her son using a walker.

I took advantage of her absence to jump on dad, "Why did you tell her about how I looked before with all the tubes and everything?"

"I didn't."

"But she said . . . "

"Son, you're a reporter. You must know that what *you say* is not necessarily what *people hear.* Their minds elaborate, expand. Remember, you told me about the day folks around NBC were laughing at what Brinkley had said on his show night before. As they remembered he had said *Yatta, Yatta, Yatta, Yatta, Yatta, Yatta, Yatta, Yatta, Yatta.* But having seen his script you knew he had said only *Yatta, Yatta, Yatta.* That's all he said but not all they heard. Your mother is like that. She has a very active crisis amplifier in her perceiving loop. Like many people, she hears what she fears."

Wise man, my Dad. Never noticed. "Oh, hi, mom, let me shuffle you two out to your car." And clop, clop, clop, hoping I could make it, I saw them off.

Returned to my room and collapsed.

What would happen tomorrow, I dreaded. I was excited by it and gratified for it -- and dreaded. It was a game I had played too often. A roomful of people most of whom knew me or about me while I knew them not. They wouldn't be wearing name tags. They didn't need them. They were mostly extended family -- twenty or thirty, Dad figured -- who'd been coming for years to these combination stockholders' meetings and family reunions . They knew my face; I didn't know theirs. I'd heard some of their names; I had never heard others. They "knew" me. I was sure mom made a point of telling them all about me once I made it on the air. Oh, she told them. They knew me. And, of course, I'd be the only one hobbling around on a walker. Their memory test would be easy. Mine? I'd see faces for the first time, hear the names that went with them and after twenty-five or thirty more, be expected to put them together, face with name. As I say, I've always hated the game.

It was even harder than I expected. The kin were not all in one room. They were strung out in adjoining rooms of a roadside motel. Not a lavish place. The somewhat concave beds had aged chenille spreads on them and, for wall art above them, completed jigsaw puzzles, cheaply framed. Each room opened onto the parking lot hard on the busy highway. The woman who was the both current president and *grande dame* of the clan stayed in her room toward the middle of the cluster so others in turn could stroll along greeting each other, starting to catch up from the year before until they reached her room to pay honor. My instant reaction: She deserved it.

My task, I and my walker, was to follow my parents along the gladding route, hearing mom brag on me, acting humble and trying, trying to fix names with faces. Though next time I saw people we'd be going the other direction and everyone would be out of order. And then what? Then we would get in cars and drive to the restaurant for the official *Dingmans Bridge Dinner*, as the sign outside proclaimed. And where was this restaurant? Not in Milford, Pennsylvania where we just were but a place called Flo-Jean's all the way back in Port Jervis, New York, near my hospital.

I had heard mom rave about Flo-Jean's for years. She told me that it adjoined the toll bridge my grandfather was asked to help build and he did help while awaiting the kit bridge floating down in pieces from up north . Now, the restaurant was the old toll house of that bridge he had worked on so its owners invented cookies to honor the fact. I never knew if that was fact or fable but the toll house cookies that night were the best part of the meal.

Whereupon, promising to see all tomorrow, I let dad take me back to the hospital and found my way back to my cell which on this night felt more like my refuge. I was tired. Social performing always wore me out.

CHAPTER THIRTEEN

BEFORE, I ASKED WOULD YOU LIKE TO VISIT THE OLD STONE
HOUSE. NOW I ASK: WOULD YOU LIKE TO LIVE HERE?
-- *Uncle Mort, Bridge President*

S trange, I thought, having known him before only as a
farmer in bib overalls out in his corn fields in Medina
County north of Wooster, the farmer in whose honor I
had been given my first name. Now, here he was in the living
room of one of the local stockholders's homes in Pennsylvania,
one of the places not yet subsumed by land-gulping
government: Morton O. Perkins. Uncle Mort, in tweed coat
and bolo tie, baggy but clean canvas pants and work boots,
wielding the ceremonial gavel as president of the Dingmans
Choice and Delaware Bridge Company.

I didn't even understand that company name. I had much
to learn.

The President turned to the Secretary, my dad, for his
report which began by announcing the transfer of ten of his
own shares of stock to his son, me, whom he was glad to
welcome to the company and to our meetings today.

There was applause. My mother beamed her pride.

There followed the reading and approval of minutes from
last year, the treasurer's report, budget discussion,

maintenance report, president's assessment of the bridge and its prospects. All looked well. Except --

There was again, as so many times before so I gathered, the haunting uncertainties about the bridge's future tied so ominously to the plans of the Corps of Engineers.

"Tick, tock, tick, tock," said Uncle Mort, an ironic fellow, "We don't know how many have ticks we have; we're still at the mercy of the Tocks."

"Still," emphasized one of the stockholders I hadn't met last night. "Any idea, Mort, when we might get some kind of resolution, any kind?"

"Oh, I do indeed," said President Mort, "whenever they make up their damned dilatory minds and not a tick before."

Dilatory, he said? I was impressed with my namesake farmer's vocabulary. Which attitude, as I immediately recognized, was damned snobbish of me.

There remained on the order of business a few routine housekeeping items quickly dismissed, and finally a motion from the floor to welcome newcomer Perk as he called himself and be sure and greet him between meetings. "Move we adjourn."

Enthusiastic approval and folks started moving toward me ensconced there in the house's most comfortable chair "for our famous visitor," it had been said by the hostess seating me. There were ten or twenty minutes of chit chat and my frequent apologizing for unremembered names. Then our President stepped over to offer, confidentially, an intriguing idea.

"After the Board meeting, Perk, I'd be grateful if you would ride with me as we all — part of the tradition — drive out to the bridge for our annual look-see. Not so much an inspection as a gratification, to see it standing proud after all these years, all these decades. Especially, I want to show you the Old Stone House right next to the bridge. That be okay?"

"I'll check with dad."

"I already did. Fine with him."

"Then I'll be ready. Thank you. "

Then the board meeting. Uncle Mort again with the gavel. The six board members including my Dad gathered around. Discussion of the need to purchase and install probably twenty-five or thirty new planks to replace or be ready to replace aging bridge floor boards wearing down. Also, it was time to do a careful check of the stringers and other structural members. Should we consider instituting a regular annual or biennial inspection by qualified engineers? Bridge is getting on, you know. Almost sixty-four years old. Next, revenue figures and talk about the appropriate dividends to pay shareholders this year. Crisp, businesslike, and yet with warmth not likely seen in large corporate boardrooms.. This, after all, was family.

Meeting gaveled to a close, I walkered outside to join Uncle Mort in his Plymouth for the trip to the bridge. I was happy when dad slipped into the back seat to join us and hear Uncle Mort's first joshing comment to me. "So, Perk, my name not good enough for you?" He knew I'd been given it and knew I didn't use it. I played with his comment.

"Too good for me. It's a name for a hard-working man. I'm no farmer, have never had to work that hard in my life. Don't know if I could. So I figure I don't deserve to wear a hard-working man's monicker."

"Yer a good talker, son. Hey, look, we're almost to the bridge.

For so many years I had heard talk about *the bridge*. Had seen pictures of *the bridge*. Had known of the family's travels to and involvement in *the bridge*. *The bridge, the bridge, the bridge*. I was ready, finally, to meet *the bridge*.

But I wasn't ready.

For years, hearing my folks talking about it, I pictured it like the only bridges I knew around Wooster, not much more than a ramp over a culvert, or a span of a simple creek, short, insignificant. The bridge they talked about, to be sure, was over the Delaware River, yes, but that couldn't be too big itself kid Perk had reckoned. Didn't Washington throw a dollar across it? Or was that the Potomac? Was the Delaware what he crossed to attack the Hessians? Young, I got legends mixed. Point was though, I always underestimated the stature of *bridge*.

Now about to meet it. I felt both eager and anxious. And strange. The mellow pills Doc had given me? Were they responsible for what seemed to me to be reality softening, melting into a fantasy forming before me? A narrow, dirt, country road. To either side, autumn trees, most leafless now, waving bare branches at me in overdue welcome. No other cars on the road, nor anything to see ahead. Why were we here? Where were we going? If to the Dingmans Bridge, where was it and why was there no crushing column of paying traffic ahead? How can we pay ourselves dividends (now that I'm a stockholder) with no traffic going to the bridge but us? Not even the horned cattle, phaetons, or bootleg hearses I'd been told about. I closed my eyes that my brain might recalibrate.

"There it is." said Uncle Mort.

Now, my eyes sharpened and for sure, still some ways down the road, there it was. I could see no river yet, but rising ahead as we approached was the complex geometry of angles and uprights gleaming iron gray against a sky filled with cotton ball clouds in a topaz sky. A man strolled out of a wooden booth on the left and took his place in the middle of the passage where dirt road became broad wooden planks. On his waist he wore a cloth carpenter's apron from which he made change as a driver paid his toll. Which Uncle Mort, known by the toll taker, did not bother to offer. Just a wave and a smile. Privilege of office, I took it. He drove us onto the bridge, drove slowly, iron cocoon surrounding us, both sides, above and for a significant distance ahead. This was no culvert-gapper, no creek-spanner. This was *a bridge!*

Dad, always the engineer, provided commentary as we drove across. "Called a through-truss style bridge, three spans, total length: five hundred forty-seven feet, (almost two football fields) Pennsylvania to New Jersey. Eleven foot clearance overhead, planks on the floor, treated southern white pine, three inches thick, eighteen feet long. Roadway on the bridge just under eighteen feet wide."

It felt tight. I wouldn't want to be driving it with traffic coming at me. A driver had to ride close to the ironworks hard beside him. There was that, but mostly, the phantasm for me was the sound: the percussive recital performed by the wooden floor boards, the rhythmic paradiddle — *rumble-clatter, rumble-clatter, rumble-clatter* — as car wheels played pine planks like a giant's marimba. You could sing to it. You couldn't help but sing to it. It was music, it was poetry.

And then you were across; you were in New Jersey, heading slowly up what Uncle Mort said was called the Old Mine Road. Dad picked up his commentary a: "Story is that this is the view my father, your grandfather, found when he first reconnoitered possibilities for building the bridge. He told his brothers he had heard a voice rising from the waters below here saying to go ahead and build his bridge and *make it magnificent!'*

"He did," I said to myself if no one else. "Magnificent."

And beautiful. As we drove back across to the Pennsylvania side, I looked up. Marveling this time at the massive intricacies of silver-grey iron whizzing through the ethereal abstraction of endless sky. Did the whizzing panorama suggest something, anything, to me?

Again, the toll taker was on his spot in the center of the road; again he let us pass with a cheerful greeting. We pulled off to a bare dirt parking area to the right, directly facing a handsome two story stone home. So this was it. The Old Stone House I had heard so much about. The place one of the earliest of the Dingman family built as his own home back when I wasn't sure but early 1800's I thought. The Old Stone House.

Set on broad lawns that sloped gently down to the river, shaded handsomely by a natural grove of slender linden trees, the grasses now sumptuously carpeted with autumn leaf fall.

"I have two questions for you, Perk," said uncle Mort.

"Okay. I'll see if I can come up with two answers."

"First, would you like to look around inside?"

"That's easy. You bet."

He led the way. Dad came alongside me should I need a hand. And continued his running commentary as we walked (or walkered) around the marvelous old manse. Downstairs then up. "Judge Daniel Dingman lived well, wouldn't you say?" Dad said this as we stepped out onto the broad upstairs balcony running the length of the house as did its twin downstairs. My mind went for a spin, flashing first on Tara only this wasn't a movie, and not the South. Thank goodness. And the South had not yet tried to find me up here. Thank goodness especially for that. Though that it hadn't yet didn't mean it still wouldn't. Disquieting if not surprising had been the latest word from Birmingham, from Ms. Palmer at the hospital there who had just yesterday passed along the update on that man who'd been arrested for the church bombing, arrested and put on trial for murder. Well, now she had passed the word, the verdict was in. What a surprise. The murderer had been quickly found *Not Guilty* of murder. Southern justice.

"Some of our bridge people have lived here over the years," Dad was saying. "Even the lady you called The Grande Dame lived here for a while."

"Not a bad way to live, I agreed. Just look out there. Leaf-speckled lawns spreading down to the silvery river. Couldn't get much more peaceful than this."

"Just what the doctor ordered, wouldn't you say ?" Uncle Mort joined us. "Perk, I said at the outset I had two questions to ask you. I asked, would you like to visit the old stone house. Now I ask: Would you like to *live* here?"

"Live here? Live here!?"

"I've spoken with Doctor Bullock," said my Dad. "He's ready to release you from the hospital but not yet send you back to work. Wants you still in this area to keep an eye on your continuing therapies and reactions to surgeries. His office is right in Milford, don't know if you've seen it, two doors from the Milford Diner — by the way, good food, great people there. So he's just ten minutes from here. He'd like to keep you around for another month or two. Living here, if you'd like. Even longer if you'd wish. Up to you."

"Is this okay with the bridge people?" I had to ask.

"Well," said Uncle Mort, "you have the president and vice president right here offering it. And, yes, we've discussed it with the rest of the board. Everyone would be proud to have you. Not that they'd be around prying. You'll have your privacy and the doctor will make arrangements for your therapists to come here or meet you at his office. In fact, we've even discussed this with a man named Arthur at your network and he can arrange occasional day trips for you into New York City so you can get working on what he says is your exciting new project."

"Seems a lot folks have spent a lot of thought and caring on my behalf . . . "

"And still are, son,' said Dad. "Still are."

CHAPTER FOURTEEN

INTERLOPERS? I'LL HAVE YOU KNOW WE WERE THE ORIGINAL
LOPERS HERE BEFORE YOU WERE BORN
--Jillian to National Park Service officer

To be a reporter, a good reporter, you need a sturdy streak of skepticism. If, instead, you tend to unquestioning credulity, accepting whatever you're told by whomever, you might better find other employment. (Though, off hand, I can't think where you'd be suited. Gullibility isn't high on employers' wish lists.)

If you are easily gulled, you can train yourself to be skeptical, you can strengthen that muscle, but there's a danger there, too. It is easy to go too far, to drive yourself unintending from skepticism into cynicism, a cynicism that sours the soul, erodes credibility and repels friends. I know; I lived there a while.

It is hard not to grow cynical about some things. Some things simply beggar cynicism. Like government. Even if we generously grant the innocence of government intentions and plans, we can't ignore how often they fail of fruition. Or worse, produce diametrically opposite results from those intended. Whenever I read of such, I hear the Scottish burr of Robert Burns regretting how he once inadvertently ran his

plow into a mouse nest in a field. Among his first instincts was
to apologize:

> I'm truly sorry man's dominion
> Has broken Nature's social union,
> An' justifies that ill opinion
> Which makes thee startle
> At me, thy poor, earth born companion
> An' fellow mortal!

Then, further on, the famous words that, for a cynic, call to
mind so many of the misthought or unthought plans
governments keep hatching. Like the one in the persistent
mind of the U. S Army Corps of Engineers in the 1960s.

> The best-laid schemes o' mice an' men
> Gang aft agley,
> An' lea'e us nought but grief an' pain,
> For promis'd joy!

The *promis'd* joy, of course had been the grand, broad, long
lake covered with happy pleasure-seekers boating and fishing
and water-skiing while surrounded by rounded mountains and
always sunny skies. Too, the inviting forests of enveloping
parklands. The promise, alas, began to *gang aft agley* first when
the people of the area rose up in fury and determined defiance.
There was a woman, one vocal and strident woman who
when a man shoved eviction papers into her hands saying her
family would have to get out of their home, saw her young
daughter come to tears. That woman, Ruth Smith, pushed the
official documents back at the man instructing him specifically
to "take these papers and shove 'em up your ass!" She said that
and proudly repeated the incident to neighbors, inciting their
own defiance. Their **Nix on Tocks** movement grew to where

the government could no longer ignore it. Spitefully, agents saw to it that the very first home seizure finalized was Ruth Smith's.

All that while fiscal realities started thundering down on America like bombs from B-52's raining death on Vietnam. Washington found itself confronted not only by war, but simultaneously by a newly emerging environmental movement, the still explosive civil rights crusade and not enough resources to justify the ever-escalating costs of what would have been the largest dam project east of the Mississippi. Oh, and a geological study that would finally report that the grounds around the proposed dam wouldn't support the earthen dam anyhow.

Accordingly — though it would take government as long to unwind the project as it had to wind it — the Tocks Island Dam, the Corps of Engineer's baby, was stillborn. Families and farms and towns and lives uprooted would never be re-rooted. What remained then, corroding all, was a deep-felt hostility by citizens toward government. Nor did government ameliorate things or make friends when, in an effort to recoup some of the monies already expended, it started offering properties in its control now for rent to *outsiders.* Longtime locals suddenly found homes their family had loved and lived in for generations until they had been rudely seized were now being lived in again but by total strangers from somewhere else. Indeed, in some cases, especially over on the Jersey side, clusters of young people materialized with their tie-dyed T's and ragged jeans and drugs and peace symbols crudely painted on houses not their own. A new culture called Hippies had moved in. Something not anticipated by the D.C. prophets.

Of the Amacher family and their Riverside Cattle Farm, there was no good news to report. The Riverside was still there but the Amachers weren't and never could be again. Their cattle had been sold, so that now with no income, they lived only on what the government had given them as payment for stealing their lives.

Jillian moved into town, into nearby Milford, rented a place with a girlfriend and settled in to continue her freelance art career. Father Chas and mother Bernadette tried to start a new cattle farm, that being all they had in their experience, in their genes, but could find no suitable lands available anywhere near. They wanted to stay near. Near home as they would always consider it. Their home.

To be sure, their property was no longer needed by the Corps of Engineers since, after all, there would be no flooding from the dam since there would be no dam. Yet, though not needing all the seized land and confiscated properties, still, as Government never gives anything back, the Corps instead transferred its ill-gotten gains to the National Park Service. Let NPS deal with them.

One way it dealt was to turn the barns and outbuildings at the old Amacher place into storage for NPS vehicles and equipment. Very convenient.

Once, feeling a bit rebellious, Chas talked Jillian into going camping with him for an overnight. "I've got a great place," he told her, "I'm sure you'll love it."

"Where," she wanted to know.

"You just wait," he said.

Strange, she thought. He never used to keep secrets from her. He really is changing. Not himself these days. Hasn't been since . . .

He told her he'd meet her outside the Old Stone House "down by the bridge." And, sure enough, right at eight he pulled up into the small dirt area between that house and the wooden shanty the bridge toll takers retreated to between cars which this time of day were few. and there she was, his dear daughter, all done up in her hiking gear, sleeping bag rolled and lashed to her familiar backpack, ready for their camping trip. It was a new moon, just rising through the spans of the old bridge.

"Hi, Pete," Chas hollered into the shanty as he walked past. Then to Jillian, "my new buddy; my new workplace." They crossed the road over to what was now an NPS parking and canoe launching area hard by the Pennsylvania end of the bridge.

"Where we going, dad? And what do you mean about your new workplace?"

"Follow me. And I meant that that's where I'm working now."

"What!?" She took a quick look at him as they walked. He was still the handsome man she had always known but there were fatigue wrinkles around his eyes she didn't remember. Or were they worry?

"Honey, you know I've been pretty lost since we had to move, give up the ranch, our lives as we knew them. I mean we're fine for money but there's just nothing to do. I made work. Got hold of our old tractor, remember, the one crushed in the storm, and started rebuilding it. Just for something to do. Finally got the old Johnny Popper all working again and wondered then what? Some days I feel there's no reason to be. Know what I mean."

"Of course I do dad, all that happening to us while we and the rest of the world are still trying to get over the assassination. JFK gone, LBJ in. Shadows layered on shadows. Calamity compounding catastrophe. So, in a way, dad, sure I know what you mean. But in another way, I don't even *know you*, talking like that. Your reason to be is the same today as it was yesterday, last month, last year. I'm surprised I have to say it because you're the one who told me so many times."

"I know, I know. My reason to be, your reason to be, is to let God use us however he wills. Always been easy to say and to believe. Till lately. Jilly, I pray about it, to find my place in His plans. Meanwhile, if for no other reason than just to get out of your mother's way, I signed on as a toll taker for the bridge. They're good people. And, happily, survivors of the Great Corps Conquest."

"Then, good for you, Dad." She stopped in her tracks, looked around at scenes she had not been blessed to look upon for too long a time. "I just realized where you're taking me. This is where you have in mind we should camp out tonight? Dad! Really?"

He smiled conspiratorially. "They may think it belongs to the government now, but, honey, who is the government? We are. The people. If the damned dam were built this would be the lake to which we would all be invited. Since I didn't bring a swimsuit, I thought I'd enjoy it while it's still dry. Ahhh," he drew a deep, fresh breath of riverside air. "Nothing like it. Nothing like being home. Let's lay out our sleeping bags over there. Don't think you'll need your revolver this time." He pointed to the site, still etched in both of their minds. The trough running through their old property, the pastures to the land side, the isolated ridge by the river, there where their cattle had had to be rescued by cowgirl Jillian back in '55.

"Remember?" her dad asked unnecessarily.

"Yippie-aye-oh," she hollered. And laughed. Improper as this outing was, if it helped her dad feel better about himself and his new life, she was happy to rebel with him. "Let's pitch camp out on the ridge, ya think?"

"Be great to listen to the river all night. Promise you won't wet your bag?"

"Dad!"

"Sorry. You're a big girl now." He looked into her luminous blue eyes. " Oh, Jilly, I do love you so."

It was a sweet, halcyon night. The moon rose over the New Jersey mountains offering a cockeyed smile at them. The air was soft, the river a gentling lullaby. They slept.

Though Chas did not sleep well. His mind kept bounding and rebounding. How could it have happened? How could he have stopped it from happening? Why would God have done this to him? He knew, he knew, it hadn't been God but didn't God permit it? Why would He permit it? To teach Chas something? *Come now, Son,* he could almost hear God saying, *are you so full of yourself that you think this whole government scheme was about you?* No, no, his mind futilely replied to the

131

unseen God he had worshipped all his life and would for all the rest of it.

Still . . .

Being back on his land was a blessing. Knowing he could never really be back on his land, a curse, the devil's own scourge.

And, to be sure, early in the morning, as he and Jillian, still in their sleeping bags, were marveling at the vivid sky beckoning the sunrise, there appeared a shadow, standing directly over them, a darkness that Chas recognized immediately as one of Satan's minions.

"You two!" it barked. "What are you doing here?"

"Enjoying God's exuberant creation and thanking Him for it," said Chas defiantly.

Undeterred, the voice persisted: "Don't you know this is federal land? This is U.S. National Park service."

"And you work for the park service?" Jillian joined the fray.

Now as the man stepped around they could see his uniform and his commanding look of authority. "That's right, ma'am."

"Which means, of course, you work for us. Well, we're not quite ready to get up. We'll be leaving in, oh, let's say an hour or so. Want us to clock out or something? We didn't see any guest register when we arrived last night."

"Now! I've had it with you two interlopers. Get up and go!"

"Interlopers? Interlopers?" cried Jillian. "I'll have you know, young man, we were the original *lopers* here long before you were born."

"And now," said Chas, "you in your official uniform — which is dirty, by the way — are telling us that we, whose family owned this land for more than two hundred years, that our almighty government is booting us out of here — *yet again!*

"Sir, please, I am only doing . . . "

"I know son, you are only doing" his voice raised to a shrill shout as he stood up at his place and acted out the line, "Only doing what Your Fuhrer commands you to do." He tempered his tone. "And, no, I don't expect you to understand that and, yes, I apologize and we will be gone in five minutes. As the Good Book instructs, 'Forgive us our trespasses,'" fixing the fellow with uncharitable eyes, "as we forgive those who trespass against us."

The Ranger left and within minutes Jillian and her dad had packed up and trudged away, unspeaking. The only thing finally said between them as they cleared the old Ranch property and headed back along the river toward the bridge was her father's one word question to the daughter he loved but could never miss a chance to kid:

"Lopers?"

CHAPTER FIFTEEN

DEAR LADY, I WOULD NEVER SAY THAT YOU WERE NOT COOL.
— *Me, decidedly uncool*

The meeting that would first upset and then transform my life came, as such moments are supposed to come, unheralded.

I was "settin' a spell," as my mom used to say. Had pulled up a camp chair in the morning sun by the end of the bridge. Willy, the morning toll taker that day, had plopped himself near me and we were having cuppa's — his coffee, mine tea, a ritual I had fallen into while living in the Old Stone house. For how long now? What had it been? Must be three weeks.

To some, the house might have felt spooky. A phasmaphobe would have curdled and fled. It hadn't been lived in for years but it had been cared for. It was clean. For my coming a broad new bed had been placed in a spacious river view room and by it a most comfortably welcoming recliner, motorized for the cripple. The bridge folk had done it, financially assisted by the network's Arthur Everywhere. The kitchen was simply stocked and the bath immaculate. As for character, it beat Holiday Inn.

Twice now, I'd been driven into New York for meetings on the new show. *My* show! Still hard to believe. We had

135

decided on an Executive Producer. Cal Johnson, the only other person I had ever told I would follow anywhere, so firm was my trust in his judgment and TV smarts. I was enlivened by the selection.

"So what's the show, Cal? How do we do it and how do we do it different?"

"We don't." He was my age, with the vigor I used to have and would again. I'd need it just to keep up with him. He'd been in TV in many roles, succeeded in all. A non-preachy Christian, dark hair, aquiline nose, always attentive eyes, taking everything in. He was a remarkably tall man, six foot seven, accustomed to ducking at doorways. He had glasses that he could never find and used mostly as props anyway, to delay a response while he selected the best answer from his catalog of reasons to deny or delay. "We don't try to make it different. We *are* different. You and the background of your life and recent heroism are different. Your style always has been. Natural. Real. That's you. That's our show. Real."

As I said, I'd follow this man anywhere. We worked to rough out some story ideas, how to structure the show, how to staff it. Arthur produced the Olivetti 22 I had asked for so I could start making notes once back at the Stone House. Actually I had already been making notes, scratching out thoughts with pen and paper although not for the show alone. I had also decided I wanted to start putting down notes on the story I knew best because I was living it and many people seemed interested. Would I write it or someone else for me? My brother? Didn't know but wanted notes for whomever.

136

As for New York and the new show, I'd be back there next week to continue.

Meanwhile, of course, back in Pennsylvania I was still in strenuous therapy and things were going encouragingly well. No more walker. Cane, but even that, less and less. Visited Doc at his Milford office twice a week. He said everything was looking good and the GI man concurred. Everybody said I was really lucky. Doc said I was really blessed. I knew what he was saying. As usual, I disregarded.

I saw them coming.

Which is to say, I saw *her* coming and because I saw *her*, I eventually noticed *him*. Old enough to be her father. I hoped he was. She was a strikingly good looking girl. Apparently just been camping, carrying sleeping bags and packs. She went camping with him? Why? Where'd they been? A lot of questions about this young woman. And I knew a reporter who'd be happy to ask her about them.

As they approached, Willy, called out to them, "Hey, Chas, come meet our new neighbor. Living in the Stone House. Like you to get to know him."

I stood up as Willy began the introductions. "Perk, this is my buddy, Chas Amacher. And . . . and?"

"Oh, sorry, my daughter Jilly. She's an artist, lives up in Milford now. We used to have the Riverside Cattle Farm just down the river there. Decided last night to camp one last time on our old place but a little Nazi found us this morning and unceremoniously ran us off.

"Dad was so mad he stood up and gave the kid a Heil Hitler salute, you know, arm shot up in the air."

As they talked, I looked. I hoped my looking wouldn't be taken as staring but given what I was seeing it was worth the risk. Nordic, she appeared. Pale complexion, a sunbright blonde, hair swinging in a ponytail to the waist of her jeans, though this morning it was speckled with twigs and leafstems from her night camping and if she knew that, I hoped she wouldn't be ashamed to be seen like that. It was charming. To my eyes, natural usually is.

"Then he apologized to the kid," she said continuing her story. "Apologized biblically, of all things saying, 'May the lord forgive us our trespasses as we forgive those who trespass against us.' Wish I had said that. I'm so proud of my dad and his cool."

"Dear lady," I flirted, "I would never say that you were not cool."

"Oh, sorry," said Willy. "Let me introduce the fellow I called you over to meet, just moved into the stone house couple weeks ago. Grandson of one of the brothers who built this bridge back in 1900. And, I'm not supposed to tell you this — he swore me not to but — is it okay?" he asked me.

"Whatever." I'd keep my humility and still hope he might impress the girl. Jilly. Nice name.

"He's a hero. Been newspaper stories about how he saved the lives of two little girls in a race riot down south or something. He's been recuperating for weeks now. He's a big time TV guy."

"Okay, Willy. That's enough."

"Well, I for one would love to hear more."

Unfortunately, that came not from her but Chas.

"Wouldn't you, too, Jilly?" her father prodded.

(Thanks for prompting her, dad.)

She jumped in." Sure would. Maybe we can all get together one evening."

"Jilly's a good cook."

"And mom's even better," the girl added.

"Let's plan on it, okay?" said Chas.

"Name the time and the place. I'd love to," I responded.

"Well, what do you think, honey?"

"I have a project due for work. Need a few more days on that. How about Saturday? And if we might be allowed to impose, Mister . . ."

"Stop," I interrupted. "Unless you're talking to your dad and call him 'Mister' you don't need that word around here. 'Perk' does fine for me."

"Okay, Perk, how about Saturday? And to be even pushier, how about we bring all the fixings for a riverside picnic, right here on your lovely lawns. I can't imagine a better place since we lost our ranch."

Her dad joined in, loving the idea.

As did I. "Saturday. I'll round up a couple more chairs."

Willy assured me they had some as he headed out to take a toll from a man in an antique Packard, a man he knew and with whom, as usual, he had a folksy chat while Jill and her dad hiked back to their car, waving as they went.

"Saturday. Here's to Saturday." I finished my tea.

CHAPTER SIXTEEN

IT'LL HAPPEN IF GOD WANTS IT TO
— Jill to roommate

So, c'mon. Tell. You've been acting strange. You're keeping something from ole Babs."

"Well, yeah, I guess I have been. It's just that I really don't know whether it is anything or not. Don't know whether it'll ever be anything. I may get some idea Saturday.

"Well, what's he like? This mysterious fellow."

"He's bright and funny and somehow he's famous, they were saying. I don't know how and ya know what? I don't care. He just seems so, so, I don't know, real."

"Is he cute? That's what I want to know," said Jillian's roommate.

"Oh yes, oh yes." She giggled as she told Babs about first the night hike with Dad, being run off the old homestead, and then all her anger and frustration melting away by the sight of the guy with a cane. And she was going to see him again at his place right on the river for a picnic Saturday evening. Only hitch: her mom and dad would be there too.

"Oh, great, you have chaperones."

"Have to see what I can do about that."

"Good luck, honey."

God's Bridge

"Thanks. It'll happen if God wants it to. Now, I really have to get to working."

Jack Perkins

CHAPTER SEVENTEEN

GUESS WHO IS GOING TO BE THERE, IN BIRMINGHAM, SPEAKING
AT A LOCAL STADIUM AROUND THE TIME OF OUR STORY
--*An excited producer, Cal Johnson*

Got to get to working. I pulled out the Olivetti, so
familiar in my hands after the years I'd been using
one in so many places. Slender, compact but with
good key action and solid build.

Looked like she had a solid build. Hard to tell in her baggies
from camping but she certainly carried herself well. I could see
her walking away across the mouth of the bridge to her dad's
and her cars. Limber, trim, a lovely thing coming or going.
Saturday!

I had a little time before I had to get in the rental and drive
up to see Doc in Milford. Wonder where she lived in Milford.
Maybe find out Saturday. What was I going to wear? Enough!

Where to start? If I was going to gather ideas for my own
story, where to start? Start "Real," in Cal's favorite word. Not a
bad exercise, I thought, to try beginning with the bombing,
just to see how much of that I could piece together from the
jagged fragments tumbling about in my kaleidoscope of a
brain. Can always go back to Wooster days and early TV.
Those might one day be part of this if it were to be a memoir,

143

whoever was eventually to write it. But let me start with what I still didn't acutely remember, however hard I had been trying to dredge up moments and string them together. Think of this, then, not as trying to capitalize on present acclaim as colleagues I know had so often done, not even bothering to write their own recollections, hiring ghosts to do that. Think of my exercise not as that but as mental therapy to go along with the PT and OT I was already doing.

And for which I really needed to get my butt in gear and in the little Ford Falcon.

Doc was not running late, a shocking headline though my remarking it did not much amuse him. "I see the dark side of your nature is healthy. How 'bout the rest of you, Perk?"

"Do you, by any chance, know a young woman named Jillian Amacher, Doc? An artist of some sort? Here in Milford? Her folks used to own a ranch down on the river, had it stolen away by the feds. Know her?"

"No," he replied, "But if it's she who has you so keen and feisty this morning I'd like to."

"So would I. And I'm going to. Having dinner at my place. Listen to me. 'My place.' But never mind. I believe I'm here for some more good news from my favorite Doc."

He had indeed, he said, gotten more good reports from the therapists. Very satisfied with my progress. Nothing much more to do, he told me. It's pretty much now up to how I feel, he said. My body was my best guide from here on.

"But, one more thing," he added. "If you and this young lady you're excited about do indeed hit it off, take it easy in bed."

"Doctor!"

"What I meant to say of course is, if you do hit it off, Patricia and I would love to have you come to our place for dinner one evening. That's what I meant."

"You, sir, are Satan. Tempting me with a lure I could never spurn. That prospect alone is added incentive to get off to a good start with Miss Amacher. For another of Patricia's meals. I'll let you know, Doc. Thanks. Again. For *everything.*

The drive "home" had me thinking. Driving is good for that. The woods and hills passed unnoticed to my right; the river giving peeks through trees to the left was ignored. The road ahead, flat and straight demanded but reflexive attention leaving my conscious free to conceive and compose. Not the show, the book. The private revealing. My story for a change, not other people's. It started flowing, forming in my mind as I headed back to the bridge.

How to recall what I had not been able to recall, that was challenge one. The moments immediately before and after the explosion that ripped me so rawly asunder. Of those, all I had yet been able to remember was that there was nothing I remembered. Wondered if a shrink could help. Must ask Doc. Talk to Bunky. Talk to the two girls. Take it on as I would a story assigned. Be a reporter, for a change, albeit of my own life. First, though start putting down whatever fragments I might uncover mining my own mind.

Setting up the Olivetti on a table on the balcony looking out at the bridge and the sweeping, pewter waters of the Delaware, I began exploring.

For most of the afternoon I was engrossed. Until at last I heard a hail from friend Willy shouting my way. "Hey, Perk, isn't it tea time?"

"Sure is, right there, friend."

Friend! How nice to say that, to feel that. After the anguished, mind-whipped months in the South, how easing to return to my roots and find a new Dick Morrison as a buddy. Here where nobody cared about "the color of his skin but the content of his character" as Dr. King had said it in his dream in D.C. just a few months before.

Naturally, once seated in our camp chairs by the bridge, and when he had poured from his Thermos our tea (he had switched from coffee, it appeared, to join my tea tastes), he had to launch immediately into an interrogation about Jillian and our dinner plans for Saturday evening. "Chas tells he she's really looking forward to it."

"Only way she could look, forward " I smart-assed. "Looking backward, she'd never find it."

"Well, if you wanta stop goofing and hear me out, Perk, you might be very interested in what else he told me."

"Speak on, oh teller of all."

"He's not coming. He has to work Saturday evening. So he's not going to be dining with you and since he's not going to he at your party, neither will his wife. Bet that makes you purty sad, huh?"

"You sure about this? Really?"

"Has Willy ever misled you. Oops, gotta go." A Ford pickup approached the toll taker's circle on the pavement.

146

So it would be just Jillian and me dining al fresco Saturday eve. Albeit with her dad right over there in the shanty keeping watch, you can bet. Still, Jillian and me on a balmy autumn eve. I wished I believed in God. I'd be thanking him mightily for this.

Next morning, I had an early pickup for the trip into the city, into New York to get my attention back to the new show. "*Perk's Journal* seemed to be the title that stuck. How could that not command my focused attention? Who, in my position would not be thrilled, excited, absolutely pumped by the opportunity. I had more ideas to toss into Cal's story stack. Was eager to hear his. And wanted to reinforce my emphasis on starting the first show with Birmingham Revisited.

There was a box on the seat of the Lincoln Town Car. "For you, sir," said the driver. "A Mr. Gradszinski left it for you."

The box inside said "Phillips Carry-Corder 150." The note from Arthur said "These aren't available yet in the States but we got one in Europe thinking it might be useful for you whether listening to your music or recording ideas. See you soon."

It was a very compact cassette recorder, smaller than I had ever seen. Be handy, indeed. With no decent music to be found on local radio around Milford, it could provide some classical in this temporary home. Something romantic for Saturday evening, for example. Great gift. I was truly being coddled. And loving it.

Cal opened the meeting at 30 Rock with a staffing update. Some of the additions I knew and was glad to have with us; others, I was happy to trust Cal's judgment. When we got to a

147

story list, I agreed to the earlier proposal to do Birmingham with the girls if they agreed. "Do that first of all."

"And we have a new twist on that, Perk. Listen to this. Guess who is going to be there, in Birmingham, speaking at one his Crusades at a local stadium around the time of our story. Billy Graham! Isn't that perfect? We're in touch with his people in Minnesota and they would like to have you and the girls up on stage with him. You game? Be a terrific way to start our first show. Couldn't ask for anything more promotable. PR's already foaming at the mouth. That'll be next Easter Sunday and the network will let us do our first show the next day. Be a quick turnaround but we can handle it. We'll set up production and editing in Birmingham and feed the show from there. Your open and close and final commentary we'll do live from back at the stadium. Film packages of the event and your interview with Billy we'll have back to New York. They'll run from there."

"Great! This is just great, Cal. Couldn't ask for a better way to launch. Or," I said surveying the room, "a better gang to do it with. Everyone up for this?"

The answer was shouts and applause. I'd never seen such from normally jaded crew members. Cal had 'em pumped.

The meeting went on with only a sandwich break for six hours. Show structure, normal order of elements, show graphics. Looked great. Fresh, bright, today. And to see my name up there in gold, well, that made me turn aside so as not to look like I was looking. Like when I was staring at Jillian that first day. First day? *Only* day so far. Till tomorrow. Tomorrow.

We talked other story ideas. One came from one of the young line producers, Beth something. She had heard a couple of singers making the rounds of the coffee houses in the Village and raved about them. They were so fresh and mellow and melodic and, she said, "they even cut their hair." Meaning not like the new group that was such a rave overseas, The Beatles. In the States we had Peter, Paul and Mary doing folk and puffing a magic dragon; there was Bobby Vinton singing everything Blue -- *Blue Velvet, Blue on Blue, Roses are red, Violets are Blue.* A California group calling themselves The Beach Boys took us *Surfin' USA,* with their *Surfing Girl.*

"But, I don't know," Beth said, "these two fellows I'm talking about are different and I think going to be terrific. They're poets. Their songs are poetry. Thoughtful, touching. There's one they call *The Sounds of Silence.* It is simply unique, and uniquely simply. I think we ought to get on them. Introduce them. Names are Paul and Artie. I'd love to do the piece if you want."

"Sounds good," Cal agreed looking to me for concurrence

"Go for it, Beth" I said. "And I'd love to meet them, hear them. See what you can set up along those lines."

Talk turned to more serious stories and it was agreed to send me off to Vietnam as soon as I could do it. I would follow Pete Wolfe, one of the network's cameramen, a guy who had already spent brutal months imprisoned by the communist Pathet Lao next door in Laos. Then, back in Saigon had been one of three American newsmen beaten by demonstrators just recently. Plus which, he warned New York that Vietnam was not going away as a story and we ought to be doing more out

149

there. "We agree," said Cal, "and this show is the way to start it rolling. If Birmingham's our first show, Vietnam has to be our second. You agree, Perk?"

"Agree enthusiastically. Actually, the way my therapies are going and the internal reconstruction, I'm just about ready to get started on more than just talking about reporting. I'll be ready for overseas travel sooner than later. We could if we chose start up the program before Easter. Do Vietnam first, Birmingham following. Possibility."

"Maybe. Great to hear of your progress. So you say you'll abandon that bridge you keep talking about and move into the city?" Cal wondered.

"That, I did *not* say. No, it's good, I think, to stay attached to my lifelines out there. And, folks, you've got to come out one day and check out my digs. You'll understand my attachment." Even without figuring Jillian Amacher whom I did not mention.

"When do we meet again, Cal?"

"Let's say Monday, same time, same place. Have a good weekend all."

At the record store downstairs, I quickly selected tapes for the new cassette machine Art had provided me. This afternoon, pumped and primed by the meeting, the prospects was clearly a Copland ride home. Then Shostakovich. For tomorrow, though, for tomorrow, some gentle Debussy, perhaps Schubert and his Trout and, to be sure, there had to be Tchaikovsky. Had there ever been a greater romantic than he? The Romeo and Juliet Overture Fantasy? Aphrodisiacal!

Tomorrow.

150

CHAPTER EIGHTEEN

YOU SHOULD KNOW, PERK, NOTHING'S GOING TO HAPPEN HERE
TONIGHT
— *Jillian's first words to me*

There wasn't much to get ready for the evening. Uneasy, I took up the folder of research I'd been given on Vietnam. I already knew that the place called South Vietnam was less a country than a cartographer's conceit, a cop-out compromise imposed on the powerless by the powerful if not wise. How the French, who themselves got bogged down there for deadly, embarrassing, financially ruinous years, must now, with Gallic gall, laugh at *les Americains* who seemed to have learned nothing from *l'histoire*. French cynicism was justified. America's impending futility seemed obvious to all except the savants (idiot savants?) of Washington, who were on the verge of spending treasure we did not have and lives we should preserve in order to "save democracy" in a corrupt little land that had never had democracy, didn't especially want it, and wouldn't know what to do with it if it had it. In both the Frenchmen's language and ours -- *farce*.

My briefing notes showed that America already had just shy of 20,000 troops in-country and had already lost 200 men.

Why did I feel that that was only the beginning of a disaster pre-ordained? We needed to get on it for *The Journal*. If Doc would clear me, maybe head over there next month latest. How about be there over the holidays. Might get good press.

"Yo! Yo there, Perk?" Willy shouting from our chairs by the bridge. "Time for cuppa's.."

I tossed on a jacket and went down, mugs of hot water and tea bags.

"Please, oh, please, Willy, don't tell me her dad changed his schedule and he and his wife *are* coming to our picnic."

"Well, if you don't want me to tell you, I won't tell you but that won't change anything, now, will it?"

"Damn you, Willie, you are a cruel man."

"Ease up, friend. No further word on that front. You go right ahead and plan for solitude and, I believe even a near-full moon. Just hope she doesn't prove to be one of those women who play coy, naive. You know how that is."

Coy? Naive? No, that girl is many things but not naive.

She'd be here at five-thirty.

She was carefully on time and about the first thing she said after I had helped her carry the victuals onto the porch was something strange. She said, "You should know, Perk, nothing's going to happen here tonight."

"I hope you're wrong. I hope something *is* going to happen."

"What?"

"A beginning. That's what I hope for. All I hope for."

"Have you had a lot of beginnings and endings in your life?" She got right into it, earnest, her mien sober yet smiling.

152

"Mostly beginnings that never got beyond the beginning. There were several of those. But my life has been notably shy of endings."

"Why do you think that is?"

"Because of me, because of honesty. Meaning honesty with myself. Too honest to let beginnings that should not have been, go further. It's not so much that I haven't wanted to string a woman along. I haven't wanted to string *myself* along. I don't choose to play make-believe by myself."

"Can I believe what you're saying now?"

"You can and I hope you will believe what I say at any time. Honesty works both directions for me. I have faults but one of them is not dissembling. Any person I might attract by being dishonest, I wouldn't want to be with."

"Wanna pet my pony-tail?"

"What?"

With a mysterious smile, she repeated the question. "Wanna pet my pony-tail?"

I laughed if merely as a cover while I tried to plumb her meaning.

"Simple question. Too hard for the big time reporter?" she teased.

"Sorry," as I played at surveying the subject more closely. "I was just checking to see if all those gnarly twigs and assorted debris had been evicted from the nest. Seeing they have, yes, I'm game."

She moved closer and turned her hair toward me. I inhaled the scent of her. I petted, I stroked, I admired.

"So," she said abruptly, turning back, "Can I see your scars?"

I stammered. I didn't know what to make of this girl. "Some of them. Just some of them."

"Why, do you still have twigs and debris in the others?" She was unlike anyone I'd known. I stood (without cane, thank you) unbuttoned my shirt and displayed the surgeons' craft in three locations.

"Ouch," she said. "Had a lot of work to do, didn't they? How do you feel in there?"

"I haven't reached in there to feel."

"You know what I meant."

"Dear Jillian, I'm not sure I've known what you meant half the time in this conversation. How about we go to the table and enjoy the dinner you've been so generous to prepare for the cripple?"

I opened a bottle of chilled sauvignon blanc but needlessly. I really didn't want it and I saw she had included in her bowls and trays of fried chicken, potato salad, baked beans, cole slaw, a bottle of homemade lemonade. Also there was what she promised was her favorite recipe for chocolate cake made with dark cocoa instead of regular.

"I'll leave the leftovers for my gracious host. Enjoy."

And we did, enjoyed the meal, the Trout on the cassette player, and, mostly, each other. It was as though we had known each other for years and expected to be friends for years to come.

Table talk was about the view and what it meant. The view, of course: the river moon-glinted at our feet, slowly rising, its ripe face smiling on us, and then the bridge, a story of persistence and survival itself. Maybe one day it might be a story for your show, Jillian suggested. I agreed. Have to mention it to Cal. And get him out here one day. Meanwhile the cake was deserving of all the accolades I hurled at it. Chocolate cake for people who really love chocolate.

"Jill, don't take this the wrong way but would you move in with me? No, wait I am serious but at the same time I don't mean it. Only that if you lived here maybe I could have this cake every day for every meal. How great that'd be."

"So you'd only want me as your house cake maker?"

"Doesn't sound good when you put it like that I guess. Disregard previous communication."

"I'll edit it out."

"I love talking with you, lady, be our colloquy playful or serious. So it's your turn."

"For what?"

"To tell me me your story as I told you a bit of mine."

"Well, let me tell you frankly . . . No, let it be as you said, I don't have to announce frankness. You may assume that anything I ever say to you is frank, open, honest. Isn't that the best way to nourish beginnings?"

"Here's to beginnings." Raised my wine, offered her some. She stuck with her lemonade.

"So I should tell you. There is only one man I have ever loved and I still do . . . "

Punch to the gut!

" . . . my dad."

Phew!

"For a while I thought maybe he was the only man I *could* love, *should* love, ya know? I've never had so much fun with

155

anyone, never so respected anyone, trusted anyone. Oedipus complex, you say? Yes, he did a marvelous job — and I've told him this — of spoiling his daughter. His answer? 'That's what I've always tried to do dear. Always will."

"Is it good to be spoiled?" I asked.

"It's absolutely wonderful! It's a love that enfolds you. Doesn't always give you everything you think you need because it knows better. It knows what you really need and provides it in full measure whether you know it or even truly deserve it. That's love. That's real love."

"So another guy will never have a chance?"

"I didn't say that. I don't think that. There have been others along the way who have tried to spoil me but they always told me they were spoiling me. You don't spoil a person by telling them you are. You don't spoil them by giving in to everything they want. I've heard it said that the best way for a gal to be spoiled by a man is to make sure *she* spoils *him*."

"Ah, yes, the old Mutual Spoliation. Also expressed by saying, 'Love is only love when you give it away without expectation of its being returned.'"

"And that," she replied, "is precisely the form of love I most desire." She reached over to the chair on which she had placed her gift-wrapped package. That's precisely why I brought you this particular Host Gift. Hoping we might get to this point in . . . in our beginning. This is the best guide book I know on love."

What? She brought me The Kinsey Reports? Couldn't be. I tore open the package. It *was* a book but certainly not Kinsey.

Nothing like that. Gilt-edged pages and inscribed on the cover: "New American Standard Bible."

"This version, this translation, just came out this year," she said excitedly. "It's a true and very readable presentation of Holy Scripture. Only the New Testament, Psalms and Proverbs so far. They're still working on the Old. I do hope that my host will find himself blessed by it. I thank him for our beginning and hope he knows that he may host this girl anytime, anywhere. Don't stand up, Perk."

She stepped over to me, leaned down, placed a kiss on my cheek, and was gone.

Tchaikovsky was still letting his lovers find their magic as I watched mine walk out the door.

CHAPTER NINETEEN

PERK, YOU'VE ALREADY MET THE PRETTIEST GAL IN TOWN?
--Doc meeting Jillian

At five in the morning I gave up. Reluctantly, I dragged my weary self out of bed. What could I do? If I could never expect to sleep after being with this girl, I'd have to stop being with this girl. And I knew damned well I wouldn't by design do that.

Washing, brushing, dressing, I saw her. Putting on water for tea I took up the gift she had brought me. Just off the presses, the newest translation of the Bible's New Testament. In my youth in and out of various churches it was usually the King James from 1611. Lots of *Thee's* and *thou's.* I never felt it was talking to me. This one was called the NASB, New American Standard Bible, published, it said, "with the conviction that the words of Scripture as originally penned in the Hebrew, Aramaic, and Greek were inspired by God. Since they are the eternal Word of God, the Holy Scriptures speak with fresh power to each generation, to give wisdom that leads to salvation, that men may serve Christ to the glory of God." And *women* too? I wondered.

I turned to the fourth gospel, to John which had been a favorite when I was dragooned into Sunday schools now and

then back in Wooster. I'd always loved how John played off
the wording at the beginning of Genesis to open his gospel.
How did this version put it?

*In the beginning was the Word, and the Word was with God, and
the Word was God.*

Always loved that construction. Engaging.

*He was in the beginning with God. All things came into being
through Him, and apart from Him nothing came into being that has
come into being.*

The repetition nailed the notion.

*In Him was life, and the life was the Light of men. The Light shines
in the darkness, and the darkness did not comprehend it.*

Life and life and light and light. Engaging! And then, of
course, a couple chapters down, the most famous verse in the
Bible, I guess. Remember the guy with bushy hair painted like
a rainbow who always showed up in the background at
televised golf tournaments holding the sign 'John 3:16'?

*"For God so loved the world, that He gave His only begotten Son, that
whoever believes in Him shall not perish, but have eternal life.*

Can never forget that sentence.

But wait. I had the feeling the bridge itself was staring at
me reprovingly, saying: "Do you know what you're doing,
son?" And I did. Instead of just reading, I was studying
wording, phrasing, appreciating word play, sentence structure.
I was admiring the writing without absorbing the written. I
was warming myself with familiar embers. Taking pride in
what I remembered while forgetting how much I had forgot.
Mine was a pleasant but superficial exercise, skimming but not
diving. Staying on the surface was safer. It let me enjoy
without committing.

I put down the book, tossed on a flannel shirt, jeans, sweater and parka, and took my tea and the book outside to one of the camp chairs on the lawn by the comforting bridge. I needed the bridge's faithful and reassuring solidity to ground me as again I opened John, starting once more at the top, this time to inhale. This time not just to see words but to hear a voice that might speak to me in the midwinter chill of this pre-dawn.

In the beginning was the Word, and the Word was with God, and the Word was God.

That puzzles people. Used to puzzle me. Then, early in my career I had occasion to interview the historian Will Durant whose scholarly multi-volume series, *The History of Civilization* – thanks to the Book of the Month Club – perched unread on countless American bookshelves. That meeting incited me to take one of those volumes down from the shelves at my home in those days and start reading. It was volume three, *Caesar and Christ,* in which he wrote about the philosopher Philo of Alexandria who introduced the notion of *Logos.* The term could be interpreted as "Word" or something more, as a voice (of God?) speaking the world into being. However conceived and translated, Durant found that "Philo's *Logos* was one of the most influential ideas in the history of thought."

If still puzzling.

And for me at that early morning moment by the bridge, distracting. I meant to read the Bible, instead I was analyzing it, distracting my seeking mind with irrelevancies. As friend Bunky often accused me: I was being analytical with a capital ANAL.

I closed the book, set it down, moved my chair away from the single yellow lamp over the bridge entrance, moving closer to the river so as to hug the dark at the side of the bridge itself. This was the Bible's latest translation. I was grateful to Jill for it. But, for a moment here in the gloom, I let my mind return best it could to the earliest "*In the beginning,* the King James version . . . as softly remembered through the fog of long-held disregard.

In the beginning . . the earth was without form and void, and darkness sat upon the face of the deep and the spirit of God moved upon the face of the waters.

Could I sense that? Here this morning by the face of these waters, could I sense the moving spirit of God? Was it here, here with me? In the dark?

And God said, Let there be light and there was light.

A switch was not flipped flooding instant luminance through the scene but slowly, very slowly did the first whispers of light suggest themselves there by the bridge, coming first on ripples in the river, catching and reflecting ephemeral sparkles dancing their praise.

And God saw the light, that it was good

Beyond the spread of sparkle lifted humps of darkness that I knew to be trees across the river. I knew that not because I could see them but because I had seen them. Memory can be our sixth sense.

And didn't a verse in Genesis speak of the creating of trees and plants on the newly forming earth? What day was that? And then the creatures of the sea, implied by the washing river in this case, and the birds in the skies, those making themselves prominently known by the caws and cries of hungering crows and jays.

And then came Man and for Man a helpmeet, and God saw that it was good, He saw that it all was good.

What was I witnessing? What had I just watched? Were I not the skeptical reporter verging on cynical, might I not, as I sat in the shadow of the sun rising beyond my grandfather's bridge, be able to accept what I had just seen unrolling historically before my eyes and mind, was a rehearsal in miniature of Creation itself?

And on the seventh day, he rested.

I knew what I needed to do. Sleep or not last night, fatigued or not this morning, I knew what I was fairly compelled to do.

Back to the house for the cold waking needles of a shower, shave, change, then, book in hand, out to the Falcon for the drive up to Milford. Many electric flashes of sunlit river on the way, and every now and then the form of a well-posed deer in the grasses along the riverside and once, just once, hurriedly spied by the tree line, a dashing red fox. Thank you, Whoever You Are, for the blessed sights of those creatures that as I recall sprang from Day Six. Just before You made me?

It was my Dad who had recommended the Milford Diner. The times I'd patronized I understood his telling me "good food, great people."

"Morning, Wanda." She was a dear older gal who tried to be blonde but didn't have to try to be cheerful.

"And how's my favorite celebrity today?"

"Wanda" I chastised gently.

"OK, how's my buddy, Perk?"

'Better. Thanks. And I bet you can guess what I'm going to order."

"Let's see, a pint of SAE 30 over burnt rye."

"Never use thirty grade oil in winter and, no, I don't think I wanna be seen comin' through the rye today."

"Then how about Two Over, bacon crisp not soggy, whole wheat and a double serving of O.J. to wash down your medicine cabinet?"

"You're why I keep coming back here, darlin'."

I settled in, opened the book at random and, as so often happens, Random knew what it was doing.

If I speak with the tongues of men and of angels, but do not have love, I have become a noisy gong or a clanging cymbal. If I have the gift of prophecy, and know all mysteries and all knowledge; and if I have all faith, so as to remove mountains, but do not have love, I am nothing. *That's what Paul wrote to the people of Corinth. What I read in Milford, Pennsylvania was this:*

If I speak with the tongue of a prideful TV celebrity but do not have love, I have become a noisy gong or a clanging cymbal. If I have the gift of prophesying the news, telling not just what has happened but the mysteries of what will, but do not have love, I am nothing.

"Here ya are, Perk."

"Efficient as you are beautiful, Wanda."

"Is that compliment instead of a tip?"

"Have I ever stiffed you?"

"Ooooh, now that's a question you ought to re-word," she said with a grin that displayed both teeth and where teeth used to be. "It's Sunday."

"Speaking of which, how's that church across the street? Thought I might drop in."

"Couldn't say but I know when their services are because people here sometimes have to rush to make them. Ought to be one in about fifteen minutes. People over there asked for their check and they're dressed for church."

"Thanks. I better get to eating. And bring my check too, will ya, dear?"

I peppered the eggs, spread the toast, pulled out my pills and began medicating between bites, not rushing but enjoying while keeping in mind that I'd like to visit that church after this. Seemed to fit my mind just fine as things had been going on this morning of revelations following a night of more dreams than sleep.

The church was historic. One didn't need the sign out front to know that. It was lovingly cared for, the red brick of its three stories bright, the paint on its towering belfry clock tower gleaming white on this hundred-thirty-year-old structure, this First Presbyterian Church of Milford, Pennsylvania. I took it in as I walked from the diner directly across Broad Street to the greeters stationed outside the church's open white doors. For the sanctuary, I was told, up those stairs, please. Finding a seat on the aisle in a pew halfway down, I slipped in, took up a hymnal, and set it down beside me next to Jillian's Bible. Quickly, I scanned the church bulletin. The sermon was to be titled Changing Lenses. Scripture reading: Philippians 4:8. I looked it up.

He knew I was coming this morning. He must have known. Or someone did. Someone?

All stood for the opening hymn, what used to be one of my favorites because it was always one of my Dad's favorites as he said it had been one of his dad's.

> Yes, we'll gather at the river
> The beautiful, the beautiful river;
> Gather with the saints at the river
> That flows by the throne of . . .

God?

I balked at even singing the word, saying the name.

If I still believed that I didn't believe, (ANALyzing again) then I shouldn't be singing the words of a hymn I didn't buy. I'd been kidding myself down by the river this morning, down in the sheltering lee of the bridge, feigning that I was witnessing Creation when it was only a murky morn aborning, normal and daily, bereft of supernatural significance meaning; it must have been simply the sleeplessness of the night before, the rushing pulse of the evening as attraction became wished-for affection that created all the flooding emotions and enticements that had bemused me, clouded my normally rational mind, so that perhaps I still was not a believer but, as I had been so much of my life, just a Wanna-Believer, or, at most, when it seemed culturally advantageous, a Make-Believer, faking the faith I thought I should have.

I sat down. All others had already resumed their pews when the hymn ended which I hadn't noticed, so befogged I was by my fervid self-diagnosis. Would I never learn? My schooling and then my profession had always worked against my learning the most important truth: that what you know is not as important as what you believe. College taught the opposite. You weren't graded on what you believed but on what you knew, and what you knew only counted if it agreed with what your professors said you should know. If that weren't indoctrination enough, then came the career in TV news where hard, provable facts were the coin of the realm, not flimsy speculation or beliefs based on bias. A struggling Wanna Believer couldn't easily fight those.

The preacher took the pulpit to read the scripture for the day, the words Paul wrote to the Philippians, and by extension, to us all. Especially, I thought, those of us reporting news. Oh, how much they – we – needed to inscribe this on our hearts.

Finally, brethren, whatever is true, whatever is honorable, whatever is right, whatever is pure, whatever is lovely, whatever is of good repute, if there is any excellence and if anything is worthy of praise,

dwell on these things.

I knew, I knew that he didn't realize I was in the sanctuary today, or even that I was I, but the pastor couldn't be hitting closer. The sermon jumped off from Paul's advice to the faithful of Philippi to speak to our own times and us. "Crucial," he intoned, "is the lens we select each morning through which to view the coming day. We have two choices. We may look through the lens of the Bible, see the world through the wisdom and spirit of Biblical truth, or, on the other hand, we may choose to view the Bible through the lens of the world."

The latter course, he explained, seeing the Bible through the world's eyes, implies that, for example, as the world is more accommodating to drugs and rampant philandering, that suggests that Bible believers and the Bible itself are out-of-date, irrelevant. If, however, we look at the world through Biblical eyes, we see the ways of the world today as aberrant and unacceptable to God.

"So what lens are you looking through today," he asked *"For me, I think Paul had it right:* Whatever is true, honorable, right, pure, lovely, of good repute, if there is any excellence and if anything is worthy of praise, dwell on these things."

It was while the closing hymn was being sung that I looked around the old sanctuary. High-vaulted ceiling, magnificent tall stained glass windows, ornate woodwork of the pulpit and chancel furniture. The sanctuary itself about two-thirds full and probably some people who didn't want to bother to dress up sitting up there in the mostly hidden balcony. Down on this level . . . I'd almost missed them. Three rows ahead on the other side were Doc and Patricia standing and singing gustily while I hadn't even bothered to look up the words for the hymn and felt a bit guilty. Hope they didn't see me.

After the benediction we all rose and started to find our way out of the sanctuary and Doc and Patricia were on me.

"Good to see you here, Perk. Hope you enjoyed the service."

"Doc, tell me the truth, you haven't told the preacher about me, have you? I mean, that reading and then the sermon were pretty much aimed at me whether he knew it or not."

"I never mentioned you, no."

I was about to respond when there was a tug at my sweater and a voice saying, "Hey, big guy, remember me? I combed out the pony tail."

"Jill! I didn't see you."

"Was hiding in he balcony. I saw you."

"Perk," said Doc, "you've only been here a few weeks and you've already met the prettiest gal in town?"

"Watch it, Hubby." It was his wife playfully contesting his designation of Jill as town beauty Number One.

"Oh, sorry, you know each other?" I asked.

"No, but he'd love to," said Patricia.

I did the embarrassed introductions and as I did, put my arm around Jill's waist. As though claiming?

"Look, you two," said Doc. "We have to run but it'd be great if you both could join us for dinner sometime."

"Anytime," I said.

"Tonight?"

I put it to Jillian. "Tonight with the Bullochs?"

"And with you?"

"Of course."

"Then I'd love to."

Doc and his wife hurried out the door. I turned to speak with Jillian but she, too, was on her way out. Catching up, I said, "Hey, you in a hurry, Jill?"

"If I'm going out again tonight, I've got to get some work done."

"Yeah, I need a nap, too."

"You didn't sleep much last night?"

"Not a wink," I confessed.

"Good," she said. "Me neither. Only thing I accomplished this morning was to wash my hair and then didn't want to bother rigging the pony tail so I just ran up there and hid away up in the balcony."

I told her she had no need ever to hide away. With her long blonde hair cascading free down her back she looked terrific. "Aren't you going to ask if I want to pet your hair now?"

"We're in church."

"Something in the book about not letting a friend pet your hair in church? Maybe this Presbyterian thing isn't for me. Anyhow, I'll pick you up at six?"

"Great." She gave me her address and said, "Babs is dying to meet you."

"You've told her about me?"

"Sure."

"What? What did you tell her?"

"The truth. Just the truth. See you at six." And she was gone.

CHAPTER TWENTY

NO NEED FOR HASTE TONIGHT
— *Jillian, teasing*

B ut what was the truth? What was the truth about me as Jill would have told her roommate? For that matter, what was the truth about me – her and me – as she believed it to be? Did it match what I believed it to be, wished it to be?

I would be off to New York tomorrow. Plenty of studying to do for that. I needed to read this afternoon. I needed to read. Or did I? Had I not already read and thought and puzzled, concentrated and cogitated enough for one long day after one long night? What I really needed now was . . .

"Perk. Hey, Perk. You in the world."

As I said, what I really needed now was a cuppa with Willy.

"Right down, man."

Since the wind was picking up, he suggested taking our tea in the toll house. There were two ancient chairs and a roll top desk in there and he had the tea all made. For a pleasant hour we enjoyed each other's company, frequently interrupted as he dashed outside to collect tolls, chat a moment with a local.

Mostly, I gathered in our conversation he was smitten as was I by Jillian. He couldn't throw enough questions at me about her, about her and me, about present and future. He was delighted to hear I'd be seeing her again tonight but even more bemused that I had run into her at church this morning, that I had even been to church this morning.

"You shoulda seen her today, Willy. Let her hair down from the pony tail I'd known and it flowed so bright and soft. She is one terrific looking woman but you know what? She is one terrific woman all around."

"So, did you . . . "

"*Stop!* Don't even ask the question."

Toll to take. Out the door he went, out to the circle on the pavement to greet and collect.

Returning, he apologized. "I ought to tell you that wasn't what I was going to ask. I ought to tell you that but I'd be lying. I was. You're right. Sorry."

He left again and this time was out for several minutes, a run of traffic both eastbound and west. While he was out, I wandered from the shack over to the lawns of the Old Stone House, was gazing out across the river when I spotted something unusual. Atop one of the rock and concrete piers supporting the bridge there was an alien object. Looked like a box, a metal box, cast there, I could only guess, by a wash of high water rolling down during last week's storm. The river breathed more calmly on this winter afternoon and though I shouldn't have risked the venture, I did. Tossing off my sweater, leaving me just in T-shirt, sneakers and jeans, I walked down the bank, stepped into the chilled water and trudged myself out toward that pier intent on recovering the waiting treasure. Though no longer a child, I childishly believed in treasures washing ashore and might this be one?

Reaching it, I found a metal ammo box, war surplus type, securely clamped and waterproof, it should be, so I figured the treasure it must hold would be safe. So I made a point of wiping off some of the mud encasing it and began plodding my way back to the shore a hundred feet away. Either the water was colder going this way (which I knew it wasn't) or I was just feeling it more, my Rational Self shouting its cursed discomfort to my Impulsive Self. The water was running above my waist, side-pushing me downstream which I had to fight against to keep my line. At one point my right foot turned on a rounded rock on the bottom and down I tumbled full into the water up to my neck. My only thought, irrational as it was: *Damn! If the U.S. Army Corp of Engineers or the U.S. National Park Service or the U.S. Coast Guard which supposedly controlled these navigable waters should see me down here polluting their waters I'll have the full brunt of the federal government down on me! As Jill had experienced! Would they seize treasure this time too?*

Willing myself the last sodden feet up onto the bank, I *flumped* down and shivered. Rational Self was right. It was even more uncomfortable now, jeans and shirt and shoes soaked, a crisp breeze I would have welcomed in other times serving now only to chill me as it turned clothes into refrigerants.

Ah, but I had the box. The Treasure.

"What the hell you doing down there," yelled not a government agent but Willy, coming toward me with the most puzzled look at my soaked self.

"Oh, hi, friend. Just sort of sitting here. With my treasure."

"Your *What?*"

"I don't know what. Was just about to find out. Give me a hand."

"You get your sorry butt into the shack. I'll get the heater cranked up."

"That'd feel good." I gladly followed him back inside scooping up my dry sweater on the way, exchanging it for my wet T-shirt.

"Now," my quick change act completed, "to see what the precious treasure amounts to. Got a sturdy screwdriver, it doesn't want to be opened."

Together we pried and forced till the clasp released and the top of the metal box, weather seal intact, swung open. And, yes, there *was* something inside. A small roll of paper, a scroll, tied with a gold ribbon. placed there by whom? Untying the ribbon, I unrolled the scroll, calligraphy carefully done by a talented hand, a small bit of verse, a precious present preserved for me by — how appropriate! — *The Bridge:*

Paean to a Bridge

To be a bridge is to rise above
To reach across
To span
Bringing together two sides apart
Affording passage where none was had

It is doing all this but seeming the while
To do naught
If Blessed be the Peacemaker
Holy is the bridge

"Whaddya know!" said Willy.

"Damn!," said I.

"Where do you think . . ."

"And who?"

"And why?"

"Hang onto it, Willy. I've got to go get dry pants, maybe a hot shower."

"I'll guard your treasure . . . intriguing as it is."

It felt good to get home, get bathed, get warm, get dry, and it felt very good to get sleep. I knew Willy was on for another few hours and I didn't have to pick up Jill till six and I hadn't slept for days upon days. Just an hour would be great.

Three and a half hours were better. But it meant that even rushing, I'd be late picking up Jillian. Better call and let her know. It was her roommate who answered and told me, "Just a minute. I'll get her, I think she may still be napping. She sure was tired coming back from church and then we talked a while. Anyhow, I'll get her. Hang on."

Naturally, when finally, all apologetic, she answered, I said "just making sure you're ready."

"What time is it?"

"Almost six."

"Oh, I am so sorry. Give he a half hour, can you. Think that's okay?"

I told her I'd be there at six thirty, wondering how her hair would be this time. I didn't tell her I was late myself because I, too, had fallen asleep longer than I meant to. I'd promised I would never lie to her but I wasn't lying, just not telling the truth by not telling anything. I took the drive up to her place slowly, stopping a couple of times just to look out at the Sunday sunset colors settling on the tops of the hills to the west. Pretty place, the run between Dingmans Ferry and Milford. Homey though distant from home; warm even when chilled.

She burst from the door apologizing. Sorry she was late, sorry we wouldn't have time for me to meet Babs, sorry to hold me up, sorry to treat my friends like this.

"Jill, it's okay. I have to confess. I, too had a lie down and only woke when I called you at six. I wasn't going to tell you but I promised I'd never lie and that would have been lying by omission. I don't want even that with you. I'm sure Doc will understand. All's well. And I stopped long enough to pick up a treasure."

"A what?"

"I'll show you, show you all. Here we are."

"Greetings, you handsome two," said Doc at the doorway. "Good to have you both."

Oh, the house smelled scrumptious. "Your dear wife has been busy, I can tell," I said.

"And I don't think either of us has had much to eat today," said Jillian. "From the smells, I'm glad we waited."

Patricia invited us into the living room saying it'd be a half hour at least. Could she offer drinks?

Jill asked for anything soft. I said, "My grumpy Doctor won't let me have anything good. Better make mine soft too. Thanks."

Doc couldn't help but see the grungy ammo box I had set down on the floor beside me. "You brought that to take home leftovers?"

"Doc, you know me well enough that when I'm invited to Patricia's cooking there ain't gonna be leftovers. No, I brought this to show all of you. Even Jill hasn't see it yet."

"Do I want to? What is it?" she asked.

Patricia delivered the drinks and I began telling them of my afternoon Treasure Hunt, a tale my physician did not endorse as recommended post-surgical regimen but done was done. I described how I'd spotted it out there and fancied it must bear a treasure for its lucky finder and, sure enough, it did. Not the sort I might have expected but treasure to be sure.

I prized open the top of the ammo box, reached down and carefully lifted out the ribboned scroll. I passed it to Jillian inviting her to unroll it and read the verse so artfully printed there.

Her first words were an artist's assessment: "Beautiful calligraphy. That's not easy. And the poem says . . ."

She read it with a gentle passion, surely getting more heart from it — or putting more into it — than I had when reading it to Willy. She made my "treasure". . . a Treasure.

The others softly shook their heads, moved, it seemed, by both the emotion and the mystery. There was silence. I looked down at the scroll and then up at Jill. She smiled at me. That smile, that smile, I understood was my real treasure.

Patricia broke the silence. "I love the simplicity. Poetry does not have to have rhyme or particular meter, iambic, dactylic. But to my mind it does need evocative simplicity. *'Holy is the bridge.'* I love it. Who would think to write a poem about something as mundane to us all as a bridge?"

"And then letting a bridge be its repository," said Doc, "safeguarding it until some headstrong, impetuous whelp disobeying his medical team's wise advice should hazard to assume the role of its discoverer and savior."

"He does get impetuous, sometimes, doesn't he?" Jill joyfully joined the cabal against me.

"And already," said Doc, "young lady, you know him so well.

"Not as well as I hope to."

"Yikes, should Patricia and I leave you two alone?"

"Doc! Please. You embarrass her. "

"No," she quickly averred.

"Well, at least me."

"Sorry, Perk, I surely wouldn't want to embarrass you, now, would I?

With which, the chef mercifully called a truce announcing that the meal was ready. And so were we.

What good people, fun people, caring friends. And one of them another Julia Child.

Understandably, there was little table talk, the food before us deserving and getting our rapt attention. We ate well and, of course, too much. Doc assured me he'd have feedback for me by Tuesday afternoon from the various therapists and physicians as to whether it was okay to clear me for duties more legitimate than salvaging ammo-box poetry. Given that, I could fix a back-to-real-work date with Cal and the show folk.

"What're you planning for Christmas next week, you two" asked Patricia and her asking startled me. I had mostly ignored the holiday coming so soon. I wasn't planning anything.

"Well," Jill jumped in, "I'll be home with my family, mom and dad. And I hope, though I haven't asked him yet, that I can persuade this fellow to be with me."

"And that is precisely what his physician prescribes" said Doc. "Got that, Patient Perk?"

"Never," I replied, "have I been more eager to please my Doc." And to Jill, "You sure the folks want me?"

"Oh, Daddy's always seen to it I get what I want. I'm spoiled, don't forget."

"How can I? Why should I? I'd love to."

"You're easy," said Patricia.

"With a gal that lovely," added Doc, "can you blame him?"

Laughing, if at the same time a bit embarrassed, Jillian and I said our thank you's, accepted the container of offered leftovers and departed the good folks.

"Just think of the intertwining coincidences," I said once we were in the car and rolling, "that brought me and them together."

"And the blessed string that led us together," she said.

"Wait. Give me a moment. Let me revel in that phrase . . . 'us together, us together.' I love the sound of that."

"So do I."

"You know, Jillian, down in the basement of our family home in Ohio used to hang a painting, a portrait of a scary woman. That's how my brother and I saw it, dark, sinister, brooding, a woman staring out at us humorless and grim. Scary. The ornate frame around her was gilded but so dark with age it only added menace. We were kids. That's how kids saw such things. As we learned more about that painting we came first to accept her and finally admire her. Her image was dingy because it had been layered by years after years of neglect and soiling air. Once she had a proper cleaning, her frame was re-gilded, and two kids learned to appreciate that the style of portraiture in 1860 when this had been done was for a woman, especially a woman, not to smile but look serious, even severe, then we came to appreciate her. And then, when we learned that she was the aunt who had raised my paternal grandmother a century ago, we almost came to love her. She was surely a handsome woman, tidily dressed, with a slender gold watch chain hanging from her neck. She was not a specter, not at all. She was Aunt Jenny.

"Lovely story, Perk. Lovely memory."

"And that's not all. Finding about her set me off on a project in genealogy, collating scraps of information gathered by this uncle and that great-aunt, notes scratched on rumpled papers in family files, clues gleaned from genealogical libraries. Painstakingly, I compiled these in a computer program that soon bulged with 460 names. More than names: history. I tracked down a certain John Sale. He had been born in the mid-sixteenth century in Chesham, England, and I knew that; I knew of his birth, and of the blessed day of April 27, 1562,

180

when he had married a woman named Agnes Parker Byrch, a union that would in course produce a son, Edward, who would have a daughter, Elizabeth, who would bear a son, Edward, who would have a daughter, Abigail — so that more than four hundred years later, I, John Sale's great-great-great-great-great-great-great-great-great-great-great-great grandson, would know this and, oh, it would please me. Please me because it placed me, and being placed is important."

"Wonderful," she said, shaking her head, her silky sun-blonde hair.

"That began — only began — to answer questions. Who was I? Who were we? Tiny tracings in a very large matrix. People who existed because miraculously, against incomprehensible odds, through uncounted centuries, there had been not a single break of genetic continuity, no premature death, no lovers denied their meeting, not a child lost to croup who should have matured to father another and continue the line. We were the product, that is, of either a divinely perfect system or a Byzantine sequence of intricately interlocked coincidences."

"And," she said, "the fact that you didn't know which, seems to me to argue the former. The divinely perfect system."

Did it? If that was her conclusion, was it, ultimately, mine? Should it be? Should the schooled skeptic relent? Repent? We rode on in silence.

"Here we are. Your dutiful chauffeur delivers you safe."

"Wanna come in. Still early for a couple of slackers who slept the afternoon away."

"I don't know, Jill. By the way, which do you prefer? Jill, Jillian?"

"Or my dad calls me 'Jilly.' That's his. Whichever you prefer."

"Then I think, in pony-tail you're 'Jill.' Hair flowing luxuriant and lovely, maybe one of your luminous blue eyes peeking through strands, then definitely 'Jillian.'"

"So do you want to come inside with Jillian?"

"I don't know if I could stand to stand inspection by Babs."

"Didn't I mention," and there was that imp in her face, "she's not home tonight."

It was a delightful place, kempt and flowery as a home for two artistic young women should be.

"Tea, coffee?" she asked.

"Isn't the classic stew's line "Coffee, tea, or me?""

"You're better than that, Perk. Plus, which, when it's time, you won't need to ask."

She went to brew tea as I looked around, admiring paintings, sketches, pen and inks displayed about on easels, draftsman's table, walls.

"These yours, Jillian?"

"Most of them," she said bringing a tray with our tea and settling us down on a flowery, well-cushioned sofa.

"Very talented lady. Run in the family?"

"No, but it's just something I've been passionate about since I was a kid."

"Passionate about anything else these days?"

"Matter of fact, yes, there is something else. Wanna pet my hair."

"I don't know. All that got me last time was peck on the cheek and a hasty departure."

She smiled, one eye teasing through wayward strands of blonde hair. "No need for haste tonight."

CHAPTER TWENTY ONE

WHAT YOU SEE, WE SEE. WHAT YOU FEEL, WE FEEL. YOU ARE
WE.
        --*Producer Cal Johnson*

I slept by myself that night, cozy at home and probably with a smile on my face. That smile would have reflected Jillian's teasing when she told me there was no need for haste in my departing last night. That was tempting. This morning, I was glad I had not let my appetites control my actions. If I had and she had acceded, I would have ended up thinking less of her and much less of myself. I was grateful a better nature had supplanted mine. What was that better nature? I wanted to talk to her about that. Maybe tomorrow. Today, New York. Car service due in forty-five minutes. Where was that Bible?

I found the passage I wanted, got out the Olivetti and started typing. Finishing, I enjoyed some cocoa, peanut butter toast and banana and went outside to wait. Chas, just arriving for work, came over to say hello.

"So, I understand you visited our little church yesterday. The Pastor was sorry he didn't get a chance to meet you. I saw him at a trustees meeting in the afternoon. He hopes you'll return."

"Oh, I shall. I and the new Bible I was just gifted by a delightful new friend. I think you know her. Though I'm not sure you know that she has invited me to your home for Christmas dinner."

"As I have said so often in this life, whatever Jilly wants, Jilly can have."

"She doesn't strike me as spoiled."

"Not spoiled, never spoiled, but luxuriously loved."

The car service was prompt. The drive, at first, was graced with the crisp winter beauties of rural New Jersey, farms and homes fondly decorated by people to whom, it seemed, this holiday time had meaning beyond commercial lust. Then, though, transition! As we got closer then closer to the city which considered itself *The City,* the meaning of the holidays morphed. The carol of the city was:

> *Hark the Herald Tribune Sings,*
> *Advertising Wondrous Things*

Who wrote that? Not I, but it fit as we cleared the tunnel and headed uptown through the heart of Manhattan (if, as my dyspeptic friend Bunky would say, Manhattan had a heart.)

I remembered. Who wrote that verse. Dr. Schreiber would be proud. It was Tom Lehrer.

We gathered in the show's office on the sixth floor. I asked Arthur if he could please take my typewritten note and have a couple dozen copies made up for me. As cards if possible. As usual, he said it'd be no problem. Nothing was for him. We were lucky to have him on the team.

"Okay, folks," Cal Johnson got us going, "I know it's hard to keep our minds on anything but the glitter and hassle of holidays, but I really wanted to meet today to nail down some things and set our minds to cranking over the season to be ready to launch early next year. We'll talk about that. Our dates. Some significant changes since just last week. Perk, you have anything you want to say as we get going?"

"Thanks, Cal. Same thing I probably said at the end of our last meeting and should be saying at each and every meeting. Thank you, each one, and thanks to the wisdom that brought you all together in this venture. I feel personally blessed."

"Thanks, Perk . . . "

"May I?" interrupted a young woman I did not know. "I want to direct this to Mr. Perkins himself."

"Nobody by that name here, I'm afraid," I said. "Only Mort if you don't like me or Perk if you do. Your choice."

"Well, Perk, I didn't want to presume. You don't know me. I don't think we've met, but when I heard this unit was forming I begged to be included and I'll tell you why. You are genuine. Not many in this business I've run across I would say that about. So thanks for saying you feel blessed by us because I feel I'm the one being given the gift."

"And your name?"

Cal answered, "Melody Grace, she's a p.a., going to work on our remotes and more I hope as we go on."

"Melody? Production assistant? Lovely. And so's your name." I smiled to assure her it wasn't a flirt but, as she had put it, genuine.

"Okay, folks," said Cal, "let's talk schedule, get progress reports and then hear new story ideas. As far as schedule, Perk do you have a fix on medical clearance yet? How ya feeling?"

"Not quite as spry as I might be if I hadn't fallen in the river yesterday morning."

"You what!

"Never mind. Long story. Hunting treasure." And I let it go at that. Called a tease. TV folk loved to tease. "I'll get my reports from the doctor tomorrow. Should be good to go."

"Call as soon as you hear."

He laid out his schedule assuming my flags would be green. "Christmas, day after tomorrow. Immediately after which PR wants to get with you, pictures, write-ups, interview to set up the Journal for newspapers, magazines. Want to schedule media, get those lined up figuring we'll be premiering in February. First show lead: Vietnam. So we need to get Perk, Bunky and a crew or two there as soon as possible, okay?"

"This was an important story before the assassination," I picked up, "Now, it's crucial. Will our new president think America should launch full scale to save South Vietnam? Indeed, does he think we could save it if we tried? And how much red and green, blood and dollars, will be expended in the effort, successful or un-? Pardon my diatribe," I concluded. "Getting ahead of myself. Cal, how do you see that first show?"

"Most of the hour, Vietnam. Your reporting, the network's men already stationed there, interviews with Vietnam authorities, US officials, touring the countryside. And a lengthy take out on our man Wolfe, who spent more than a year locked away in a communist prison camp. Want you to speak extensively with him, Perk."

"More than just a minute soundbite. I really want to get a good feel for the man. What he went through. Must be a

Jack Perkins

profound fellow and with experiences none of us should ever hope to know."

"Most of the show made of that. Lots of looks at the countryside, feel of the people, and most importantly, your thoughts as you witness all of this. What you see, we see. What you feel, we feel. You are we. Don't preach at us; inform us, share with us."

"How journalism ought to be," I agreed. "No preaching, no teaching, sharing."

"Then after Vietnam, to close out the show, the regular segment we'll be calling "AfterWords." Maybe an essay by you, maybe an inspiring vignette of some sort. In this case, I'd like to propose a brief introduction to those coffee house singers we were talking about, the two balladeers and their song *"Sounds of Silence."* A couple of us went down to the Village Saturday night and caught them and they are really good, mellow, thoughtful, poetic. Make a good counterpoint to Vietnam and a sweet way to sign off. Any problem with that, Perk."

"None at all. You've spoken with them? Their people?"

"That's the thing. They don't even have people yet. We're catching what I think will be stars when they're still un-peopled."

"Sounds good. Though I can hear the critics now after our first show: "The new *Perk's Journal* could have used less *sound* and more *silence.*"

A bit more chatter and we took a break for sandwiches and conversations, my trying to get to know as many of the show staff as I could on this brief social basis. Andrew returned at

189

this point to deliver — already! — the cards I had asked for. When we returned to the meeting room, I set them up for everyone.

"Friends, in my recuperative time I've doing a lot of thinking about our project, about television in general. Thinking about the young genius, Philo T. Farnsworth, in his lab in San Francisco so many years ago inventing what would come to be known as the image orthicon tube, the instrument that would eventually give us, for better or worse, television. When he was running tests between rooms he needed something to project, some design on a piece of paper, simple, graphic and he chose one and scratched it out on a tablet and held it before his lens to project it to his colleague. And it worked. And thus it was that the first object ever "shown on television" was a crudely-drawn image of *a dollar sign!* Of course, they didn't see that as a harbinger, an omen. We, today, know it was. Actually, young Farnsworth hoped his invention would redound to the great benefit, intellectually and artistically for us all. Cal, an aside: Let's look up that old lab and do an "AfterWords" on it one show."

"Good idea. Kim, make a note would you please," he asked his secretary.

"Anyhow, before I led us off track, I was getting to these." I held up the stack of cards. "Last few days I've been going through the newest translation of the Bible. NASB. And was struck by one verse that I asked Arthur to have made up for us to carry in our wallet or pocketbook or simply in our mind as we undertake this project. This was St. Paul talking to the people of Philippi and, I think, to us as well.

190

Finally, brothers and sisters, whatever is true, whatever is honorable, whatever is right, whatever is pure, whatever is lovely, whatever is of good repute, if there is any excellence and if anything worthy of praise, dwell on these things.

"Arthur, if you would, please." And as he was handing out the cards, "Dwell on these things. You all know what TV is like these days, too much of it. Not worthy of dwelling on. But I hope that we can make our program worthy. Let us be positive, not by slanting or ignoring but by emphasizing. Let's use Philo's invention more as he intended and hoped it might be used. But importantly, let's never tell anyone that's what we're doing. Let *The Journal* be known not by its pronouncements but by it's spirit; not by saying we're being positive, but by being positive. Finding and heralding the good. Never proclaiming to critics that that's what we're doing. Just doing it. That's the most powerful brand of positivism."

"Perk," said Cal to affirming nods around the room, "I think you have just served our meeting today with its perfect *AfterWords*. Merry Christmas, all, Happy New Year."

The greetings ran through the room, and hugs and handshakes.

Merry, true, honorable, pure and lovely Christmas.

CHAPTER TWENTY TWO

SOMETIMES YOU JUST HAVE TO TRUST — HER, YOURSELF, THE
SPIRIT OF LOVE.

--Bunky's advice

After the meeting, Bunky detoured me down to
Hurley's. Or as he called it, "The bar, the grill, the
legend!"

Smack on the corner of 49th and Sixth, at what seemed the
pivotal base of the towering block that was Rockefeller
Center, Hurley's had been there, against odds, forever, so it
seemed.   When Prohibition came, the owners simply filled
the front windows of their speakeasy with flowers and kept
pouring. When developers conceived the massive structure
that would absorb the whole block, the Hurleys refused to
yield their lease forcing builders to construct Rockefeller
Center around their place. Hurley's became the haven for
those from NBC, Associated Press and other denizens of the
complex, but especially NBC-ers who, whether coming from a
show just completed or fortifying themselves for one to come;
whether wangling for a new contract or wriggling out of an
old one, took refuge at Hurley's. Any NBC type you wanted to
see, or any NBC type who wanted to be seen was there.

We bellied up to the sixty-foot-long black granite bar, I and my favorite cameraman/producer/friend. Hadn't seen enough of him since moving to the Bridge. A lot to catch up on and I didn't have to drive home. Still, when the bartender asked, and Bunky ordered a tap beer, I said, "Could I get an iced tea, ya think?"

"I'm sorry," Bunky said to me. "I thought I was drinking with my pal, Perk. My mistake."

"I just haven't had much taste for it lately, man. The meds and therapy, I guess." Not mentioning what was probably the principal cause, Jillian. With her, I never felt need for alcohol, didn't want to blur a moment with her.

Bunky and I went through a couple of rounds at Hurley's, catching up, talking the show, Vietnam, our trip there hard on us already, talking our hopes and concerns and, underlying it all, my wellbeing. "We've got to take care of you whatever else we do or don't."

"You've been doing an exemplary job of Perk-caring. I appreciate it, Mr Google."

"You're welcome, Mr. Doogle."

"Seriously, friend," I said, "I wanna ask you something."

"Shoot."

"Nothing to do with business but important to me. Okay, how long was it after you met Suzie and started going out that you knew she was the one?"

"*Knew?* A long time. In fact, I still question it sometimes, I hate to admit. But if you asked how long before I *sensed*, or *believed*, or *thought maybe* . . . that's different. Sometimes, I think, that's all there is. A possibility yearned for. A likelihood that suffices without sure knowing. Sometimes you just have to trust — her, yourself, the spirit of love."

"Spirit of love?"

"Yeah. Some call it God."

"Bunky . . ."

The barman came by asking if we wanted refills. Both of us declined and asked for the check.

"Bunky," I persisted, "I've known you for how long now? And I never heard you talk like this. About God and such."

"My mistake. It's just something that's easier to talk about once you know the other person is already on the same wavelength. Like love itself. You always hesitate to be the first to declare it to someone until either she does first or you're damned sure she will. Don't want to be hung out declaring your love and she doesn't reciprocate. 'I love you' you get up the nerve to tell her and she replies, 'You want to see that new Hitchcock movie next week?' Ouch! Hung out to dry and cry. That's kind of how it is talking God for the first time with a friend, even as close a friend as you are. It's just easier and less risky to steer away from the subject. You know?"

"Oh, I know, I know."

The barman brought the check but we told him we'd changed our minds and would like another after all. As he went off to fetch them Bunky and I continued our probings and self-reflections. We had never talked this way before. It felt good to open to a friend with whom I had assumed I already was open. When finally, he left for home and I rang up the car service and headed to the bridge, it occurred to me what I should have said to him but hadn't. I never had. But I meant it. *I love you.* I really do, Bunky. What took me so long and I still hadn't said it? It's a cruel waste to leave an *I love you* unspoken, unheard, unrequited.

It was love's season. Christmas Eve tomorrow. Dinner with the Amachers Christmas Day. Oh, and lest I forgot. I have some desperate shopping to do. My dad always held off as long as he could. I got the bad habit from him and doted on it. Always scoped out my late night Christmas Eve options. An all-night drug store could offer at least boxed candy. Maybe costume jewelry. How late did the local Woolworths or Kresge's stay open? Of course around Dingmans Ferry there were no stores and I had not seen a five-and-dime in Milford. Up in Port Jervis? What were my options? Limited, that's what they were. If not non-existent.

Why didn't I do this in the city? Especially for Jillian. What the hell could I get for her. It had to be special. A box of Whitman's Sampler was a cliché. Jillian was no cliché. What was she? What was she to me? If I didn't know, maybe, as Bunky was saying I may never *know.* I might sense or come to believe or think maybe . . . But *know*? Perhaps never. Maybe I'd just have to trust — trust myself, trust her and, as he put it, trust the spirit of love.

"Some call it God."

CHAPTER TWENTY THREE

"IT'S LIKE SHE'S HOARDING YOU. HER THOUGHTS OF YOU, HER
MEMORIES, HER FEELINGS.
Jill's roommate to Perk

The bridge was strung with colorful garlands of light.
That was my way of waking on Christmas Eve morn.
More reflective and calming than my day ahead
promised to be. What should have been a blessing of peace to
set the mood for the celebrations of tomorrow was going to be
more like my dad's kind of frantic day-before. Frantic, hassled,
desperation day. Why did dad ever think this a good idea? As a
kid I went along for the challenge of last-minute shopping but
shopping then was for people I sort of cared for but that caring
was never like this. Never like caring for Jillian. I had known
her for, what, a matter of days; I had known her, it seemed,
from time's beginning. For her parents I could always find
something to gift. I had already sent some little things back to
Ohio, apologizing that I wouldn't be able to get there this year.
They'd grown used to that.

But Jill! What in the world could I think of, find, get for
dear Jill, already spoiled as she claimed to be? Maybe Willy
could come up with an idea. After dressing, I wandered over

to see if perhaps he was on duty but hit it lucky finding that it was Chas himself wearing the carpenter's apron, taking tolls.

"Chas," I called out. He turned.

"Perk, you ready for Christmas?"

"Oh, man, am I glad to see you. First, I need to know when I should show up at your place? When do you do your Christmas?"

"Have breakfast first. You're surely invited for that. Say nine, ten? Whatever Jilly says. Then exchange gifts, slowly, acknowledging the day's greatest gift. Dinner's early, maybe three or so. That help?"

"Great. And then, too, I need other help. An idea, please. I need an idea."

"For Jilly?"

"For Jill. And something I might be able to find somewhere around here. Today. "

"That's all you need? Instant Christmas gift for very special girl?"

"And very spoiled by her mom and especially dad, she claims."

"I'll plead guilty to that. So an idea. Hmmmm!" He pondered, ran out to the circle, wished a couple of motorists holiday greetings as he collected their tolls, came back. "She likes jewelry. Simple. Especially handmade. A couple of jewelry makers are here in town. You know the Waterwheel Market?"

"No."

"I can steer you. Or actually, as I think about it, you might be better off going to Peters Valley, over on the Jersey side, just a couple of miles from the bridge. Artists of all kinds gathered around there, in the process with the Park Service of forming their own co-op and teaching facility for crafts of all sorts. Where the old town of Bevans used to be. I'll give you directions. I'm pretty sure you'll find something from one or another of the artists there."

"Sounds perfect. Don't tell her."

"Not much chance. I think *you* see her more these days than *we* do. And, by the way, I want you to know, her mom and I heartily approve."

The directions he gave were helpful but it was that last remark — *heartily approve* — that lifted me up to the colored lights atop the bridge. This was going to be a memorable Christmas.

I found the area he told me about. Looked in on a couple of painters. Nothing. There was a printmaker, quite talented but not for me this time. Then I found a young glassblower who showed many beautiful pieces, crafted there in his own garage. Those I liked, though not for Jill. I bought a couple, he wrapped them and I asked his guidance to the best jewelry maker. He didn't hesitate. The best around, he said, the finest working in Peters Valley those days was a young woman named Priscilla. Could he direct me to her? He certainly could, he said, and walked me out of his garage and next door to his house where he said proudly, "My wife, Priscilla."

For most of an hour we talked, she showed, I admired, we talked more. She was delightful, her jewelry whimsical, original, fetching. The piece that naturally struck me most of all was a necklace with a delicate chain remindful to me of

Aunt Jenny's. The golden ornament it bore was gleaming and certain. Delicately drawn with fine gold wire, it was a side profile of the bridge. Her homage to the Dingmans Bridge.

"If you'd like," she instructed, "the bridge could be made into a pin instead."

"No," I assured her though she didn't know what I was talking about, "I'm partial to Aunt Jenny. I'll take it as is. I love it. And, by the way, you might be interested to know: It was my grandfather built that bridge."

"How perfect, then. I'm glad to know it's coming home."

Crossing back, I thanked Chas so lengthily that I held up traffic and he had to move me on. Apparently many others were out shopping on Christmas eve. Hope they all got guidance as good as I had.

While I was at it, I drove back up to Milford, stopped by Doc's place to leave one of the blown-glass pieces, hastily scribbling a card the artist had provided me.

To Friends and More!

Christmas love,

The Real Perk

Naturally, I had no excuse to on the way back from Doc's place to miss the opportunity to say hello to . . .

". . . Babs? Oh, hi. I was just on the way back home from dropping off a gift to my Doc and his wife. Hoping I might catch Jill."

"And I'm sure she'd love to get caught but she's not here and I don't know when she'll be back. Sorry. You're welcome to come in unless you're still afraid to stand inspection by the roomie."

"Nothing secret, nothing sacred around here, is there?"

"A lot sacred."

As for secret, though, she went on to say, there was a lot lately her roommate did not share with her. Like me. She had been unusually mum on me. Which, for me, she thought, was a good sign. When Jill did talk a lot about her dates they never amounted to much or lasted long. But when she clammed, Babs figured, she must be serious. About me, she had clammed.

"It's like she's hoarding you. Her thoughts of you, her memories, her feelings. I'm left out and that's never happened before. And, if I may add a personal note," she said. "I am very happy for her. She's been Daddy's Girl too long."

"I like him. Haven't met her mom yet. Will tomorrow." We chatted a while, about Jill some but also about Babs, her own art works and background and aspirations. I had other things to do but, just on the chance ...

After a half hour though and Jill hadn't returned, I had to get going.

"Tell her I dropped in and that I hope she's sorry she wasn't here. As for you, dear Roomie, I'm glad you were. Thanks for the hospitality, good finally to meet you. Merry Christmas."

CHAPTER TWENTY-FOUR

IT'S JESUS' BIRTHDAY BUT I GOT THE BEST GIFT OF ALL.
— *Jillian, after Christmas gift-giving.*

Merry Christmas," I called as the Amacher door was flung open next morning by a beautiful blonde. "Especially, you."

She grabbed me for a hearty hug and soon another blonde lady, her mom I assumed, made it a three-way hug.

"I'll just offer my hand," called Chas, reaching to shake. "And indeed, a Merry and God-blessed Christmas Day to you, son."

"*Dad!*" reprimanded Jill.

"I mean 'Son' as in 'young man'. That's all. Nothing more. Sorry."

"You're sorry you called me 'son.' That's not a good sign." I laughed.

Jill's mom jumped in to ease the embarrassment. "You fellows, don't forget the Son we are really here to honor today. *Happy Birthday, Jesus.*"

All echoed the wish, including – I think it surprised Jill to hear — me. And to me, saying it felt not ceremonial but genuine. Real.

I have raved in these pages about Patricia Bullock's cooking. That day I realized that Patricia had a worthy rival. Bernadette Amacher with her daughter's help brought forth a parade of breakfast that seemed to consume most of the morning as we merrily consumed dish after dish. I couldn't restrain myself from remembering Tupelo, Mississippi, and telling about it.

"No idea why we were there but our first morning, early morning, trucker's time, we hit a roadside dinner, Bunky and I, and the waitress, all bleached and pumped up, came for our orders and I had to ask, 'So what is this item at the bottom of the menu, *Heavy Duty Rig?* She said, 'what's that? Oh, honey, I couldn't tell you everything."

"I mean, is it eggs or pancakes or sausage, bacon, ham, grits, potatoes, sweet rolls, toast?"

"Yep," she grinned, head bobbing excitedly, "Let's just say that there's a whole buttload full o' breakfast.'

"So, I ordered it and it was."

"And the point you're making?" Jillian teased.

"If serious, the point is insulting; if not, irrelevant. Sorry. I missed the director's cue to shut up."

With which it was moved and seconded that we take ourselves into the living room for the stockings, four of them hanging from the mantel, vivid and bulging with candy canes and oranges and apples, with small trinkets, packs of Beeman's Pepsin Chewing Gum (family joke?) for some, Snickers bars, but for me, a Jolly Jack. And no, she told me she didn't know it used to be my favorite candy bar but I hadn't seen one for years.

It was a happy time but for me more than that. It was a family time. I hadn't known many of those lately.

After the stockings were emptied Chas moved over by the tree, a handsome seven-foot fir decorated with history and love and, beneath it, an overflow of presents gaily ribboned and bowed.

"Don't get the wrong idea," cautioned Jill, "many of those gifts go to our church, the old Methodist on the hill in Dingmans Ferry, one of the few survivors of the Blitz. Anyhow, we take them there before our dinner here so they can be distributed to town kids late afternoon. Let them share in His birthday."

"Nice idea. Could I see that?"

"We'll make it happen," said Bernadette. "but now!"

"Now," declared Chas, "in my official role as Santa in this house, I have the privilege of passing out the gifts."

"If I may." I went back to the table by the front door where I'd left two boxes and brought them over to add to the pile.

"Thank you," Santa said "and as it happens the first package is for Perk, the card says. Here you are, er, friend."

Wrapped in silver foil paper and silver ribbon it was a small, flat package and the greeting read "To help you to know us better." I tore it open to find a sizable stack of cards, picture postcards, each one a different view of the sights and relics around Milford and Dingmans and the river.

"Very nice. Good primer to my new – if only temporary – home," I said. "Thank you."

"I don't like that." It was Jillian speaking. "I hate that."

"I'm sorry," I said quickly, "hate what?"

She answered with a smile, "Your saying this may be only
'temporary.'"

"Now, Jilly," interrupted her mother, "as we ourselves have
so painfully learned lately, everywhere is only *temporary*. Until
we get to *finally*. But that's not talk for Christmas morning."

"Mom, I hope one day to grow the kind of wisdom you
have."

This was real, this love, respect, mutual caring. Not a
Christmas affectation, not a show performed for a visitor.
Sincerity does not need to perform, it just *is*.

We took probably two joyful hours opening gifts, admiring
them, thanking for them and now and then taking a break to
join the singers on the record player in a rousing carol-sing.
Finally, and not coincidentally I was sure, there were just two
packages left beyond those for the Christmas kids at their
church. I recognized mine for Jill and the other must be hers
for me. It was a large, flat package as a framed picture might
inhabit. One of her pieces of art? I could only guess as it was
handed to me by her Santa-Dad. First, of course I had to open
the card, silently read it, swallow hard to stanch emotion, put
it back in its envelope while turning to Jill that my eyes could
take upon themselves the entire task of thanking her. Words
would wait. Carefully, I began removing the wrapping,
respectfully as though not wanting to risk a tear or wrinkle of
the precious paper, precious because she had selected it, her
hands had placed it carefully on the package to give to me.

It was a frame which I quickly turned over to see her art
but, no, surprisingly, I found not a piece of her art but
something of my own now made *ours*. Carefully flattened,

decorously framed in a molding mocking driftwood was the poem, my treasure from the ammo can. *Holy Is The Bridge.*

"Dad sneaked it out of the tolltaker's shack," she explained excitedly, "while you were in New York the other day and I had my friend who frames my pieces for me do it up. I hope you like it."

"I love it. I love . . . "I was that close to saying what she had already said to me in the card she had put with it, but I didn't. Instead . . . "it."

A tinge of disappointment came to her eyes but, after all, this was her folks' home. Neither the time or place, I thought. Although . . .

As her father reached for the last little box, mine, he said he didn't know whom it was for as there was no card attached.

"Oh, sorry," I said apologizing, "here's the card; I forgot to put it on." I took it carefully from my right blazer pocket not the left one where the message inside said only "Merry Christmas, dear Jill." I handed it to him.

And he said, "Guess what, it's for my dear daughter."

She chose to open the gift first, knowing it was from me and she found inside, swaddled in soft cotton, that delicate, gleaming gold replica of the bridge. "Oh, it is beautiful." She studied it in her hand and then said, "Help me." As she turned her back I decoded the catch, fastened it at her nape, and she swirled around, facing me to display the golden bridge lying on her Christmas-red cashmere.

"Dazzling, Jilly," her mother said.

"Beautiful," said her dad.

"So is your daughter," I added.

Conversation whirled. Where did you ever find …. Thank your dad … Exquisite craftsmanship … Who made it … How did you ever …. I love the driftwood frame … Perfect … We sure had a bridge-y Christmas, didn't we?

It was hours later, Christmas ebbing, the joyous trip to the church to do what the holiday was meant for, giving, and then back to the Amachers for a dinner that was not an overflowing feast nor should it have been but a gentle celebration of intimate family love. I felt blessed to be included. The meal and pretty much the evening were capped with the lighting of candles on a white-frosted, silver-beaded birthday cake. "Jesus' birthday," Jill reminded. And then, with the fireplace down to remembering embers, Jill's parents excused themselves and at last I had a chance to respond to the message Jill had written on her card. *Dear One, On this day of loving, I want you to know, my love is yours. Jillian.*

"But you didn't respond," she said with disappointment. "You just stammered about how you loved *it.*"

"I know. It was awkward with your parents and everything and never having said that to you before. Never having said it, best I recall, to any girl. I was reluctant. And, anyhow, I was going to say it privately in another way."

"How? When?"

"Jill, my dear Jillian, you never did look at the card in the envelope attached to my gift to you, did you?"

"I don't remember."

"You would."

Off she scurried, back to the living room to excavate search through discarded wrapping papers until she found the card I had carefully taken from the proper pocket and belatedly attached. It was really more of a letter. Unfolding, she read:

Dearest Jillian, this is our first Christmas. But how can that be? I have known you for years. I have known you since long before we met and have spent the time intervening, it seems, just waiting.

So why is it now that having found you, I hesitate. There is something I want to tell you but how painful it would be should I declare it only to find it not reciprocated. I have mulled the matter, not the first to do so I'm sure. What I have concluded is this: As painful as it would be to proclaim my love and be met by apathy, even antipathy, what a wounding waste it would be to hoard a love unspoken, because a love unspoken and unheard is destined to be unrequited. Jillian Amacher, I here proclaim my deep and I believe God-given love for you.

As we sealed our requital with an embrace and a kiss, the first words spoken were hers.

"It's Jesus' birthday but I got the best gift of all."

The second were mine:

"My dear, we're about to have our first disagreement."

CHAPTER TWENTY-FIVE

THE GUYS RIPPING MY NAILS OUT, STRIPING MY BACK WITH
LEATHER STRAPS TIPPED WITH NAILS AND PULVERIZING MY
INNARDS APPARENTLY HAD THEIR OWN GODS WHO AT THE
MOMENT WERE DOING MORE FOR THEM THAN MINE WERE FOR
ME.

-- Former POW

The next few weeks were cathartic. The holiness of the holiday, the ego-pump of being fawningly interviewed to plug the new show, retelling over and again the pains of the 16th Street Church, how did I feel now? That so many seemed to care would have flattered, were I credulous.

One evening, I brought Jill on our first big-city date, a club in Greenwich Village, smoky and close, to meet the singers that producer Beth had been taken by. I had not heard of them. Not many had as yet! But Jill and I quickly agreed with Beth's buildup. This Paul and Artie pair were special. In recent days, they had started billing themselves by their last names, Simon and Garfunkel. Young Simon was as poetic a writer of lyrics and melody as I had known and his partner sang like an risen angel. You wouldn't say much for their appearance, especially in this village venue, but their music was always, as Beth had assessed it, uniquely simple, simply unique.

Talking with them after their performance was to speak with two lads humble and hungry. They were going to make it, they knew, and were grateful for any leg up our show might afford them. For me it was a gratifying evening made vivid by sharing with Jillian.

Sharing with Jillian. That had become a sustaining part of life. Until now.

Until launching onto a tedious excursion cross country, cross ocean, cross dateline, cross thirteen time zones before setting down finally at Kai Tak Airport, Hong Kong, British Crown Colony, gazing out wearily across Victoria Harbor to the starlit hills and glittering skyline of the Pearl Of the Orient which I would never have called it had I been sentient which after all of the cross-cross-crossing, I most certainly was not.

Limo and ferry transported us through the night across from Kowloon to the Hong Kong side and from the ferry terminal there to the Hilton where we would bed down for the night and in the morning at NBC's offices up on the hotel's 12th floor be joined by Pete Wolf.

He was gaunt after sixteen months in a communist prison camp in Laos, *At the Mercy of the Unmerciful,* as a friend had encapsulated his ordeal. Externally recovered now (though not internally; that would take a long while yet), he was tall, tanned, white haired, a handsome man not reluctant to exhibit a zest for his life recaptured. Nor to jibe about his name and former condition. "You gotta understand, my full name is

Peter Oswald Wolf. Maybe my future was pre-ordained by my very initials."

He was a facile story-teller and surely with stories to tell, though, it seemed to me, he was always guarded, never admitting hearers into his inner self.

We talked at length to prime me for the interview we planned to shoot the next day out at his home on the far side of Hong Kong Island, by the fishing village of Stanley. And we talked of what we should do, whom we should believe, whom not, in Vietnam. He wouldn't be going with us – too close to "the unmerciful?" -- but would brief us with names and places. I filled a small notebook.

Lunchtime, he took us a few blocks to another Hong Kong high-rise at the top of which, looking grandly down on the Tai Tam section of the city and, notably, the Happy Valley racecourse, green among the gray towers of expensive living. We would take our spoiled ease at the widely known Foreign Correspondents' Club of Hong Kong. Pete ordered Pimm's Cup #1 for us all, a gin-based English must-have at cricket matches and Wimbledon; perversely, I opted for tea.

As the drinks arrived with the formally dressed waiter, I asked Pete a question, a question that started him talking as he would for most of the lunch hour, frequently refueling as he went. My question was simply this: What sustained him through those terrible months imprisoned, much of the time kept in solitary in a stifling and dark bamboo hut? How did he make it? I guess what I was hoping to elicit, given my own changing perspective on things, was his witness, his acknowledgement of faith, a belief that it was God who got him through his terrible test. I posited that possibility. His tongue was free.

"Why the hell would I ask God to help me through that time? Yeah, why the hell would I ask him to get me out of hell? If there was a God who could get people through, even out of, such places, such times why would he let them get into them to begin with? No, I had buddies who spent a lot of time praying and I guess it didn't hurt them. If it made them feel any better at all, as they claimed it did, then good for them. For me, I'd be a hypocrite even to try. If there was a knowing God, I figured, then he knew I was not a subscriber. Why would he even listen to me? Heed my hollow importuning? Anyhow, the guys ripping my nails out, striping my bared back with leather straps tipped with nails, pulverizing my innards, tromping on my legs till they broke them both apparently had their own gods who at the moment were doing more for them than mine – if he'd been mine – was doing for me. Why not pray to their gods?"

There was no answering him nor did any of us try, focusing instead on our burgers or tuna sandwiches, staring out at the city, sunlit and sparkling, while he ordered another Pimm's and kept right on going.

"No, gentlemen, I know it'd make it a better story for you all if I could say different but if there's one thing I decided in that hellhole, it was that if I came through it and one day was back here at this club . . . Thanks, Ming," he interrupted to accept his new drink from the server, "the one thing I promised myself was that I would never pretend that I had been really brave or stalwart, that I prayed and that's what

214

sustained me, or that those months were not really that bad – because, believe me, *they were!'*

The hardness was etched in his face; hatred burned there. Had his cruel captors transformed him into one of their kind?

"You know the only time, through all that time, I felt anything but terror and dread? It came at one moment, right at the end. Right at what we had been told was going to be the end, but could we believe even that? Was that too one more frightful trick they were playing? Get up our hopes then send them crashing down on our pathetic selves? Was that what it was? But no, they had marched us several miles through the heavy heat – not really marching; none of us was up to that -- but walking, stumbling, supposedly to be repatriated at last. There was a river crossing ahead of us, several meters distant, and we figured if indeed we were being set free that's the kind of geographic divide negotiators might have chosen for the swap point. As we came nearer, stumbling, one man falling, another helping him back to his painful bare feet, I began to discern a silhouetted form at one point on the river. And you know what I thought? My first, crazed impression? It was the Bridge on the River Kwai. Just like it. Was somebody going to blow this bridge up just before we got there? I trembled and shook at the image. But then something happened. Maybe the way clouds and sun were playing in the morning sky, but the bridge came to appear to my eyes to be glowing, enwrapped in a brilliant cloud. Now, my eyes weren't good. They hadn't fared any better than any other part of me these sixteen months (which at that point we didn't even know had been sixteen months). But that's how they interpreted the visions they were recording. Almost as though the bridge was wearing a halo. The bridge, somehow, was holy. As I say, my eyes and my brain by then were quite capable of conceiving chimeras. Was that what this was? But, no, across the bridge we could begin to make out American army trucks and ambulances, bold red crosses on top. This was not eye-tricks. Not commie tricks. This was real and it grew more and more real each step the closer we got until finally we were walking, not just stumbling, so that best we could we marched across that bridge, the bridge that on that day delivered us from captivity, degradation and agony to freedom, honor and before long home and family."

Pausing, he dropped his head, drew a deep, thankful breath, raised his head and finished his drink. While, I, to myself alone, said silently, "Holy is the Bridge."

CHAPTER TWENTY-SIX

LET'S GO HOME AND SEE IF WE CAN CHANGE SOME MINDS
--Reflecting with Bunky

As the Air Vietnam flight climbed out of Kai Tak, reached cruising altitude and leveled off, I was thinking about two distinct human qualities -- innocence and arrogance. Which was which? Which was to be our curse in Vietnam, we Americans?

Certainly arrogance. Understandable, perhaps. America had never lost a major war. Our Revolutionary War earned us our nation; the War of 1812 preserved it; from the Mexican-American War we got California; in the bloody, internecine Civil War both sides lost but the nation won; World War I gave democracies including us victory over dictators; World War II did it again; the Korean War was at worst a stalemate. We were emboldened to consider ourselves invincible.

Ah, but now came Vietnam. This War we were inexorably getting entangled in, to many thinking people – journalists, diplomats, historians – was destined to be a foolish, arrogant blunder.

Arrogance I was thinking as the stewardess delivered a plastic cup filled with ice and canned pineapple juice. Wasn't that the inevitable consequence of continually telling ourselves and anyone who would listen that we were a Superpower. Superpowers could do anything. How far we had come from the humbler era when Lincoln described our nation not as a superpower but as, simply, "the last, best hope on earth." Yes, there was arrogance involved in our butting into Vietnam.

But innocence too, I thought. As a people, we were woefully innocent, unknowing of both Vietnam's history – the artificiality of its national boundaries, the long, futile years of frustrated French occupation – and the driving personalities involved on both sides. In the North, the man about whom powerful nationalist stirrings coalesced, a man schooled in New York but returned home to lead the fight for promised reunification. In the South, the corrupt and corrupting crooks who ran what only pretended to be a democracy. Just in recent months they had assassinated their leader, perhaps with our goading, a new one slipped into his place. We didn't acknowledge religious fervor as a driving force in the land, the militaristic Roman Catholic government crushing the pacifistic Buddhists. We knew little of these. In that respect we suffered from precisely the sort of innocence novelist Graham Greene had warned about in *The Quiet American,* innocence "like a blind leper who has lost his bell, wandering through the world, intending no harm."

We intended no harm.

Our innocence could engulf us. Did we know that at the time? Should we have? Or, for that matter, would we understand in time to step around the quagmire before it was too late?

Mr. Long met us at Ton Son Nhut, eager and obsequious. "Your plane good, Mister Perk?" he asked. I would never learn his real name because everyone in the network bureau called him just Mr. Long. The cheery, moonfaced fellow had been working for the office for several years.

"And I'm told he always seems to know more than a mere driver should know." It was Bunky coming up behind me, joining my silent conversation with myself. "He knows the news before it happens. I've been talking with some of our people from here. Mr. Long knows the war and the enemy. How does he get his information? How much of *our* information is he passing back in return? That's just one of the unanswerables about this place. I'll say this for him, though, he can sure get us expedited through customs, gear and all. Here we go."

I took the front seat to get the best look at this country-less country I'd been reading so much about. French, very French it was in the broad, tree-lined boulevard streaming us into the city, past grand colonialists' mansions, past The Club where French gentlemen and their ladies (or someone else's) disported themselves. Down to the center of the city, the open air market to the right, a stand of office buildings to the left, one of which housed the network's offices. Passing that by, we turned left a block to find the Caravelle Hotel, our homes for the coming days. Checked in, we headed up to the roof garden dining patio, already filled this noon with mostly Americans and Europeans. The six of us ordered and I slipped away to greet one of the most experienced reporters in this town, Wally Knudsen, foreign correspondent for a chain of

Midwestern newspapers. I had met him in the States and greeted him familiarly.

"Wally, good to run into you on my first day in-country."

"Perk, welcome to our beloved little hell-hole. What can I do for you?"

There was a seat open beside him. I slid in. "Wally, for all your efforts, those of you and Halberstam and Sheehan and Arnett and the rest, do you think Americans realize we're about to sink into quicksand here? Do they get it?"

"Some of the people, maybe. Our people's national leaders, I don't think so. You know that American reporters are not honored in Saigon and certainly not in D.C. I write what I believe is the foreboding truth, I say it, so do my colleagues, but does the message get through? I don't think so. I believe our national cause in Vietnam is both vain and in vain. We're like horny GI's about to crawl into bed with whores only to wonder later how we got the clap."

"You don't waste words."

"Every report I write, every column I put out, I wonder if that's not exactly what I'm doing – wasting words. Anyhow, good luck on your visit, Perk. You give it a whirl. Any help, just ring me. We need you."

I returned to our table pumped but frustrated. Do the job best we can and, in Wally's experience, it'll make no difference. So why do the job? Because you have to try, you have to keep trying. Eventually, the lying South Vietnam leaders and the cowardly politicians of our government have to learn, don't they?

That evening, having looked in on network offices, I sent a cryptic cable message to Art Gradszinski's office in New York as he had arranged for me to do to forward notes through to Jillian. Then Bunky and I took a walk, just to see what we could see, and think about what we saw. From the hotel, we walked sadly down infamous Tu Do Street, bar after bar, teeming with baby B-girls, rouged and calling out "I love you too much, you buy me drink" to French contractors or American "advisers" or some of the twenty thousand GI's America admitted were in country. The barely pubescent little whores tried hard and made themselves hard as though to refute that they were still children.

Walking down Tu Do street I could not but recall stories of how French soldiers, departing after their failed war here years back had marched down this very street to their waiting ships singing the popular song of their time, Piaf singing *Je ne regrette pas rien. (I do not regret.)*

"Bunky, what do you suppose GI's would be singing when they walked down Tu Do a futile decade from now?"

"The Stones' song. I can't get no satisfaction."

We headed back up Tu Do to Lam Son Square by the National Assembly building, too grand a structure given that the assembly had mostly nothing to do with running this dictatorship, *our* chosen dictatorship partners. We Innocents.

It was near here only a few months earlier that terrible and blazing headlines were made. We were on our way to meet the man who had sent the frightful pictures worldwide, Mal Browne of the AP. He had said eight on The Shelf. Half hour yet.

The "Continental Shelf" was the broad terrace around two sides of the Continental Palace hotel. Across its cool tile floor were arrayed tables already filled with men, mostly men, who thirsted with a thirst unquenchable. The heaviest drinker could never hope to drink enough here in Vietnam to forget that he was here in Vietnam.

If the war was just on the verge of becoming an American war, it had been a cruel and butchering thing already for many people and many years. Just not *us*, but *them*. Some of the blind and twisted reminders gathered each evening around the Shelf. A young lad with pretzeled legs from a bombing or battle somewhere, sometime, swinging his torso forward with only his arms, his pitiful propulsion tearing at hearts assuming they were tearable; two children – 4? 5? -- here in January trying to sell packets of Christmas cards; working too among the tables, lithe Vietnamese girls in long, slender silken *ao dai's*, the native dress, high-necked, slit to the thighs, flowingly attractive. More discreet and older than the children of the Tu Do bars but engaged in the same sorry trade. Cesspool of broken bodies, lives, hopes and expectations. Forced jollity to mask empty souls. America, I thought, this can be your future too.

"An *Orangina*, please," I told the inquiring waiter, knob-headed fellow clearly of long service, his French fluent, his English needing work for the next wave of intruders. Bunky ordered a *Ba Mui Ba,* local beer. And here came another vendor. This, a gnarled, twisted, yet strangely dignified looking gentlemen, the effect heightened by his carrying a walking stick or cane, also somewhat gnarled and twisted. He

222

homed on us. "You like?" He gave the stick a debonair twirl. "Fi'e hunerd P, tha's all." Five Hundred Piasters . Less than five bucks. Still . . .

"Give you two hundred," said Bunky negotiating for something he didn't want but loving the sport.

"No. You see." The salesman whipped the cane around again, this time taking one end in each hand and pulling, exposing the stick's secret. It was a sword, the innocent stick merely its sheath. "Fi'e Hunerd," he said again.

"Sold." Bunky handed him an American five and the man was thrilled.

"A walking stick to kill with. Just what you needed, Bunky. You notice how it seems that everything around here is either a weapon or the victim of one. Or, down on Tu Do wanting *us* to be. Clap docs must be pretty busy around here."

"Well, as your friend Wally was saying, America is crawling into bed with whores and before long we'll all be wondering how we got the clap."

"You got the clap?" It was a new voice. "Hell, guys, you just got in-country. You work fast." He grabbed a seat as I made introductions.

"Bunky, AP Saigon Bureau Chief, Malcolm Browne. Mal, my journalistic better half, er, call him Bunky."

Handshakes and greetings around, another beer ordered, and the man whose powerful photographs had appalled the world just a few months ago slowly told us the story. He had told it many times and would for years to come. It was a pivotal moment in those early days of the war which our nation would burn into its consciousness and conscience for years to come.

Thích Quảng Đức was his name but no one would know that, no American certainly. He was just "that crazy Buddhist monk over in Vietnam who set himself on fire, self-immolation. Hell, for many Americans it was the first time they'd heard the word "immolation" let alone seen a ghastly picture as Browne had taken there in the Saigon street as it happened. The new Catholic government in Saigon had begun a severe crackdown on all things Buddhist. This was one holy man's gasoline-doused rebellion.

"He never cried out or screamed," Browne said, "but you could see from his expression that he was exposed to intense agony, and that he was dying on the spot — and then, in the end, when the body was rigidly burned, they couldn't stuff him into a casket because he was splayed out in all directions. As shock photography goes, it was hard to beat. It's not something that I'm particularly proud of. If one wants to be gruesome about it, it was a very easy sequence of pictures to take. Work is a great panacea for the horrors of that sort of situation, or of a battle, for that matter. I think combat photographers are very conscious of the idea that the real fear comes later, after they get home and develop their film and have a look at what they were through. Then they are aware that they nearly died."

In coming days we heard others echo the thought, great reporters and cameramen, including one for whom most of his colleagues had unanimous praise and respect: NBC's Vo Huyhn. No man in the country knew better the wrinkles and enigmas of this war than he. He had filmed it, he had directed greenhorns through their coverage of it. At one point he had taken over command of a South Vietnamese unit being overrun in the dark as its commanding officer, panicked and lost control. Huynh took over, ran a counter attack and saved the post. Now, for ten days he led me on a tour of the war he knew so well, guiding me, frightened, into skirmishes, battles, and only after trembling trepidation on my part but never his, safely out. Asked by the network to get some publicity pictures of me, he produced one quite impressive shot, I thought, me lying flat on the grasses along a jungle path, cautiously staring ahead to spy whatever danger portended. When he developed it a few days later I was proud of my heroic self as he had captured me. Bunky, on the other hand, noted the anomaly. "Perk, consider the angles. You're lying there, hugging the ground, cautious and alert while the cameraman is standing up in the open to photograph you. Who's brave and who's posing?"

"Bunky, have I told you lately . . . "

". . . How much you hate me. I know, I know."

"No," I corrected, "How much I love you for hating what's happening here and, unstopped, going to happen even worse. Let's go home and see if we can help change some minds."

CHAPTER TWENTY-SEVEN

DID YOU FEEL HIS PRESENCE WHEN YOU WERE IN COMBAT?
--Jillian to Perk

"Jillian, it's so good . . ."

"Wha?" Scratchy, intermittent voice, "Wha? Who..."

"I say," I spoke loudly and deliberately, "IT IS SO GOOD TO . . . "

"I can barely hear you. Is that you, Perk?"

Phone service wasn't reliable Hong Kong to the States. Soon as I had been sure we would make the flight from Saigon, I had the bureau there wire the Hong Kong office to book with Cable and Wireless a phone call for me statesward. I was eager to talk to my dear friend as soon as possible but was thoroughly frustrated. Sent a cable instead.

Again, the flights, this time Hong Kong to Tokyo to Anchorage to Newark, were tedious and tiresome. Bunky was next to me and we spent the time profitably, going over our notes on everything we'd shot, the interviews, the scenic visuals, the visits ranging the countryside, as we began laying out our show. We had more than enough, the challenge being to distill, choosing fairly to cover the spectrum from our American ambassador and the new South Vietnamese premier to the GI's already in-country to the skeptical reporters and

227

historians, American, British, and French who almost universally saw frustration in America's future, defeat in Saigon's.

It would be good for us, for the new show, to be among the early clarion-callers for caution in a distressed part of the world Americans barely knew. Dial back both arrogance and innocence.

Seated across the aisle from Bunky and me was a young American woman with a baby. "Born just a few months ago in Hong Kong where my husband and I are serving a tour with his company. The American Consulate, bless them, arranged a passport for Jillian . . ."

"Jillian?" I blurted, interrupting.

"Born just six months ago."

"Nice name. I like that name," I said. "Dear Jillian." Mostly, I liked speaking that phrase.

Cabin lights darkened as we flew through the night, Bunky and I disregarding the movies they would be showing, preferring finally to sleep however many hours we could before we would see Anchorage rising ahead of us with the sun.

Mother and baby were immediately ahead of us as the uniformed immigration agent took their passports, scanned them carefully and then, speaking warmly to the baby, said simply, "Young Jillian, welcome to America. Welcome home."

That scene, those words blew dust from my sleepy mind: Wasn't that what American men in uniforms ought to be doing? Not going off to fight and kill people they don't know and don't understand; not risking their lives and sanity to save democracy where it's never existed? Rather, like this uniformed American, let them be trained and informed, caring and while still doing thorough screening, also modeling the open heart of a country that is great not because it can beat up the small but because it doesn't want to.

Thus sleepiness swayed me, to hollow palaver one might say, or perhaps to that uncommon thing called common sense. Whichever, we still had many miles, many hours to go so Bunky and I got back to ideas and plans. Which is to say exercising our own innocence and arrogance.

She was there at Newark Airport at the appointed hour, even before time as that last flight of ours arrived a half hour early. Hers was the first face I saw when exiting immigration and she was my Jillian; her hair, down, quite pettable as we embraced.

"What's the line," I said as we headed toward luggage claim, "If I'd known what a greeting awaited I'd have come back long ago?"

"Or never gone," she prompted.

"But then, there would have been no welcome home," I reasoned, unreasonably.

I introduced her to others of the crew whose looks I interpreted to mean hearty if not jealous approval of my choice. Or, I had to wonder, was *I* her choice? Or, maybe, as she might say, were we both God's choice?

Once in her car and on the road home, I got not only thinking such things but discussing them with her. I'd known her less than two months but we always had so much to say to each other and so much to hear from each other. I was glad the drive home took most of two hours to allow conversational intimacy. I was glad she was driving, giving me time to absorb her, the blonde hair flowing onto a purple cashmere turtleneck which displayed on her bosom the delicate golden bridge. I envied the bridge.

"What did you learn?"

"Pardon."

"On your trip,' she said, "the days and nights, the people and places. What did you learn for yourself that's worth passing to others? That's your purpose doing this work, you told me once.

"Frustration. Purveying the frustration of those honest brokers of journalism who, reporting omens, are ignored. Of the GI, the corporal who cannot fathom the unfathomable ruses of this game that isn't a game. Of the maimed trying to survive by demeaning themselves. Of those of honest religious faith driven to suicidal desperation by those abusing their own religion to justify mass murder. The frustration, I can only imagine, of God himself to see all this happening."

"Was He there?" she asked softly.

"God? How would I know?"

"Did you feel Him? His Presence when you were out in the midst of the combat zones?'

I pondered. Did I? Had I?

"Honestly, I don't think so. But you know what? I might have. Several times, I might have seen Him. When staring into the blank faces of farmers out in their paddy fields wondering which band of murderers and destroyers would be trampling their fields next. I might have seen Him when staring –

230

without seeming to be staring – at the mangled young man trying to make his way up to the hotel bar where the people with money might share the pitiful pittance he needed for simple survival. I may have seen God hovering around that fellow. I hope I did. I hope God was somewhere there."

"Did you give anything to that crippled fellow?"

"I? No?"

"Well, isn't it possible that God was hovering not around him, as you thought, but around *you?* Wanting *you* to serve as His loving hands to the cripple?"

We had driven past the little town of Layton, New Jersey and were coming down the hill toward a welcoming glow in the crepuscular sky. It could have been the glow of God or it could have been the lights of His Bridge. Or both?

She left me in my exhaustion at the Old Stone House saying she'd love to see me tomorrow. "Church at ten?"

"Diner at nine."

I couldn't sleep in. I'd made the mistake of leaving a light on in an upper room and that was all the signal he needed.

"Perk? Hey, Perk!" Friend Willy.

Groggily, "Ahoy. Get the tea going. Right down."

Willy wanted to hear about my travels, what that place was like, are we really getting into a war there? Should we be? What did I think? What I thought was I didn't want to think. "Sorry, Willy, I'm tuckered. How're things around here?"

"Well, tell ya. Been starin' at that doggone poem they got framed for you, been starin' at it and thinkin'. How it says all those wonderful things a bridge is or can be but those are all it says. So, I been coming up with more. I mean, a bridge is a lot more than just those."

"Like what?" This man had a curious mind.

"Like: For some folk, a bridge is their roof. Underneath's their home, their only home, maybe a slab of corrugated on top of their makeshift room but mainly just the bridge itself. Make their fire there to cook their grub, lay a blanket or whatever they got for their bed, that's home."

"Glad, as ours is configured, there's no room underneath for that."

"I've got more," he insisted. "A bridge is also a great makeout place, a great site for non-conjugal conjoinings."

"Man, Willy, you're going highbrow with your language now."

"Trying to talk like a poet."

"Well, a poet who feels need to use fancy words and weld together crazed convolutions, isn't my kind of poet anyhow. Got more?"

"You bet. I've been thinking about this while you were gone. Which was a long time, by the way."

"As I've been told by someone else, it happens. Hey, Willy. Especially nice tea this morning. Thanks. What is it?"

He grinned and reached out to show me the package saying, "I got tired of that tea called Orange Pekoe. Didn't either look or taste orange and I have no idea what a Pekoe is, so ... "

"So, Lemon-Mint. Refreshing change. Like it." Sipping. "So what other ideas you got?"

232

He hesitated. "You won't like this but it's true. For many folks a bridge is either a gadget you wear in your mouth ..."

"Not fair, Willy."

"Or the thing you jump off of when Jillian dumps you."

"Now, that is really not fair. Surprised you didn't include the Bridges at Toko-Ri or the one over the River Kwai. Man, I got home just in time."

We laughed and enjoyed our tea, in between his poppings out to greet people and take their tolls unless they were gong to church which still, as always, meant free passage over the Dingmans Bridge.

When he got back, I had to ask: "So, have you any other literary criticism?"

"You bet. That thing framed there is supposed to be a poem, right?"

"Right."

"So why doesn't it rhyme? There's not a single rhyme in the whole thing." He gave a look of triumph.

Which I chose not to squelch with a discourse on blank verse, examples of unrhymed classics, opting instead to remind him of what I knew to be a favorite song. "Whom do you prefer singing "Moonlight in Vermont?" Sinatra, Ella, Jo Stafford?"

"Ella, of course. She's my people."

"You are such a racist," I joshed.

"Nah, it's just I love her record of that. As I love that song."

"And it doesn't bother you that in that entire song, that lyric, that poem, there's not a single rhyme?" *Gotcha,* I thought.

"Sure there is," he insisted as he began singing to himself. "Pennies in a stream," he began singing, "Falling leaves . . . or something."

"Of sycamore" I prompted"

He made his way through the rest whereupon he muttered, "Be damned!"

I showed off. "Ohio fellow named John Blackburn who wrote that poem felt no need for rhyme and you and most people all these years have never missed it. As I don't miss it in the Bridge poem."

All he had left to say — once more — was "Be damned!"

It was during breakfast at the diner that Jillian told me, "I have an idea for your show, Perk. Am I allowed to do that?"

"Of course you are."

". . . He replied, perfunctorily," she interpreted, "Meaning, 'I really wish you amateurs wouldn't bother us professionals who know what they're doing where you don't."

"No, not at all. That's not what I'm thinking. (It was.) You *are* an amateur, to be sure, but an amateur meaning someone who does something for love not for money. And I do and always will welcome any idea you have, my dear, about anything. *Mea non culpa!*"

"I love you, Perk. Of that, I am very, very *culpa.*"

"Alright, you lovebirds." Waitress Wanda, handing us the check while asking, "You want something else? More coffee or tea?"

Jillian answered. "No thanks, ma'am. Have to go. We have a date across the street with our Father."

"You have the same father?" she said not understanding, her words trailing behind us as we went up, paid out bill and hurried across the street. To our Father as I was growing ever more comfortable thinking of Him.

CHAPTER TWENTY-EIGHT

"THIS WAS SOMETHING I NEVER EXPECTED TO SEE, CERTAINLY NOT HERE."
                    --Me, astonished.

What a comfortable morning!

I and my companion-become-spiritual guide, a few new friends scattered around us, hymns (that rhymed), responsive readings that had me softening my voice as to not stand out, scripture readings parts of which I did not understand but noted their citations for later study in my Bible, choir singing not belittled to be accompanied by a single piano instead of the magnificent pipes of cathedrals, a time of congregational greeting, everyone seeming to appreciate the opportunity to 'share the peace of Christ' among friends and strangers equally, and then the preacher ascending the pulpit for his weekly challenge of finding ever new ways to refresh old wisdoms. I had an advantage, of course; most of those ancient truths were all freshly minted to me. A preacher's wish, I imagined, was that at least one person listening to his sermonizing would somehow be gently touched, maybe moved, even in the long term changed. I was touched and intended to take home the notes I had made to study, consider, perhaps myself to be moved.

It was a joy to meet and greet him on the way out. It was another joy to have my dear Doc and the best cook in Milford welcome me home with another invitation for that evening to the finest eating place in town – their home. Call me foolish (or feeling guilty to be yet again mooching) but I, instead, said that having been away from my beloved bridge too long I would rather invite them to dine with us, Jill and me, at the Old Stone House, an invitation they happily accepted leaving me, as we walked out of the church asking Jillian, "What did I just get us into," a question she answered with a single word.

"Us?"

"Well, I assumed . . ."

She let me hang long enough for us to cross the street, get the car from the diner parking lot and be on our way, whereupon she let me off the hook. "I think it's a great idea. Let's start figuring what to have."

The rest of that day was figuring and fun, shopping, chopping, searing and simmering, yes, but also donning coats to go for a hike. It was brightly cold; river waters, wherever they pooled along the shore, showed the frosts and skim ice of winter. Looking up we could see a frost-halo rimming the sun. In our noses were no smells but tickles of ice. We walked without speaking or feeling a need to. Until Jill, looking inland said only: "There it is."

It was my first time to see it although clearly the dark brown sign by the path identifying everything beyond as the property of US National Park Service was a recent addition.

"A blight those blighters just added," Jill sniffed. This was an important moment for her, showing me her past, opening herself to memories we now might share.

"Our only home," she said softly, sadly. "And I don't mean just my mom and dad and me. I mean this was the only home for my grandparents and their folks before them."

"Sizable place, it appears."

"Now, yes, but only after Gramps and then my dad added on. Grandma used to talk about how when she lived here, they didn't even have a bathroom. Gramps called the little shack out back the KYBO. That's where you went to Keep Your Bowels Open. Sorry for my language."

"A bit crude but so was that kind of living."

"Grandma never had a real bath till she was twenty. Until Gramps finally had a bathroom built right attached to the house they didn't have a bathtub or shower, anything like that. She said they had to take what they called Possible Baths."

"Possible Bath?"

"Get a number 2 galvanized tub, fill it with water by the wood stove, get a wash rag and starting at the top, you wash yourself down as far as *possible*, then starting from the bottom you wash up as far as *possible*. And then you wash your *Possible*."

I burst. "Jillian, that is the funniest, saddest, most poignant thing I've heard in . . . *Wash your possibles!* You folks are hilarious."

"Makes up for being morose lately."

It was tough for her to see home forevermore out of reach, her past never to be her future.

"Tough with but one compensation." She was still looking back to the mirror of her life.

"Compensation?"

She turned to me as we paced ourselves back over the fallen leaves that autumn had lain on the path for winter to frost. "You."

"What?"

"My sole compensation. It was coming back from my last visit here that I met you. Remember? I've talked about this with Dad. He says that that moment, he felt and still believes, was the moment, the instant things changed. That's how he put it. Things changed. Daddy's *girl* started her butterfly transformation to becoming someone else's *woman*. Oh, I'll always be Daddy's girl, you know, but. . ."

"I know," I said hoping to rescue us from the awkwardness.

"So. I have a question for you," she said as we neared the bridge and saw that it was her dad on collector duty.

"Chas," I hollered. "Look who I've got and guess where we just were."

His smile was instant and infectious, quite like his daughter's. He greeted us, came over to embrace each and was quickly back on his circle doing his duty. Two cars collected and passed, he yelled back at us, "So what're you two up to today?"

"Getting ready for dinner guests," Jill answered, "his doctor and wife at the Stone House and before long. Great to see ya, Dad. When can we get together sometime."

He said he hoped it would be soon, wished us luck on our party and was back on duty.

And Jill was back to our conversation. "I have a question for you."

How to describe her look at that instant? Quizzical? Winsome? Teasing? Was she going to test me somehow?

Or another question: if this was the woman I loved, who loved me, why was I fretting? "Ask away."

"Well, I was wondering. You know my family. Today you saw where I used to live, where I grew up, my old home."

"Right. It was fun. Interesting."

By now, we were sitting in the living room, having tea and some store-bought cookies, a peaceful break before we would get to finishing dinner.

"So," she continued, "when do you think I can meet yours? See yours?"

"In Wooster? Go to Wooster?"

"It's not that far."

"No, not that far. Though, in a sense, a world away."

"Think about it. No rush, but I'm at that point of wanting to see, meet, hear everything and everyone I can in your life now and then. I love you, fella."

Dinner with the Bullocks was dicey if only because I let it be. Constantly, I was comparing my cooking with Patricia's and coming up short. So that at one point she complimented something, I felt maybe I was being patronized. Talk about insecurity. Which was also compounded by the earlier importuning of Jillian to push things on to the ominous Meet-His-Parents-and-Visit-His-Hometown stage. Much to think about, too much. These thoughts nagged as I should have been basking in dinner with dear friends.

"Something wrong with my patient this evening?" asked my always perceptive physician. "Seems somewhere else."

"Sorry. Just thinking … "

"Couldn't blame you," he said to comfort me, a worthy trait of the good doctor. 'The new show coming soon, the trip around Vietnam — must have been a full immersion journey. Eager to hear more about that."

"Yeah, that's it. Lot to think about." I'd let it go like that. If he would.

"Well, friend, before we leave, thank you for this lovely evening. You have quite a place here, great location, always remindful that you yourself are a bridge and you know what that means; you showed us that poem." He and his wife rose and made their way to the door but the Doc was not quite finished.

"If I may, my often impatient patient, one last thought. As you rush and frazzle through your every day and night, never forget to take time to be grateful for the blessings of the God who loves you. And, from what I see, the young woman who does too."

As I drove Jill home, neither spoke. I don't recall we ever spent so much time together wordless but it was right. Only arriving at her doorstep did she speak.

"He's right, you know."

"In many ways, so many ways. See you in the morning."

"Ah, yes, our adventure. My idea for your show. Get me at ten?"

I *shouldn't* have humored her because how many times did professionals have amateurs offering them "a great story you'll just love" and have to wriggle out gracefully, likely displeasing if not insulting the person when the "great story" isn't worth thinking about.

I *should* have humored her because she was right. This *was* worth thinking about. Might make a fascinating little "AfterWords" for a show sometime. Maybe soon. Yes, soon. The anniversary was approaching. When? Have to check.

April 14th, 1865, it would be. Centennial of that awful day, that deadly night, fast approaching. That time no one expected and no one would ever forget. Actually, there was one person who did expect it. In omen and dreams, the President himself, Abraham Lincoln intuited the disaster-to-come, hearing one night what he believed were the wailing and moaning that seemed to fill the White House such that when he found himself leaving his bed and going downstairs to investigate, he would find, there in the East Room it seemed, mourners gathered around a grand catafalque positioned there, a covered corpse laid upon it. "What, pray, is happening," he asked in his vision and was told it was the body of the President who had been assassinated. Days later he recounted the dream to some friends and his wife who was appalled and insisted he never tell that again.

Five days later, his own body lay in state in the East Room, victim of the assassin's bullet.

We all knew the story: Ford's Theater, John Wilkes Booth, single Derringer shot to the back of the President's head, lingering death, nation thrown into mourning. Perhaps we had read one of the accounts that kept coming with ever more detail. How theater owner Harry Ford, to honor the President's attending on what was basically the end of the Civil War arranged American flags to adorn the presidential box. How one of those flags had literally caught up the assassin as he leaped from box to stage yelling *Sic semper tyrannis,* and caught a spur on the flag, the awkward fall breaking his leg. How, later, one of the players in the evening performance of *Our American Cousin* took one of those flags, folded it lovingly to serve as a pillow beneath the dying president's bloody head.

"Here we are," said Jill, excitedly.

We were in the very heart of Milford, Pennsylvania, corner of Main and Broad where a stately structure housed the local library.

"Gonna read books," I asked querulously.

"Going to read history," she said. "They have a special exhibit I want you to see."

We turned into a side room, to discover, lovingly mounted on the far wall, an American flag, an older one, only 36 stars. The sign above it read: The Lincoln Flag. Indeed, this was the very flag. And, yes, you could see it, the blood stains. How? Why here?

Jill told. "One of the actresses in the play that evening, the one who had folded the flag as the death pillow, had taken the flag and years later retired to this very town, bringing a bit of history here to the safekeeping of the local historical society."

I was awed, standing there staring at the reddish-brownish stain about the size of my hand, there on this century-old flag.

This was something I had known nothing about, never expected to see, and certainly not here.

"I need time, Jillian." I took a seat, she sat beside and we simply stared, speechless.

CHAPTER TWENTY-NINE

THAT'S WHY I TELL YOU, THIS IS GOD'S BRIDGE."
--Willy, toll taker and volunteer evangelist

Some people when confronting a calendar crammed — too much to do, too many commitments, promises made that must be kept, appointments unbreakable, wish lists demanding fulfillment – confronting these, they panic.

Some with no fewer pressures attack them and thrive. It's a choice.

Over years I've gone both ways and discovered an irony: Panic doesn't help; it enervates. Attacking doesn't hurt; it energizes.

Much of my own congestion those February days was my own fault. I worked differently. Most reporters, preparing a story for TV would either have someone else write it and the film editor put it together, or the reporter himself would lay down a script, hand off his track to the editor or a producer who would take it from there. I wanted more control. Needed it for my style which, intentionally, was more conversational than journalistic. Greatest compliment I could get was when a viewer would say, "Perk, you never sound like you're reading the news, just telling me a story!"

To get to that place, I had to write it myself and not only write it but sit there with the editor as the film was being edited, shots selected. If he spotted a shot he'd really like to use and it would add to the mood or meaning but it meant more work, I could immediately alter my script to accommodate the change and the piece would be stronger. That was important to me anytime, especially now, crafting the first program of our new show. I happily traded my time for quality of product and the process enlivened me.

Juggling the work, the long days in the city along with my determined courtship of Jillian (old-fashioned term for old-fashioned girl) which brought me eagerly home each evening; thinking and tapping on the faithful Olivetti while traveling to and from; musing what to do with the Lincoln death flag; Jill's gentle urgings that we find a way to go to Wooster and meet my parents. All these plus, still, my need for occasional physical therapy and gut checks. I made the conscious choice: I would ride this bronc however fiercely it bucked and I would love it.

(Where that analogy came from just now I have no idea. A whirling mind sometimes spins out of control like a rodeo bronc. I covered a rodeo once in Reno that was all females. The people, I mean, not the animals. Of course not the animals. Imagine eight seconds trying to stay on a bucking *cow*? I'm falling. Help! Send in the clown.)

Withal, there was my a-borning faith. Why was it that I felt different about God depending on where I was? Did that mean my faith was not real, but dependent on wherever I was? When home, out in the shadows of the bridge, the solidity of

248

that structure seemed to firm my belief. Even just its shadows solidified. That contradiction I could not explain. But most certainly, as I left behind those shadows, left behind the reality of the bridge, I seemed to leave behind as well some of the conviction of my faith. How, why, would that be. I turned to my counselor in matters of weight.

"Wait," he said.

And then, with a break in taking tolls, here he was. No tea this time for Willy and me; it was his mind I needed. I explained my quandary and he calmly replied. "Not surprising. Not at all surprising, Perk. You've got to remember the singular truth about this bridge: It isn't yours. Your kindly kin who gather with us each fall need to understand. Sure, your grandfather and his brothers are said to have built it – everybody says that! The records claim it! But you have to understand: They didn't. They didn't build this. Not by themselves. Way I figure it, they were the workers, the expediters and supervisors and I don't diminish that, but it never was or meant to be *their* bridge. They were just the instruments the good Lord used to accomplish this miracle for the people hereabout. That's what I mean. That's why I tell you this is God's Bridge."

"God's Bridge?" I numbly replied.

"It isn't called that, of course. Heck, it's called Dingmans Bridge but have you seen any Dingmans around lately?"

"No, of course not. They had their chances, built their bridges and they failed, every one. Ours hasn't and won't . . ."

". . . As long as God wills," he injected. "And that's my point. This is always in His control. You folks provide the maintenance it requires given wisdom as to what those needs may be, but you are doing it for Him. For His Holy bridge."

Cars came. Back to his circle went Willy leaving me alone in contemplation. I was still mulling the matter next morning as the car arrived to take me once more to the city. As we clattered over the bridge to rise through the woods of New Jersey, I had the poignant feeling I was leaving something, something important behind. I'd never thought of it in that way. I loved passing the small white-steepled churches scattered among apple country along the back roads of western Jersey but then they disappeared in the interweaving of highways and thruways. Had the faith of the people dissolved there as well? Did they need their own God's Bridge? Creeping through traffic on the non-God bridge named Washington, arriving in the city and coursing its thoroughfares, I sensed in the architecture itself a challenge. Churches, few as they seemed, were grandiose. Had buildings grown more important to God's people here than God? The rest of the buildings standing at parade rest along the boulevards and streets seemed to be sanctuaries too but devoted to other gods. Temples to commerce and greed, hustle and hype, to worldly worship of gods profane. Perhaps too many New Yorkers had slid away in the night to these new gods who dangled promises of rewards more important to them than service and sacrifice. Maybe the harvest they now sought was to be found in the here, not the hereafter.

Never before had I thought in this way but never before had I really been comfortable in New York. I always felt myself to be in other people's way and treated as such. This day, I found myself thinking: *Willy would never speak of New York as God's City, now would he?*

That day at work when finally, we broke away from writing, editing and plotting, I hijacked friend Bunky to Hurley's for burgers and God. Share with me, I asked and finally, sensing time was ripe, he shared, opening himself to me as never before. In those moments, we became closer than ever we had been. We came to share the great gift of an intimacy we had never known. Which, more than ever, hung with me as finally the day's work was wrapped and I was headed home.

My mind was a-jumble. Can a wrought iron construction of stringers and spans truly belong to the Creator of all? Should the Dingmans structure, in any real way, be called as Willy had described it? Almost home I wondered: was the music our car played on the the bridge's marimba a hymn? Sitting out on my upstairs porch in winter's crepuscular light I heard a voice inside me that made no sound speak softly:
O, God of the Bridge, God of the golden glow suffusing it, suffuse in the same way my heart. If this bridge is yours, let me be as well. As I commit myself to this bridge, I give myself also to You.

The phone rang. Muttering about how could someone be so thoughtless . . .

"Jill. Just the person I hoped."

"Am I interrupting something?"

"You certainly are. My loneliness. Or more truly my newest companion. I need to see you soonest."

Fifteen minutes later we were at a pizza house in town and I poured out my mind and my heart. She took it all in without speaking and when I was finished, still mid-pie, she took my hands, we dropped our heads and prayed and cried together there at the table, mindless of who might be watching, who might be hearing. As long as He was.

Finally, raising our heads, wiping our eyes with paper napkins and pretending we still had appetites, we finished the pizza in silence. In which tender moments I saw more of her smiling eyes than pepperoni.

"Oh," I interrupted the spell, "I have news. News that fits right into our hopes."

"So? So tell. I love news when it comes from my Perk."

"Your Perk? Yours?"

"That's how I figure," she giggled. "Any problem with that."

"Just want to understand. So the bridge is God's and I am yours? You and Willy have things all worked out, it seems. Except, my dear Jillian, you guys have left out the most important part of the equation."

"You're right, of course" she replied. "The part that says *I am yours!* Doesn't need to be said. Obvious to all. Shall I ask those folks over there if they couldn't tell that I am yours and happy to be."

She started to get up to go over and ask them when I stopped her halfway with just four words. "Wanna go to Wooster?" It's not that I had expressly been delaying the news but had been so immersed in my matters of faith that Wooster had seemed inconsequential. But the network's PR people had requests for any background on me they could get, especially my small town roots. Network agreed that'd be good to highlight. This show wouldn't be just another product of the

252

initial cities, NY, DC, LA, like most everything else on air. The host was real and the show would be too. A photographer and writer would meet me in Wooster on Saturday morning for the weekend.

"Wanna come?" I asked unnecessarily. "I figure to drive. About seven hours, I'd guess. Stay with my folks. They have two unused bedrooms, my brother's and mine. Be interesting to be back there a couple of days."

"They wouldn't mind my dragging along?"

"They'll love it. My mom'll be sizing you up to see if you're good enough for her son. Dad will assent immediately, just seeing you."

"Wearing my golden bridge . . ."

". . . And red turtleneck, I hope."

We were still discussing our plans when we were interrupted by the soft-voiced couple who had been sitting across the room, the table Jill was headed toward when I had called her back.

The woman apologized for interrupting but just wanted to tell us something on their way out. She spoke softly with a catch of a smile. First she said that it always warmed their hearts to see people bowing and praying before a meal in a restaurant. And second, she wanted to tell us that while they hadn't meant to eavesdrop, they couldn't help but hear when it appeared that Jill was set to approach them. So if we really wanted their opinion, yes, they could indeed tell that she most assuredly was mine. Whereupon the husband added that, yes, and I was one lucky guy. I concurred. They left. Soon we left.

God's Bridge

And that was the sweet conclusion of as transforming a day and lovely an evening as I had ever known.

CHAPTER THIRTY

'A LOT OF US AROUND THIS TOWN ARE PROUD OF YOU, SON.'
--*Wooster barber Dick Morrison*

Overlook Drive didn't change. (Though I swore each time I returned 1526 had shrunk.) Drive up Beall Avenue past the College of Wooster, hang a left at the Presbyterian Missionary apartments, then first right off Bloomington to Overlook and there we were. A five house *cul de sac,* the one at the upper left, the Perkinses. White clapboard, small front porch, two decorative columns supporting a porch roof unneeded. White front door which opened as I pulled the Falcon into the gravel drive to the right of the house.

"And we're here," I told Jill, stating the apparent.

"And these would be . . .

Dad and Mom on the porch, Dad coming down to greet us, Mom hanging back as though not wanting to commit with premature effusiveness to this woman she suspected was intent on stealing her son.

"Hi, Dad, and hi up there, Mom. Want you to meet my dear friend Jill. Jillian Amacher, a friend and neighbor down by the bridge. She's an artist, Mom, a very good one."

"She is also," Dad chimed in, "a beautiful young woman. Isn't she, Ruth?"

Not taking the bait, Mom answered only to say, "Well, bring in your things. You made good time."

"Yes, ma'am," said Jill, "He's a good driver. And we sure hope you have two spare bedrooms we might use for a couple of nights."

Mom was relieved, I could tell in her face. *Two bedrooms.* There'd be no hanky-panky these nights in her house. What she couldn't know, and wouldn't have believed if she'd been told was that there hadn't been any anywhere yet and wouldn't be if and until...

The place was immaculate and Jill remarked the fact to my mother, pleasing her though her reply was self-deprecating. "Oh, I do my best; we don't have a maid, you know."

"Well, I wish my roommate and I could keep our place this clean and neat. She's an artist too and we blame that. I understand you were a schoolteacher and social worker. Your son is quite proud of you." This girl was good! "Told me lots about you. Even how you got him in one of your little theater plays where you were a stumbling drunk though in real life you don't drink. Quite a portrayal."

"Oh, yes, I made a fool of myself and he played a shy kid and was really good himself. We've always been proud of him . . . of both of our sons. Have you ever met Jack?"

"No. Ma'am, not yet. But, as for Perk, I do have trouble thinking of him as shy."

On and on they went, Jill engaging mom as a suitor seeking approval. Which, of course, she was. But she was playing a

256

role she naturally lived. Meanwhile, dad and I went down to the basement so I could check on our layout, the HO gauge model railroad we had built on a platform next to the old coal-storage bin. Dad kept working on it when he had a chance, adding trackage, emplacing new buildings he had designed to scale and constructed. There was a new Ford dealership at the edge of the little town, I saw. Dad had always been partial to Fords, even back in the forties when his new one came with bumpers made of oak, chrome having gone off to war, as they said. And, sure enough, the tiny Ford he had modeled and placed outside the dealership had tiny wood bumpers. Oh, and its license plate read US 123, the number they had been randomly given years before and would keep the rest of their days. Jillian had to see this.

"See," I bragged when she answered my call and came down, "this is an engine called a Docksider, an 0-4-0 switching engine. I built it from a kit." As she seemed to marvel at that I bragged on dad saying "And this beautiful brass engine, a GE E-7, Dad made, not from a kit but from scratch, just photos, metal and his hands. *That* is terrific."

With which she eagerly agreed, giving him strokes as she'd been administering to Mom upstairs. None of this happened by plan; no insincerity involved. I had never seen or heard insincerity from Jill.

She wanted to see the railroad in action and so did I, so dad plugged in the system, took the throttle, aligned the various switches and off moved my little Docksider, slowly, trying to keep to scale speed as it worked its way in and out of the yard, from this siding to the next, gathering cars to assemble a "consist," a string of cars to make up a train. He engineered with dexterity but then handed controls over to me and I was doing fine running my engine but missed switching a switch at one point and ran the Docksider off the track. I wasn't in practice. We laughed; I made humble and turned things back over to Dad. He got to running both engines at the same time, keeping switches in line and taking the consist all the way around the layout, over the river, past the town, into the tunnel through the mountain, then up the slope and around to come back at the mountain, this time ascending to cross over its top and slowly take the run down to a line of industries, to each of their sidings to spot one of the freight cars destined to them and then on to the next. He put on an expert show then back to the yard to the call of my mother from upstairs: "Time to wash up."

Dinner in the dining room, not the kitchen, was one of the predictable "wheel" of meals Mom cycled through. She had scores of cookbooks and doted on cooking magazines but she had her standbys and she was loyal. Meat loaf with ketchup glaze, tuna-noble casserole, pot roast with vegetables, Sunday chicken and dumplings, often followed in sequence by chicken hash with poached egg and ketchup next day, macaroni and cheese, and my favorite, ham loaf and succotash.

Tonight was pot roast. Followed by dad's favorite desert, warm Gingerbread slathered with whipped cream, the real stuff not sprayed from a can. The table bubbled with cheerful conversation, compliments, and queries. How long had Jill and I known each other? What were our plans? Did we have any plans? That last one I dodged by telling our plans for the next couple days. My work schedule. Starting first thing in the morning at the college library. Something I wanted to look up before we started our filming tomorrow. Even Jill didn't know what that meant but didn't pursue it.

Mom and Jill started to clear the table but Jill was not permitted to work in the kitchen, instead, retiring with us guys to the living room where the bookshelves testified to a brief membership in the Book-of-the-Month Club. Also, as I had told Jillian, there was always a Bible on those shelves but I never knew it to come down from those shelves. And there it still was, wedged incongruously between *Guadalcanal Diary* and *John Gunther's U.S.A.* The King James Version of the Bible. The one I could never understand, the little I tried. There was also, there on the shelves a book I had often been drawn to, a small book of American poetry. "Lyrics of the Hearthside" it was called, published, I noticed about the same year my dad had been born at the turn of the century. One poem especially had engaged my searching mind. It was by a certain Paul Laurence Dunbar, a name I had no reason to remember but remembered. As I would never forget the key line of the final verse: *I know why the caged bird sings.* What a beautiful, memorable image.

Mom, always proud of our having a piano, had to brag to Jill how I had written a rhapsody once and it was really wonderful. I ought to play it for her.

"Mom!"

"Would you, Perk. Please." Jill's importuning might have availed had I had any pride in my "composition" which I had extravagantly if unoriginally entitled, "Rhapsody in Deep

Purple." It was a pale parody of classical music. Childish and definitely not something I wanted *anyone*, especially my *Everyone*, to hear.

"I really don't remember the piece," I lied. Not to Jill: I'd promised not to lie to her. But to mom whom I'd never promised.

"Meaning," insisted Jill, "you don't want *me* to remember it."

"I didn't say that."

"Oh, come on, Perk. This is me you're talking to."

"You mean, 'This is *I,*' and you shouldn't end a sentence in a preposition, you know."

"How about a proposition?"

"Truce," I called. Mom and dad seemed amused by the badinage but I turned to easier talk. How was I healing? Almost complete. What had I been doing? Hong Kong, Vietnam, lots of New York. Dad asked how it was going living in the Stone House. Getting to know the bridge people. It was heaven, the only thing saving my sanity with all else I had going on. Whereupon Jill had to ask did I really mean the house was the only thing saving me and I had quickly to recant. We laughed and chatted on for an hour or so before I pleaded fatigue and off we were shown to our separate rooms, me back in my own, Jill in my brother's room. Kiss goodnight and we'd see each other in the morning. Breakfast at eight.

My mission to the college library had two purposes. First, to show Jillian my favorite schooldays haunt, doing research here in the cloistered peace of the place for my various debate and

260

speech tournaments; second to do some more. I asked the librarian where I would find anything of or by Arthur or Karl Compton. I'd seen quotes I really wanted to nail down in my own continuing personal research on faith. It took a half hour to unearth what I wanted. I copied passages into my notebook and we had to leave the cloisters for our appointment with the producer and crew.

The crew included a favorite cameraman, George Sozio, and a soundman I didn't know and the bright young p.a.who had been so complimentary to me back in New York, saying how she'd begged to be put on our unit. Melody Grace, I remembered as I introduced Jillian around to them all.

First stop: college band practice, the kilts, the pipes. Then downtown to Liberty Street lined on both sides by the buggies and bonnets of the Amish come to town for their once-a-week shopping. These stops, color for the piece about me the crew was assigned to do, my background here in the small town. I insisted we stop by Dick Morrison's barbershop and was glad to find both it and him going strong.

"Perk," he welcomed as the camera rolled and the customer in his chair filed no objection. "Heard you might be coming to town. Ya know, a lot of us around this town are pretty proud of you, son.'

I introduced him to Jillian and assured him that the humane gentleness I had witnessed as a kid in this very shop were still with me. And, oh, yes, the color-blindness. Must have been in my unconscious mind back in that church basement in Alabama. He had read about that, he said.

Everyone had. Nice to see our local boy standing up to the racists down there.

"Well, Mister Morrison, don't ever forget that you and your friends here were my lasting lesson in tolerance. Awfully good to see you again, sir."

The producer gave me an excited thumbs-up at that bit of dialog and we moved on. They shot me getting one of those special ice cream cones from Isaly's where the ice cream was scooped conical echoing the cone below. Butter pecan always my favorite. Walking along Liberty, passing the movie theater they had me wired for sound to reminisce about the weekly cowboy double features. Alas, I could not introduce them to Grandmother Perkins up in her dim hotel room; she was several years now deceased. We went to the high school where they'd arranged for us to use my old home room for a sit down interview with me about the values of a small town childhood and youth. About growing *with* parents and *without* drink or drugs or the pressures of acquiring those. I tried not to sound corny but I was sincere and if some thought me hypocritical, that would be their problem.

In to surprise me strode Bob Pollock, my old speech coach, wanting to say some praiseful things and jibe me a bit about cribbing an oration from a magazine to win one tournament. It was true but I hoped that bit of film would not be used.

Our last stop was back up on Overlook Drive. Mom didn't want to be interviewed so Dad would forego the chance as well but they reluctantly agreed I could take the cameraman downstairs to see the railroad layout. Producer loved it. Had me run my Docksider and reminisce.

Then, we went next door to see our longtime neighbor, Elinor Taylor, columnist for the *Wooster Daily Record.* I had often baby sat for her two sons she told the crew and the camera and whatever part of America might eventually see.

It was a full day, productive and gratifying. As it always is when you get to listen to people say flattering things about you.

We'd told my folks that Jill and I would have dinner with the crew at the Wooster Inn on the college campus. We invited them to join us there but, Mom's feelings hurt, she declined. We'd have an early dinner and see the folks after.

Actually, the producer and crew had spotted a pizza and wine place in town they wanted to try, leaving Jill and me with no complaints having dinner at the Inn alone. We had a flood of thoughts dammed up waiting release. Most immediate, for me, were the notes I had taken back at the college library, notes on Wooster's Compton brothers and their contemplations on Science and God.

Scientists, it is often thought, are not likely to be believers. Oh, believers in science, yes, in what can be established through equations, formulae, hypotheses, theories and proofs. Which is to say, believers, with a small "b."

But not true, capital "B" Believers! That's how many assume. That's how many *wrongly* assume. It was good to be reminded there in my small hometown of two profound exceptions: the brothers Compton, Arthur and Karl.

"They grew up here," I told Jillian as we awaited our dinners at the Inn. "Went to this college and then moved on.

Oh, did they move on!" These were the notes I had researched
in the library this morning.

"Older brother Karl became president of M.I.T. Younger
brother Arthur helped develop both radar and the atomic
bomb and was awarded the Nobel Prize for Physics."

"Impressive family," said Jill. "Congratulations, Wooster."

"Indeed, but what is most important to me right now is not
what they accomplished in their fields of science but what . . ."

"Here you are, folks," the waitress said delivering our
dinners at the inopportune time.

"Thank you, miss. Looks great," Jillian smiled as we settled
into our meals and I held my thought.

The food was worthy. Maybe I enjoyed it more knowing
that I wouldn't have to do the dishes out in the kitchen as I did
years back working at Babcock Hall, the women's dorm down
the street. "You don't want to know," I told Jill when she
asked what thoughts had taken me away from her. "But as I
was saying about the Comptons, especially Arthur, how did a
graduate of this fine little Scotch-Presbyterian College, this
son of a Presbyterian minister, speak of his science and his
God? Here's the quote: I read from my notebook.

"Science is the glimpse of God's purpose in nature. The
very existence of this amazing world of the atom and radiation
points to a purposeful creation, to the idea that there is a God
and an intelligent purpose in back of everything.

In their essence, there can be no conflict between science
and religion. Science is a reliable method of finding the truth.
Religion is a search for a satisfying basis of life. By enabling

men to see more clearly what those values are and to work for them more effectively, science has become an ally of religion.

Jill was transfixed, taking it all in.

I told her of a series of renowned lectures he had given, reaching finally this profound and agreeable conclusion: If indeed the creation of intelligent persons is a major objective of the Creator of the Universe, and if, as we have reason to surmise, mankind is now His highest development in this direction, the opportunity and responsibility of working as God's partners in His great task are almost overwhelming. What nobler ambition can one have than to cooperate with his Maker in bringing about a better world in which to live?

The concluding line I had copied from Dr. Compton's lectures was the one that finally clinched things for Jill and as well for me. It was a line that burned into the memory and made one wish that every single atheist and agnostic, doubter and disbeliever in the world would remember and recite it aloud each remaining day of their lives:

An orderly universe, wrote Dr. Arthur Compton of my hometown, testifies to the greatest statement ever uttered: '**In the beginning, God . . .**'

CHAPTER THIRTY-ONE

"NEXT MONTH — READY OR NOT
   --Ad promoting our coming show

My wakeup call next day back home was one I'd hoped for and downstairs and over to the tolltaker's hut I happily hurried. For tea, yes, but also, as it turned out a continuation of heavy thought from friend Willy who had been thinking, he said, a lot about bridges. For the next half hour, between sips and tolls, he discoursed.

"About bridges. Not so much this one, though I've told you what I think about it, being God's Bridge. But more generally, thinking more broadly, I've got to thinking this way." And he laid out his latest equation of aphorisms.

"Start here. To bring us together with Himself, God gave us Jesus. Right? And then later, Jesus, to keep us in touch after His earthly death, sent the Holy Spirit to us, okay?"

He wanted me to agree so I nodded and he continued.

"To put all that in a different way, we could say that Jesus was the first bridge we were given to span between God and us. And now the Holy Spirit continues to serve as our bridge between us and both Jesus and God. The greatest blessings we could ever receive, in other words, come to us over bridges. We thrive the more we open ourselves to bridges."

"Very interesting, Willy," I said and meant it.

Really meant it. This man was a philosopher in a toll collector's apron. I owed him more than my toll as I was soon crossing our Dingmans Bridge being transported again into the city to wrap up our first show due on air later that week. I had done all the recording for the Vietnam segment, the body of the show, still had to write and lay down the track for Simon and Garfunkel. I'd shoot the in-studio stuff tomorrow to get the whole show to reviewers a couple days before it would air to get all the publicity we could. The network was promoting it on its own programs and buying commercials and ads in papers and other TV, on billboards with my mug and the words "**Perk's Journal: "Real" Happens,** day and time. They were giving us tremendous support.

Now our program had to justify it. Whereupon, even before our first show made air, we'd be fully immersed in the next, the program I was most anxious about.

The last thing I did for this first show was go into the studio and record the closing on camera. Cal and I had talked about my script. He loved it, he said, but wondered if while plugging our visit to Birmingham next month I shouldn't mention specifically the two girls whose lives I had saved, and while we're at it, how about Billy Graham, being invited to participate, the three of us, in his Crusade that weekend? I argued that those things we can and should trumpet in promos during the month but I was concerned it might endanger the girls or the Crusade to be promoting them already. Anyhow, my closing copy I felt was strong as it was. I fell back on a line I often used. *Less is More.* He acceded and I went to the studio, script intact.

Never comfortable with coat and tie, and Cal had said he wanted *Real,* I wore khakis, blue button-down shirt, no tie, no coat, no pretense. And said simply this:

On this first hour of our new Journal, we have ranged from the perils of distant war to the fresh, lifting sounds of not silence but blessed music.

It is important to know those things, both the far away and the pleasant, but it is all too easy to be diverted by them.

Next month, we'll come home, reflect once more on the awful war raging in our own country, the war we must never stop fighting. The war for dignity and sanity, which both — need we remind ourselves — are Civil Rights.

Next month: back to Birmingham.

Good night.

CHAPTER THIRTY-TWO

SO WE'LL HAVE TO BE OUR OWN CHOIR
--Billy Graham at home with us TV folk

"Reviews are great," exulted Cal, his call waking me the morning after our first show aired. I had screened it at NBC a few days earlier and then watched it broadcast at Doc and Patricia's house with Jillian and my bridge buddy, Willy. All were praiseful. I felt good.

"Actually, let me correct that," Cal continued, "*Some* of the reviews are great." Here it came, I thought. He couldn't hold the moment, blurting "Others are absolutely *Terrific*. Listen." And he began transplanting bouquets into my morning mind.

"Engaging, informing . . . Television as it ought to be . . . Important stories told by a master storyteller. . . If Perk was a hero in Birmingham a few months back, he's a hero on the tube today. . . As good as TV gets . . .and next month's Journal promises to be even better . . ."

"And you know Bob Doerr, master critic and prophet in his own mind? Here's what he prophesied."

"Decades hence, some TV geniuses will invent a new genre they'll call Reality Shows. And they'll be wholly contrived frauds. If you want Reality, friends, don't wait. Start watching Perk's Journal now! This is real."

"Oh, c'mon, Calvin, you wrote that one yourself. You must have."

"Well," he confessed proudly, "I did have lunch with Doerr last week and might have mentioned the word 'Real' once or twice in my plug. And, I'm damned glad he picked up the idea. PR folks are going to have an orgy with all these quotes. Congratulations, Perk."

"To us all. I have to get a staff memo out immediately, before we take off Monday for California and then Montreat and then, and then, Birmingham. Very excited about this one, as you can imagine. And nervous."

"As I can also imagine. Bunky and the crew will meet you at Newark tomorrow morning. And, again, congratulations, man. This is great, *real* great."

Next thing I did, of course, was call Jill. Good news cries to be shared with those you love. She could tell, despite the calm, almost offhand way I gave her the news that it meant the world to me. I was excited, thrilled, and didn't want to show it. With her, I couldn't hide it. That's part of being in love.

We arranged to have dinner that evening at the Dimmick. Going away dinner. It'd be weeks before I'd see her. That would be when she joined me down in Birmingham. That, she had said, she would not miss. I was ambivalent but acquiesced.

I hadn't dined at the old Dimmick Hotel dining room but it seemed to be the special occasion choice for Milford locals and Jill didn't wave me off so here we were. Heart of the town. Walk in through the bustling bar to the much more quiet and sedate dining room, tablecloths, lit candles, servers silent until called upon then promptly attentive. The menu was expansive

272

and varied, the prices reasonable. It was the perfect setting to forget TV but who could?

"How do you go from here?" Jill asked. "Not geographically or story-wise, but how do you all continue to justify those exuberant reviews?"

"Always the challenge, usually self-defeating. You're tempted to start changing things when it's already what you wanted it to be, what press and viewers have applauded. It's the cliché. If it ain't broke . . . But there are some producers, some execs who have to get in there and put their own stamp on it when it doesn't need any new stamps. It already delivers".

"In other words," said Jill unfurling her going-to-get-you smile. "If you have a good thing, keep it, don't lose it. Right?"

"Especially, don't lose it if it's as beautiful as the lady sitting across from me in the candle flicker tonight."

"You say, you've always said, the secret to your show is keeping it real."

"As is the purpose of my being with you. Real. Real love."

"Really reciprocated."

Our flying to San Francisco, Bunky, the crew and I, was to shoot an AfterWords piece in an old, mostly abandoned but astonishingly historic building. It was here, at 202 Green Street, back in the year 1927 that an intrepid twenty-one year old named Philo T. Farnsworth, experimenting with something he called an electronic image dissecter managed, for probably the first time anywhere, to transmit a crude image from one room into the next. Thus was born what people would come to call electronic television. And the first picture transmitted that day? A single line on a piece of paper. A couple years later, though, when potential funders of his continuing research asked what was in it for them he sent a more prophetic "television" image, that dollar sign.

As television programming later developed, he became less sure of the true value of his quickly commercialized creation. Until, one day late in his life he watched Neil Armstrong standing on the moon for the world to see live. And, turning to his wife at his side, Philo said, "Pem, this has made it all worthwhile."

We spent a day and a half shooting in Farnsworth's old digs, two evenings dining on the wharf and clubbing on North Beach. Had to see Carol Doda and the newest fad (which we would *not* be featuring on our show): The Monokini. It was a topless women's swimsuit from designer Rudi Gernreich. The nation was variably gassed or aghast by the scandal.

From San Francisco, then, we would make a complete change, heading back east again to wind our way up into the North Carolina mountains, to the hillside town of Montreat.

It was a well-loved, well-lived-in log cabin there on the mountain. Secluded as a man so popular, so often traveling, so rarely home, profoundly appreciated. A gift from God to a man of God. Billy Graham's mountain hideaway.

He towered in the doorway as we approached. "Welcome, Perk. Fellas. Good to see ya."

Then, as I took his sturdy hand he cautioned: "Watch your head. I'm six-two. You look taller. The door isn't. But that's how the workers cut it, it didn't bother Ruth, so I figured there are worse ways to enter or depart a home than by bowing." He ushered us in and I thought, *It's real. The man is always preaching.*

He was 46 and for years a religious icon, his Crusades in cities across the country, in countries across the world, having awakened thousands after thousands of Seekers. There was no one like him in the Gospel world.

We talked for hours. Ruth graced us for a few moments, bringing iced tea and homemade fudge. That eased our conversation, Billy raving about his beloved life-partner and asking us abo ut our wives if we had them. Which set it up for Bunky who teed off.

"Great question, Billy. Great because our friend here," pointing at me, "is on the verge of making the Big Decision. He wouldn't ask, I'm sure, but I know he would welcome your wisdom."

"So, Perk, is your love coming with you to Birmingham? If so, let's make a point of setting aside some time, you, me and her and talk about things. Okay?"

We agreed, my gratitude expressed to both Billy for offering and Bunky for prodding us into it.

Mostly, then, our conversation focused on the coverage we would be doing at the Crusade Easter Sunday in Birmingham and about what he wanted me to do as part of that event.. He knew all about me and the girls and the church bombing.

What I did not know was that when Dr. Martin Luther King, Jr. was jailed in Birmingham around that same time, who had quietly bailed him out? Billy Graham. He didn't just preach it, he lived it.

When finally, reluctantly we came to take our leave, Billy guided us all to our knees beside the burning rock fireplace and led us in prayer. It was a moment that I think none of us – believer, skeptic, undecided – will ever forget. All I said when it was over was, "I miss the choir singing '*Just As I Am*.'"

"So we'll have to be our own choir," he said enthusiastically, standing, hand in hand, he led us:

Just as I am, without one plea,
but that thy blood was shed for me,
and that thou bidst me come to thee,
O Lamb of God, I come, I come.

Leaving the house, I bowed.

It is one thing to meet someone you have long admired but never met. Quite a different thrill to meet people you had never heard of but whose lives, apparently, you saved. That would be our next stop.

Yes, it was unsettling enough just to be returning to Birmingham, that social fester which harbored and in many cases encouraged those who killed innocent kids, tried to kill me and tried again, until they drove me fleeing in the dark of night out of their town in pain and fear. I would never again not feel pangs of those.

But two young girls made up for all. Beatrice and Camille. I knew just their first names. And their generosity, that handmade blanket, handwritten note. I didn't *know* them but I loved them. Now I would meet them.

"I'm Carmela Jones, "said the handsome black woman who answered the door. Short-cropped steel-grey hair in tight curls, incandescent smile, a large, statuesque woman and proud. She was certainly proud of the beautiful, shyly smiling girls tucked behind her apron. "One of you gentlemen must be our saver. Note, I didn't say Savior; that position is already filled. So which one of you gentlemen is . . ."

"That one. There. I just know," said one of the girls excitedly, pointing unmistakably at me.

And I said, just as excitedly, "and you – I just know are Camille."

She giggled, saying shyly, "I'm Beatrice. She's . . ."

"Let me guess," I said, affecting great concentration. "She, I am certain, is the real Camille. Right?"

"And how did you ever figure that out," laughed their mom and all of them together.

I introduced the crew, we went inside the small house, the mother apologizing that her husband, the girls' dad wasn't home yet from church. He worked at 16th Street Baptist now, got the job when he volunteered to help clean up and rebuild after the bombing. Was hired to keep working there when the repairs were done. "Got something good out of all that," said the mom, "That's how God works sometimes, you know?"

"Ma'am, I guess I could say that the bombing while it grievously injured me, also accorded me manifold blessings: meeting Beatrice and Camille, gaining public acclaim undeserved but welcome, bringing me closer to my own family, and finding the woman I hope will help me create *our* family's next generation."

"Oooooh," oohed Camille, "will we meet her?"

I assured them I hoped so. I wanted her to meet them, too. "We'll have plenty of time. I'm really happy for that."

At which point, their dad got home and we went on another round of introductions, his thanks, my gratitude for being able to meet them all. I asked if I might say a prayer before leaving, noting that before the bombing I would never have thought of doing such a thing . That was the greatest gift I got out of all of this. As you said, Carmela, that's how God works sometimes.

We agreed to meet down at the church next Monday morning. But first, off to my brief but never forgotten Birmingham home.

CHAPTER THIRTY-THREE

I DIDN'T KNOW <u>WHERE</u> I WAS BECAUSE, AT THAT POINT, I
DIDN'T KNOW <u>THAT</u> I WAS
--Recalling for TV my months-ago hospital bed

The sign reads Saint Anthony's Hospital. I never saw it before, either entering or departing this place where my life was saved.

Standing here now, I imagine the ambulance delivering the tortured mess of me to this hospital that Sunday morning not many months ago. "Another from 16ᵗʰ Street" calls the driver. "Grownup guy. Dunno what he was doing there. Maybe one of the bombers, ya think? If so, there'll be people wish we hadn't rescued him. For me though . . . "

Hospital personnel take over, wheel the gurney inside to Emergency, to the medical men and women whose sworn oaths pledge them to save – whoever, whatever, however. Thank you, Hippocrates. "Unconscious," notes a nurse. "Said one thing as we first got him. Kept repeating 'My name is Doogle, my name is Doogle.' Had no ID. His buddy grabbed his things and headed directly to Ms. Palmer's office. Secretive. Dunno what that means but for now our only concern is this poor fellow. Part of that church bombing and quite the worse for it."

Bunky, by that time was on his way to see the woman we are both headed for right now.

Dr. Eugenia Parker, Hospital Director, her sign reads and it is good to see her again in these much more amiable and stable circumstances. The greetings are effusive all around. She quizzes me on my health but already seems to know the answers. "I've been keeping up through our Dr. Bullock to your Dr. Bullock and thus to your condition. Glad to witness their good reports confirmed in the flesh."

"At least what flesh you can see," I josh. "Yes, ma'am, I'm feeling pretty good."

"And doing well. We gathered staff around in the rec hall the other night to watch your first show. Sure made a quick transition from St. Anthony's to Saigon. A lot of people around here are awfully proud of you – of the strange disappearing patient they thought of as Mr. Doogle."

Bunky: "And we're grateful to all of you for keeping this guy anonymous and, thus, safe. Any later repercussions?"

Her face takes on a serious cast "Hard to say. But with your coming here now, and it being so widely reported – oh, I don't know, maybe I'm being hypercautious but I confess I'm concerned. Leary, wary, call it what you will. Sure, some of their people are in jail but the Klan has a lot more wackos *not* in jail. They saw that picture of you and the two girls in the paper, the paper calling you a hero and they don't forget, and they don't forgive. Please, fellows, be careful while you're here. Now, come on."

And she leads us on a tour, greeting and my being greeted by nurses whom I might not know but who want me to. Dr.

Zack of course I remember and exchange both medical and social chat. Here's a nurse who looks most familiar, the one, I believe, who first cracked my identity as Mr. Doogle and called Ms. Palmer. Memories rush of times mostly beyond memory. That white featureless fog I lived in for how many days and nights?

Bunky takes over, plotting where and with whom he'd like to shoot over the next few days. He works things out with Director Palmer as I just wander and wonder. I never knew this place. It's people, mostly, never knew me. Now here we are inexorably bound for better or worse. They owe me nothing. I owe them everything. Or should I say I owe everything to the God I didn't yet know when I was here. Didn't know that it was He working through the skilled hands of these caring people that began my transformation, a transformation that would prove to be far more than physical.

'Wanna see your room?" Ms. Palmer asks. "No one in it at the moment."

Before I can answer, Bunky does.

"Definitely. We want to shoot there, Perk recalling lost moments, hours, days – whatever they were – in what I've heard him call his white fog. Gonna shoot it soft focus, whirling, abstract, his voice playing over. Can we do that in the morning?"

It was agreed. Ms. Palmer and I walked on, Bunky staying behind plotting angles and morning lighting, assuming that this will be a crucial turning in our drama. And drama it will be.

"OK, Perk. Rolling."

Next morning. Hospital room dim, the scene surreal as pale light shafts slant through partially open Venetian blinds casting prison-like bars on murky walls. I'm perched on the edge of the high bed. In the camera shot, I'm in focus, all else vague, spectral. I speak softly, evenly.

"This is where I lay, on this bed, not knowing it. I didn't know *where* I was because at that point, I didn't know *that* I was. For those moments, hours, days, whatever they were, in the sense people use the word 'know,' I didn't. Pharmacists had seen to that. That I should neither know nor feel."

"What was happening in this tortured time? A war. A battle raging in my body as organs and bundles of muscles and nerves fought to hang on even as alien forces fought to continue the destruction the bomb had begun within me.

"The body is fragile, yes, but in the end, the body is tough. And I realize now that another power, too, was at work. A greater power which many physicians acknowledge even if they cannot or do not define it. Nor would I for a long time. Today, I define it as spiritual. I knew none of this at that time. And those caring for me knew not even who their patient was. They thought my name was Doogle. In this hospital only one woman knew the truth."

At this point in the piece, we will cut to the interview we'll do with Director Palmer telling how she'd been informed of my true identity and kept it secret as she and the hospital kept getting queries from townsfolk she knew to be KKK apparently trying to find and punish me for daring to interfere with their black-child massacre.

Back to me on camera.

"Nurses kept calling me Mr. Doogle but still foggy I angrily denied that name. Why were they calling me that? I didn't know who I *was* but I knew who I *wasn't*. Until, something snapped and vaguely I came to remember the code word my buddy and I had made up should we ever be in danger in this alien land. He'd be Barney Google; my name: Doogle. That was it. That was I.

"Whereupon, puzzle solved, all seemed well until the evening yet another KKK type stomped into Ms Palmer's office demanding to know where not Mr. Perkins as they'd asked for before but where Mr. Doogle was and she knew the charade was over. Almost immediately the emergency evacuation plan was set in motion.

"When they wheeled me out of this room late that very night, I knew not where I was bound. I simply had to trust. It was trust well placed."

From there our piece will quickly retrace the flight from Birmingham to Stewart Air Force base in upstate New York, then on to the hospital in Port Jervis and leave it at that. No use giving a still vindictive Klansman any more.

"Good take, Perk." In those days of film, we couldn't check it on the spot so, "Let's do another for safety then move on."

We worked hard that week. Shooting with Director Palmer and Dr. Zack there at the hospital, taking Camille and Beatrice back into the bowels of the 16th Street Baptist Church, along with a demolitions expert to explain how the bomb had been placed and triggered, how the wall had fallen on top of me as I had thrown myself over the two girls, reflexively, unknowingly, but likely saving their lives. Then, Bunky. He came in to describe how he'd rushed inside from shooting exteriors to find the miasmic hell of the bomb's destruction. How he had pulled me off the stack of bodies and fireman-carried me up and outside." I didn't know if I was doing right," he confessed, "I just did it."

His just doing it likely saved my life because after he had hauled me out, and other men had lifted the two girls beneath me to safety, another whole chunk of ceiling and wall collapsed right where we had been.

"Only when we'd begun the cleanup a few days later did we realize how much worse it might have been." The man describing that phase of things would eventually be identified as the father of Beatrice and Camille. He had gotten his daughters' lives saved and in the end a full time job with the church, a job he had sorely needed. The piece would end then with the girls regretting the deaths of their friends, thanking God for sparing theirs and vowing to use their remaining days in His service.

Oh, and forgiving the KKK bombers.

All that filming, all that re-living, exhausted us. Weekend loomed. Jill was due to arrive Sunday afternoon. I had tomorrow off and a hunch. I went for a drive.

It was only a couple hours drive from Birmingham over to the little town of Selma and something I wanted to see. A bridge, such being my bent of those times. A reporter friend had warned me about the Edmund Pettis Bridge spanning the Alabama River just outside Selma.

"It's already known some minor hassles, blacks hounded by black-haters," my friend told me. "But the big one is still to come, I fear. It's right on the highway what leads to the capital in Birmingham that demonstrators keep threatening to march to one day. Across that bridge, a comparative kid compared to our Dingmans, this one not built till 1940, not the length of my grandfathers' bridge and, most ominous of all, named after a former Grand Dragon of the Alabama Ku Klux Klan. Not a shining omen. It sickened me to think of what might happen here one day. As it encouraged me to know that Billy Graham's Crusade coming here to Alabama might spur a social transformation in this tortured state.

The most hopeful sign of all, for me, of course, was Jilllan"s arrival tomorrow.

"Miss me?" she asked.

"Not a bit, Susie, er, Sally, er . . .I forget."

Mock-mad, she pushed me aside from our hug, trying to look angry but instead breaking into laughter and assaulting me with a clinging kiss, finally coming out of it only to whisper "Thank God for you."

"For us," I added softly as we headed out into the mellow Birmingham night.

CHAPTER THIRTY-FOUR

WHENEVER YOU DO IT, WHEREVER, I HOPE I'M INVITED.
--*Billy Graham on our wedding plans*

"Cliff, it feels disrespectful."

"What?"

"To call him just 'Billy.'"

"Well, Perk, what can I say? Is my calling you just 'Perk' disrespectful? Would you rather I called you 'Morton Liberty Bell Perkins?'"

He answered my grimace, "Didn't think so."

"You've done your homework, you folks," I allowed.

"Security checks carefully on special stage guests. But as I was saying, you've met him. You were in his home. Did that log house appear to be the abode of a Reverend Doctor William Franklin Graham or just plain Billy? As for respectful, if it's what he wants wouldn't it be disrespectful *not* to call him Billy? Perk?"

Cliff Barrows had been with Billy from the beginning. It was good to be briefed by him before getting together again with the man himself. Jill and I would soon be at the temporary Crusade office to talk not about Crusade or TV but as he had kindly offered, marriage. *Our marriage!*

"This must be the young lady – both lovely and from all I know about this young man, lucky." His Carolina drawl bespoke sincerity. Jill verged on a blush, something I had never seen of her. Her reply was a simple nod, a smile, and an agreeing "I think so too."

"So what can I tell you?" Billy said, asking himself it seemed, not us. We were seated comfortably around a small conference table in the Crusade's trailer office. "To start, think about this. In Satan's first appearance in the Bible what is he doing? Trying to break up a marriage. That's still one of his specialties. He wants our marriages to flounder and fail because he knows that few things will discourage us more."

"How to thwart him?" I asked.

"Simple. Let God be the party of the third part in your marriage contract. And, yes, marriage is the most serious long-term contract a couple will make in their lifetime though many enter into it with a lack of maturity and knowledge. The growing number of divorces shows how imperative it is that young people be adequately prepared for marriage. Are you?"

How does one ever know? Is there a way to be sure? These were questions we put to him but, instead of answering, he rather urged us to answer for ourselves. Jill looked to me, I to her and our eyes agreed.

When Jill asked Dr. Graham to whom he turned for spiritual guidance when he sought pastoral assurance, he didn't hesitate. "Ruth. When it comes to spiritual things, my wife has always had the greatest influence on my ministry."

Jill said how great it was to hear that. She hoped, whatever my calling became or continued to be, I could say the same about her.

"Do you have a date? And a commitment to abstinence prior?" he asked forthrightly. We told him that, no, we had not yet made wedding plans but that, yes, we did, *we do,* believe it is God's plan for our lives to be forever together. We have remained sexually abstinent and shall until the vows be sealed in the presence of God and witnesses. We talked about these things, replied to his loving questions, surprised by both his directness and our easy candor. It was uplifting and somehow cleansing. And then, inviting us to kneel and placing his hands on our shoulders he prayed for us and our future, whenever God ordained it to begin.

"Young people, look to your Bibles when whining about any matter, including – especially – marriage. Then, lifting his hands he surprised us by saying, "And whenever you do it, wherever, I hope I'll be invited."

"Billy," I heard myself saying, "Would you really. . ."

"We never know the future, now, do we?"

From there, we were joined by Cliff and a couple of other staff members for the briefing on my role in the event, what they wanted me to do when called on stage. Basically Dr. Graham and I would converse, he eliciting from me my tale and my testimony, the bombing, my unintended, unaware heroism and the slow recovery during which I slowly began to understand the power that brought me through it and why. At that point on would come the girls, Beatrice and Camille to tell their stories and, all of us together, praise the God Who had turned Satan's destruction into our salvation.

This would be the first time in public I would ever make such confession, give such witness.

"Will you be nervous for that?" Billy asked.

I hesitated. Would I?

"You shouldn't be, Mr. Perkins." It was darling Camille. "We'll be with you."

"That's right," said Beatrice. "You won't have to be scared."

I looked at the two of them, then looked over to Billy whose face reflected the glory of the girls' childlike faith.

All I could say was "Sometimes, girls, that thing people call heroism is easier as it happens than having to deal with it afterward. I'm glad you two will be with me."

"And don't forget," said Camille, "So will He."

She didn't mean Billy Graham.

In all, it was a soul-warming day. Until we got back to our hotel.

"Put a package for you up in your room, Mr. Perkins," said the desk clerk whose tag named him Buford. "Came this afternoon 'bout two. Dunno from who. No return address. Guy just brought it and said put in your room for you. Gave me a fiver. So I did it. Hope that was alright."

"So *you* put it in the room? *He* didn't go up there?"

"Right. That okay?"

Was I paranoid? Or prudently cautious? "Sure, okay, Buford," I mumbled though not convinced.

Jill read my caution and shared it. "Let's find Bunky. Ask him. Maybe he had it sent."

Back to the clerk I went. "Tell me, is Mr. Buncombe around, do you know?"

He didn't. Hadn't seen him since morning.

"And how was the package you put in my room addressed?"

A puzzle darkened his face. "That's one thing strange," he said. "He sure enough told me it was for you, for Mr. Perkins. Sure enough. But on the address label I could plainly see it was made out to a whole other name. Sure was. Was made out to someone named 'Mr. Doogle,' sumpin' like that. Strange. But he'd given me that fiver. So . . ."

"Get me a phone." Whom to call? Police? In this town, was that safe? For me? Could I track down the Graham Security people? Wasn't their problem. Riffling through my notes, I hastily dialed St. Anthony's and got Director Palmer.

"Eugenia. Have a problem. Need advice." I filled her in. She, on another line, placed a call, got what she wanted and told me that some reliable men from her own security force would be with me in ten minutes. Don't even go to my room in the meantime.

They arrived in seven, just as Bunky himself was returning from some shooting. I filled them all in and we headed upstairs, Jill hugging hard by my side. I let us all in and there, lying on the bed was a box sized to hold a basketball – or a bomb – and addressed, sure enough, to "Mr. Doogle/Perkins."

"Don't touch it," demanded one of the hospital security men. "I trained in IED's in the army. Rest of you, leave the room. I need to. . . Wait. Better yet. Clerk carried this up here with no problem, right? Not likely a timed device or the maker wouldn't have known when to set it. I'm going to carry it out of here, down to our vehicle and back to the hospital. I want to X-Ray this baby."

We followed, the clerk watching in amazement as we headed out to waiting vehicles and sped off.

"Nothing to it," the security guard reported, coming out of the X-Ray room. "Basically empty box." He ripped it open. Nothing inside but a brick. "To give it weight I guess. Look."

The brick was actually a cement block chunk, size of a couple of bricks, clearly having been damaged somehow. Instinctively, I knew how. And it wasn't in the box just to give the package weight but to send a message. Chalk scrawls on it confirmed.

"Here is part of the wall that almost killed you, Hero Doogle/Perkins.

"The next one will!

"Stay away from picaninnies.. Get out of B'ham! And take that nigger-lovin' preacher with you."

CHAPTER THIRTY-FIVE

IT TOUCHES MY HEART WHEN I SEE WHITES STANDING
SHOULDER TO SHOULDER WITH BLACKS AT THE CROSS.
--Billy Graham

Billy Graham loved negroes. As he loved whites and Hispanics and Orientals and Indians and all men and all women created by the loving God he worshipped and preached.

Years earlier he had set down a rule — against the wishes of some of his team in BGEA, his organization headquartered in Minnesota. He decreed that from then on he would not speak before any audience that was racially or ethnically segregated. This was before the landmark Supreme Court decision of 1954, before the slow societal inching toward equal facilities. He just knew it was the right thing to do.

"We have some of the finest civil rights laws in the world," he would come to say, "but they have not solved our racial problems. Why? Because we need a change of heart and attitude. The closer people of all races get to Christ and His cross, the closer they will get to one another."

Accordingly, the Crusade meeting at Birmingham's Legion Field on this Easter Day, 1964, would be equally open to all,

Dr. Graham saying "It touches my heart when I see whites standing shoulder to shoulder with blacks at the cross."

So it would be.

But would Danger be standing there with them at the Cross?

The Crusade security team had called in local police after all, what with our "bomb" scare. They in turn had enlisted the help of the local office of the FBI. Agents wanted to speak with me. Before that though I had one thing I wanted to check, a hunch to play.

The guest log lay open on the hotel desk. Names and hometowns of guests checked in. I paged through recent entries and found what I was looking for.

"Pardon," I asked the clerk currently on duty. "I'm Perkins in room 322. I know you weren't the one who checked me in yesterday afternoon. Forget his name. Bubba or something like that."

"Yesterday afternoon," he said. "That would have been Buford. He was on then. Every afternoon."

"So he would have done this check-in a couple of afternoons ago, too?"

He checked the date and time and agreed. "That's him. That's Buford."

"And is this the way he usually abbreviates the name of your city?"

"Yep. Can always tell when a local checks in and Buford's on. He writes it that way. *B'ham.* Don't know where he got that. He's the only person I've ever seen do it that way. Lazy, I guess."

"Certainly distinctive. Personally, I *have* seen it spelled that way though just once before."

"Once before," as I explained to Bunky on our way downtown, was yesterday on the cement block inside the "bomb" box. *Get out of B'ham!* So Buford might just be our man. If so, was he working with others or going lone wolf? See what the FBI thinks.

Federal Building, eighth floor, room 812. Special Agent Rudolph Riggins greeted us with "Call me Rudy." Tall, bronzed, close-cropped sandy hair, and solidly sculptured frame. He could handle trouble. But could he nail our "bomber" before the sick bigot bombed for real? I filled him in, he took notes, checked the photos he'd already received of the "bomb" box, the cement chunk message it bore and said, "Good deductive work. I'll get a search going with locals for him immediately. See who he's in this with or if he's solo-ing. Meanwhile, you fill in Graham's people. Crusade's tomorrow. Have to work fast. Keep in touch."

I went to the Crusade's trailer and let them know. Police would furnish them with mug shots of the suspect from his employment file. Put them on alert. "And I'm just thinking, if you or they figure this sicko is more after me than the Crusade, maybe I should disappear."

"Don't even think of it," said Graham's aide. "Billy wouldn't hear of it. Not for us. If you wanted to do it for yourself, your own safety, that'd be different. But for us, Billy wouldn't have it."

"You sure?"

He got up, left the trailer and returned in three minutes with Billy himself who said precisely what his man had said he would say.

"Don't worry for us, Perk. God will take care of us and you too if you're willing to stay. Your choice."

"The police and the FBI and you and your team — and God? Pretty good odds," I agreed. "See you tomorrow."

Back at the hotel, Jill was less sanguine. She found no solace in the *maybe's*. Maybe they'll be able to catch Buford before tomorrow morning. Maybe he is the only one involved in a planned bombing. Maybe it's all bluff. Maybe, maybe, maybe.

"Or, maybe it's real. You know what, Perk, I don't know how you do all this. You are stronger, braver . . . I'd be headed home. Don't you miss that beautiful bridge, that Holy Bridge?"

"I do. I truly do. And I'm not being *macho* or anything but there's a helluva story to be told here. An important story. Rarely are the lines between good and evil so starkly drawn. Between hate and love, God and Satan." I was rambling, preaching and I didn't like myself doing that. So I veered.

"Speaking of which, Satan, I mean, you know how people love to knock television, how it diminishes us as a people? And you know how the Emmy Awards are given each year to counteract that attitude by honoring TV's best?"

"And how you're going to win this year, dear one, because you *are* the best!" She unfurled a smile.

"Impartial judge, you're not, love. But thanks. The point I was making, was going to make, was that the organization that gives the Emmys is the National Association of Television

Arts and Sciences, N.A.T.A.S.. Which, you might notice, if spelled backwards ... "

"Right," she countered, thinking fast. "And if you win one of those awards you'll know you've really lived. And *lived* spelled backwards ..."

With which we agreed to change subjects and go to dinner. Distraction: successful.

The message awaiting at the front desk on return to the hotel was a number for me to call. I didn't recognize it but we went to my room to call. Or was that safe? Privacy not guaranteed on a hotel phone especially when the suspect works for that hotel. Back downstairs, out into the street and a couple blocks north we found a pay phone in a bar. Ordered two Dr. Pepper's while I slipped to the back to place the call.

No mystery. It was FBI agent Riggins with the heartening news that Buford had been found, taken into custody, was being vigorously interrogated. Police were at that moment at his house checking things. Call again later this evening for more info. I assured him I would and thanks for the update. Great relief.

After dinner we took in a movie that could not have been a greater diversion: Stanley Kubrick's newest, *Dr. Strangelove.* Peter Sellers-times-three. Brilliant film and somehow watching the world about to be destroyed by atomic war put Buford's pitiful bomb stunt into perspective.

Or did it? I called agent Riggins. He said that, yes, it was clear that *I* was indeed the target. Buford's plan had been — and it was only a one man derangement —to build the bomb in his basement where police had found it now ready to go, secrete it in the makeshift Green Room back stage at the Crusade facility for tomorrow. He meant to have it wired to just outside that structure with himself stolen into hidden position nearby at the trigger switch. Why? Because he had come to see me as the symbol of dreaded northern nigger-lovers threatening the South's way of life. He had several versions of the picture of me and the girls, Beatrice and Camille, pinned to the wall of his bomb-making room. How thrilled he must have been to find me checking into his very hotel the other day! Must have taken off, run home and put together the bomb-scare threat box then come back seeming so innocent to tell me it was waiting for me in my room. He played it so straight. Might have worked if only he had spelled out "Birmingham."

"By such quirks are many-a-plot derailed," said Agent Riggins. "We just have to discern them. Or, in this case have a *You* who discerns them for us. Good work, Agent Perkins." Whereupon he added a line I had surely not expected, not from him, not, I guess, from any government guy. .

"It's after midnight, Perk. Easter. *He is risen!*"

CHAPTER THIRTY-SIX

"I HAVE NEVER SPOKEN LIKE THIS BEFORE.
NEVER IN PUBLIC. I OWE A GREAT DEBT AND AM HERE BEGIN
TO PAY IT."
--Speaking at the Billy Graham Crusade

He is risen, indeed! Alleluia! So Cliff Barrows exulted before some thirty-five thousand gathered in Birmingham's Legion Field, blacks and whites, devout or merely curious. Just a year earlier what the press took to calling the Birmingham Campaign had begun — protests, demonstrations, attacks and finally, just six months ago, the church bombing, with deaths of four black children, the total that might have been six had it not been for a TV guy's timely if only reflexive intervention. Now, he and the two young girls whose lives were saved would appear with Billy Graham before the people of this hoping-to-heal town.

Billy was with the girls and me in the green room which would have been wired to a bomb were it not for police and FBI. "Doing God's work, for sure," he said to no rebuttal from any of us. His longtime friend, George Beverley Shea, was onstage, singing "How Great Thou Art." After which Cliff Barrows would introduce his boss and the crowd would erupt with praise and honor. He would greet the crowd with a prayer, reflect on the the tumult of their times and introduce me.

There were a few scattered *boo's* at my name as I stepped forward but Billy responded immediately. "Friends, this pulpit welcomes divergent opinions but not discourtesy. These three people are here at my personal invitation. I respect them and God, I am sure, loves them – all."

That would be the only hint of controversy. Rev. Graham introduced me, embarrassingly effusive, and asked me something about how it had happened six months earlier.

I looked out at the crowd, not the first crowd I had faced but the first I had ever faced to not just tell a story which I was comfortable doing but to give testimony, proclaiming my faith, which I had never done in public. Silently, I asked for His help.

Rev. Graham stepped back, took a seat. I began:

"I don't know," I said simply. "The more important the story, I had come to believe, the simpler should be the telling. I just don't know. Terrible thing for a reporter to confess. We rarely do, do we? But that morning I can describe to you only because people have told me. I recall only being in the basement of the church, a familiar place for me having covered many meetings and prayer sessions there. But as to what happened to me, around me, that deadly morning when Hate exploded I know only by hearsay. And I didn't even hear the hearsay till days later when, finally and slowly, I regained senses.

"I was told that my life was still in danger, not from the many injuries I had already suffered but from those that were

300

still darkly and menacingly threatened by those agents of Hell I knew to be completely capable of imposing them. If not death itself.

"Good and godly people here arranged my hasty departure to safer climes. They who medically had saved my life now saved it again. I shall be forever indebted to them. But more, I came to appreciate in my painful recuperative time, that I owe ultimate gratitude to the Ultimate Giver of Good. God. Who has given me restored health and work I love and – His greatest gift – the woman who will be my wife."

I heard a murmured gasp from the stands. I imagined I could hear it from my mother.

"I have never spoken like this before. Never in public. My network may not appreciate it, nor some of my viewers across the land, but they cannot be my main concerns any longer. I owe a great debt and am here begin to pay it." With which I raised high my hands and bowed my head. "Thank you, dear Jesus. Thank you, God. I am Yours."

Camille and Beatrice were introduced, diverting on their way to the podium to give me hearty hugs. My eyes filled, my mind whirled and I couldn't tell you what they said but the audience, white and black alike erupted in applause; Billy Graham embraced the girls, and held them as he moved prayerfully into his usual altar call, and the choir started to sing "Just As I Am."

I found Jillian just offstage and hand-in-hand we joined the hundreds stepping forward across the grass or threading down from the high reaches of the stadium, Graham's continuing call guiding them. "Way up in the top rows, come on down, if you're with other people, they'll wait for you. Come. You who came in buses, they won't leave without you."

Clergy met each man, woman and child responding to the call, prayed for them, handed each a paperback printing of the Gospel of John. Jill and I took ours, bowed for the prayer and, with rapturous hearts there on the floor of an alien football stadium surrounded by hundreds of other pilgrims, we formally, publicly, devotedly gave our lives, ourselves, and our futures together to God.

Alleluia! Amen!

CHAPTER THIRTY-SEVEN

PERK, I'M A DIAGNOSTICIAN. YOU CALL US BURSTING WITH
BLESSINGS, EAGER TO SHARE. A = B AND B = BETROTHED
— *Doc, spoiling our surprise*

Producer, crew, several editors and I worked through the night Sunday and most of Monday there in Birmingham to weave together our show from many threads: twelve interviews, my hospital reminiscences, the account of the bomb plan thwarted, highlights from the Billy Graham Crusade. Once the tapestry was complete, my sparse narration laid in, and the show aired nationwide, we heard encouraging *Attaboys* from New York whereupon, thanking and farewelling colleagues, my new fiancée and I eagerly if wearily began the journey home.

Home.

Back to the bridge that Willy, inspired by my ammo box treasure had us calling the Holy Bridge, although he, by now, had graduated to calling it simply *God's Bridge.* An early morning flight set us down at Newark, the car service picked us up, Jill curled to doze as I settled back with a cup of tea to ponder.

Why had it come to mean so much to me, that overgrown Erector Set over the Delaware? Why? Sure, it was part of my family heritage, something my own kin dreamed and did, bestowing a gift on this early heart of America. I was proud of that.

But there was more. After my tortured times, soul and psyche twisted and torn, the bridge was refuge, my place of solace and remove from the evil that assaulted me, just now tried once more (and might again?) After the surreal sterility of hospitals and surgeries, the bridge and now the Old Stone House offered what my heart needed. A *place*. Solid, sure, surrounding and safe.

And, of course, one thing more, maybe the most important ultimately: the bridge brought me Jill by that blessed coincidence that only with her guidance, I came to understand was not coincidence. The bridge brought me Jillian, Jillian brought me God. Not just the Bible she gifted me on our first date but, more, her own cheerfully infectious faith and that of her welcoming parents, a faith I had never heard acclaimed in my childhood home. Without it now, would I have found myself layered against the wintry chill at the foot of the bridge one recent dawn fancying that before me I was witnessing nothing less than a re-creation of Creation?

I overstate things at times; I overthink them. But to this day when gazing upon the Dingmans Bridge as I'm soon to do, I see my life as for too long it has seemed. Structured. Its iron geometries patterned and fixed. Reliable, yes, but confining. If I stand at one end staring down toward the other, I feel encaged. Like the caged bird that poet Paul Laurence Dunbar sympathized with in the little book on my parents' bookshelf:

I know what the caged bird feels, alas!
When the sun is bright on the upland slopes;
When the wind stirs soft through the springing grass,
And the river flows like a stream of glass;
When the first bird sings and the first bud opes,
And the faint perfume from its chalice steals—
I know what the caged bird feels!

The bird feels as I feel this moment approaching the bridge beneath which the river flows like a stream of glass, the wind stirs soft through the springing grass, sun is bright on upland slopes. I feel it.

But, too — and too often — I feel myself severely encaged. Beating against the iron trusses of unyielding commitments and responsibilities. What can I do? Learn from the bird.

I know why the caged bird sings, ah me,
When his wing is bruised and his bosom sore,
When he beats his bars and he would be free;
It is not a carol of joy or glee,
But a prayer that he sends from his heart's deep core,
But a plea, that upward to Heaven he flings—
I know why the caged bird sings!

The magic comes for the bird as for me when a prayer upward to heaven he flings, I fling. And the prayer sails upward through the bars of his cage, the iron trusses of my bridge, to the cloud-puffs above of springtime sky, the azure assurance that the blind hymn-writer Fannie Crosby called the *Blessed Assurance.* We sang that last time we were in church here.

"We're here, Jill," awaking her softly. "The bridge."

From now on, when feeling encaged, I can burst free with simply a change of focus. Out of focus: the gray iron bars. Into focus: the blessed assurance that always lies beyond.

And the floor-plank marimba plays *This is my story, this is my song; praising my Savior all the day long.*

Dropping my things at the Stone House, I use my little car to take Jill back up to her place, planning to take her folks to dinner tonight to give them our big news. And I want to let Doc know and, of course Willy. Better hold off on him though so word doesn't get to Chas prematurely. Tonight is Revelation night.

Well, not really. Word's already out. Babs comes running out of their place to swarm Jill and me with hugs and excited babble asking when and how and all that and hoping she'll be invited, could she be a bridesmaid, maybe maid of honor? That'd be, well, such an honor she bubbles. She is so glad Jill told her which she hadn't really but Babs had decoded the hidden message from Jill's exhausted-excited phone call this morning and couldn't wait to hear all about it. Where and when? Honeymoon?

"You know, Babs," I say gently, "getting engaged I always thought would be hard. It was easy. Talking about it now, all the questions we haven't even asked ourselves yet, this is hard: give us time."

"But as for bridesmaid," Jill quickly adds, "count on it. I shall."

Dinner with her parents — who have not heard — is as it should be, scripted by a caring playwright who accords us all the appropriate moments of beaming surprise, joyous

306

exclamations and blessings and at one moment here at the table, salads already delivered, a handholding, heads-bowed time of prayer to God for our future together.

From there, calling to ensure they're home, we drive to Doc and Patricia's place and — how can it be? — they know! They're out on the stoop to greet us with ebullient congratulations. "How, how, how" I inarticulately mumble.

"Perk," Doc insists, "I'm a surgeon, sure, but first of all I'm a diagnostician. Take the clues, the patient's obvious state of mind, analyze and reach your reasoned conclusion. So you two have been away for most of a week. With a holy man. You call us with undisguised excitement, bursting with blessings you're eager to share. . . A = B and B = Betrothed. Simple."

"So come inside and tell us," says Patricia, leading the way.

How transporting is the evening I can only hint by telling you that Patricia whips up a magnificent desert which I devour and will not remember. They had seen our show so knew about the bomb that might have been and they ask a lot about that. Also our impressions of Billy Graham. Did we call him just Billy? What did we think of him? Is he genuine? Then more about how it felt to relive the story and so baldly, proudly bespeak my faith. How did that feel?

A delightful evening with dear friends and then take Jill home and happily get myself back to my haven by the bridge.

And before sleep, much yearned-for sleep, I take Jill's Bible off the side table and as I have come to do, open it randomly, put down a finger and read the verse it touches. Sometimes this yields gibberish, at least meaninglessness to a Bible novice.

God's Bridge

Tonight, though, my finger fortuitously finds these lines in Proverbs:

> *An excellent wife, who can find?*
> *For her worth is far above jewels.*
> *The heart of her husband trusts in her,*
> *And he will have no lack of gain.*
> *She does him good and not evil*
> *Her children rise up and bless her;*
> *Her husband also, and he praises her, saying:*
> *"Many daughters have done nobly,*
> *But you excel them all."*
> *Charm is deceitful and beauty is vain,*
> *But a woman who fears the Lord, she shall be praised.*

Praise you, Jillian.

Thank you, Lord.

CHAPTER THIRTY-EIGHT

"I HAVE HEARD THEM SPEAK OF THIS STRUCTURE BEFORE US AS
HOLY. I DIDN'T UNDERSTAND. BUT TODAY HERE WITH YOU
ALL, I FEEL IT.
— SURPRISE GUEST AT WEDDING

I woke with just enough time to bathe, shave and dress before hearing the welcome call. "Perk, cuppa's or not with old Willy? Forgetting yer friends, Mr. TV Star?"

I called down. "Gotta leave for the city in half hour, but get things perking for Perk. Right down."

We talked about my trip, of course and, yes, he had heard already from Chas about our engagement and thought it one more blessing settled upon me by my newfound God. Which prompted me to tell him about my Caged Bird hypothesis, which discussion was finally cut short by the arrival of the car service and I was on my way. No time off, no rest, for New York.

That's how it would go, and keep going, month after month. Plotting shows, traveling to shoot them, returning to write and edit while plotting the next batch. It was called working.

And being more than amply rewarded by employer, press and audience. So much so that the network begged us to expand the show from monthly to bi-weekly. Could we do that? Promised additional staff and funding, we said yes.

But I wondered.

Partly, because at this same time I had a persistent swarm of bees buzzing in and out of my mind-hive. Jillian and I had chosen a date. We would be married at the bridge in October while the extended family was in town for annual meetings and while autumn leaves quilted the woods around the Stone House where we newlyweds would be living for a while. Between now and then, there would be so much to decide, to plan, most of that burden necessarily weighing on Jill while TV Bird busily beat on the bars of his cage.

Swamped but never drowned would be our summer. And then, so soon, it was fall. Fragrant, apple-y, crisp-aired fall, the waters under the bridge floating red, orange and yellow flotillas of oak and linden leaves, coloring miles in the annual celebration of the river's remaining heroically undammed.

"So," asked friend Willy one afternoon as I returned from the city, "Are you guys ready for the big day, Perk."

"Willy, I'd be scared if I thought we were. Thinking you're ready, I figure, guarantees you're not. We're not and we know it."

"Which may mean you *are*," reasoned my charmingly unreasonable friend.

"Good morning." It was my surprise overnight houseguest emerging from the guest room to the aromas I had working in the kitchen, bacon and biscuits, eggs to come. "How're you doing this morning, Perk, on your first and only ever wedding day?"

"I'll feel better after a prayer."

"Well, it's your day. Should be your prayer, don't you think?"

"I'll feel awkward. With you here, and all."

"You're not talking to me; you're talking to God.

Nervous, unnecessarily, I spoke a simple prayer, unadorned, giving thanks first for my soon-to-be-bride, the blessing of her in my life, and then for all the friends and family gathered for our wedding this day. Especially the man who surprised me late yesterday with his arrival for the occasion. Weeks back, I had sent him details of our plans just in case though doubting he'd be able to make it. But here he was. Not to be an official part of the service, but a friend of Jill's and mine who had said he'd like to be here if schedules permitted. I thanked God that they had. And hoped Jill wouldn't mind my keeping him a secret.

Not for long. Her car pulled up and out she popped, she and Babs carrying the wedding dress and frilly accoutrements. "Hi, husband to be," she called cheerily before seeing our guest to whom she rushed, arms wide. "Doctor Graham!" she enthused as she embraced him.

"There's a doctor here? he joked. "You sick?"

"Sorry. Billy." She turned to Babs, proudly introducing her friend to "America's pastor." Babs burbled.

Whereupon I had to fill them both in on our honored guest's surprise arrival and desire not to be a part of our service. Our pastor would still be doing that here on the bridge, Billy was here simply as one of our friends and family to witness and wish us well on our way.

"Something's burning," called Babs and she was right. The biscuits were still in the oven becoming charcoal briquettes.

"Totally forgot our breakfasts Billy. Sorry."

Not surprisingly, he had a graceful way to let me off. "Perk, you're not the first worshipper to sacrifice with burnt offerings."

As Billy retired to the guest room for his devotional time, while Jillian and Babs took over my room to prepare the bride, I went outside to greet early arrivals. My Best Man was first. Willy had been thunderstruck when I asked him. "Ought to be your brother or someone, don't you think? Or are you trying to make points with the Lord asking a black man?"

"My brother's in Ethiopia or somewhere. Wouldn't have to buy all those plane tickets to get him if I could get you. Anyhow, are you really a black man, Willy? You never told me."

My dad arrived, dapper in camel's hair sport coat with a vest sweater beneath against the autumn chill, especially here by the river. Dad arrived but . . .

"Your mother is terribly sorry. Please forgive her, she asks. She has her new dress for the occasion hanging on the closet door back in the room but was taken down with a bug of some sort and just isn't up to it to be here in the cold today. She's bundled in bed but hopes you might stop by and see her after everything. If it isn't too much trouble."

Her folks were among the next arrivals, her dad taking me aside to ask, "Perk, I got thinking. You, a big TV guy and me scraping by collecting tolls — is it too late to ask for a dowry, you think?"

"Chas, check your dictionary. I think a dowry is what *you'd* be offering *me* if you weren't already giving me the greatest woman God ever created."

"I heard that. I resent that. I thought *I* was." Jill's mom.

Badinage, greetings, wishes. The flood had just begun. Doc and Patricia showed up with the other Doc Bullock and his friend from Birmingham, Hospital Director Dr. Eugenia Parker. And look who was with them! My dear young friends, Beatrice and Camille and their folks. Their arrival made Billy's emerging on the scene perfectly timed. Others, spying him tended toward him. A New York contingent – Bunky, Cal, several editors, organizer Arthur Gradszinski. And the high boss himself, Bill McMurphy. "So this," he said, "is what keeps you at a distance from the city, Perk. Can't blame you. Beautiful spot. And your granddad built this bridge?"

"He and his brothers, yes."

"You have reason to be proud, Perk."

"Plenty of reasons. And you haven't met the best one yet."

I worked the crowd best I could though it was not easy getting anywhere close to Billy, so thick were the admirers around him. Only when our own preacher arrived did I clear a way for him to meet Dr. Graham, as he insisted on calling him.

It was time. Time for the moment that would change forever my life.

Jill was nowhere to be seen. Nor was her dad. Good.

Music danced from outdoor speakers suspended over the bridge. Mendelssohn's classic from "A Midsummer Night's" Dream. Hushed, people turned toward the bridge, no doubt wondering as the preacher took his place in the tolltaker's circle, I and Willy flanking him, where the bride was. The bride and her father to give her away. Where were they? Mendelssohn insisted: *Dum-dum-da-dum, Dum-dum-da-dum.* At the far end of the bridge something appeared. Couldn't be traffic. Bridge was closed for an hour, townspeople understanding and excited to join the celebration themselves. No, it wasn't traffic approaching from the far end of the bridge. It was the most peculiar marriage carriage most had ever seen, bright green and yellow, it's driver suited in blue bib overalls, his passenger a white cloud of radiance, proud atop a platform built by the tractor's seat on the old Johnny Popper, so lovingly restored for this holy moment.

Her dad helped his bride-daughter down, her sparkly white sneakers stepping to my side; the music dimmed, and the pastor began his ritual, slightly nervous he confessed later, what with Billy standing there.

What is a wedding for? Jill and I had asked ourselves. What and whom is it for? Sometimes for parents, wanting to "do right" by their daughter or son whether son or daughter care. Sometimes to show off. We can afford all this, yes, we can if with the bank's help. Sometimes because people love to dream and fantasize big, festive occasions, taking years to create. Bride magazines offer three year subscriptions, not one issue of which will suggest a bride arrive on a rebuilt John

Deere tractor. A wedding, done right, we decided, was for two people. For *us!* For that indelible moment when *she* and *I* formally, in God's eyes and man's, become *we.*

The pastor's ritual words did it. And, in a way, Jill's whispered words as I lifted her veil to kiss my new wife, did it too. "You'll never need to ask now."

"This was not planned," spoke our pastor, "but sometimes our loving Father surprises us with a blessing unexpected. I'd like to invite one of the bridal couple's friends to offer our closing prayer. If you would, Doctor Graham, please."

With grace and gratitude, Billy stepped forward, was handed the mike and invoked God's great blessings upon these, His blessed son and daughter, on their day of lifelong commitment to each other and to His holy service.

He concluded with this: "I have heard them speak of this structure before us as God's Bridge. As Holy. I didn't understand. But today here with you all, I feel it. As a bridge has the power to bring together one state with another, one community with others, these people with those, I'm told it brought together Jillian and Perk themselves. God works through people; we know that. Why should we not accept that He can also work through a physical structure such as the one before us? That he used men and women of devout belief to construct it so many years ago and care for it lovingly ever since. Let all of these who enjoy it continue to take pride in it. It is their bridge, yes, it is yours, but let each acknowledge that it is also and always will be His. God's Bridge."

Service finished, Jill and I joined everyone for the picnic set up across the front lawns, mingling, sharing laughs and love.

Then, as inconspicuously as we could, we disappeared. Stealthily, we found our way back out to the tractor, I hoisted Jill onto the seat while I took the bench behind and off she drove, wheeling it around and bucketing back across the bridge to the Jersey side, hanging a sharp right up the Old Mine road, up to where a small clearing opened to the water, the gentled river below. Sitting there, we gazed and we listened. Was this exactly the same spot? Probably not but close enough. Imagination accommodated and I could hear, we *both* could hear, the whispering voice of the river as my grandfather told of hearing it decades before.

*Gaze upon us, you up there. Gaze and see for yourself, we are waters of peace. And it is naught but peace we wish for you in your days and years together. As to your grandfather long ago we blessed his plan for a bridge across us, we now bless your commitment to bridging yourselves together in marriage. Echoing what we told him then we urge you now: **Make it magnificent!***

Author's Afterword

In what would become known as Psalm 39, King David
asked God to reveal to him how long he would live.

Millennia later, my brother Perk was tempted to ask
the same thing. His life was so good, so *magnificent* I should
say, how much more life might he hope to be granted?

Neither man — David or Perk — got an answer.
Unknowing can be God's kindest gift.

Perk still had the Bible Jill gifted him years before. He read
on in Psalm 39.

Surely every man at his best is a mere breath.
Surely every man walks about as a phantom;
Surely they make an uproar for nothing;
He amasses riches and does not know who will gather them.

Perk had amassed relative riches over TV years and soon
found himself asking weren't those enough? Weren't other
things more important now?

Reluctantly but realistically he and Jill moved from the Old
Stone House to a house they built just a few miles away, still
on the river but closer to Milford. Children came, a girl they
named Beatrice Camille, a boy baptized Fred after our Dad,
and one more girl named Bernadette for Jill's mom. By which
time, Perk felt ever more the burden of so often packing,

leaving, going away to yet another somewhere that wasn't home for a story that was not of his own family.

More demanding than ever became his job as competition mounted. CBS' brilliant young producer Don Hewitt created a new program called *60 Minutes,* not just monthly or semi monthly but weekly, every Sunday. Could Perk's show match that schedule? CBS had two anchors, Harry Reasoner and Myron (Mike) Wallace. Perk had Perk. His network could add more faces, changing the very character of the program. Or . . .

Perk made the choice for everybody. With the same fervor as he had entered television news years back, he now left it of his own choice, rare in our profession. TV writers, network execs and certainly the public were astonished.

Jill, on the other hand, was grateful and thanked God. Her husband had chosen her and their family over the life, the work she knew he loved. He would still write, occasional newspaper or magazine pieces which he could do from home. He would pop into the city for occasional guest appearances on this show or that, and while home undertake another challenging form of writing, as far as one can rise above journalism – poetry. That would never yield much income but this was his time to graduate from making a living to making a life.

Their lives would know the inescapable heartaches and challenges. Both lost their parents. Their two sons and daughter eventually moved on to find their own odds to beat, encouraged to follow their own paths, albeit while permitting God to guide them.

As for Jill and Perk themselves, they kept the sacred vow they pledged that October afternoon so many years before as they stood upon the tractor on God's Bridge. Death has not yet come to part them

Finally, regarding this manuscript which I ghost-wrote for my brother in, of all places, dreary Moscow, my posting at the time, once he received it and had gone through it carefully he cabled me his profound appreciation. With a twist.

"Brother, dear, thank you. I love it. Even the parts that are true."

Made in the USA
Middletown, DE
11 August 2022

71180977R00196